Praise for the novels of John Shannon

"Tough and engaging ... [a] fine contribution to the L.A. novel—hard and real and full of heart."
—Michael Connelly

"Shannon is a fine writer. Make no mistake, this is the real L.A., real people, some of them you cross the street to avoid, looking everywhere but at them. Take a walk with Jack Liffey, a brave and decent man."
—Kent Anderson, author of *Night Dogs*

"A fine, interesting read."
—James Crumley, author of *Bordersnakes*

"Like Graham Greene—and there are other admirable resemblances—he is an explorer of that shadowy area in which, as spurs to positive action, abstract idealism and personal psychology merge. The author has achieved one of the most stimulating of the form's uncountable possibilities."   —*Sunday Times* (London)

"A serious adventure ... [that] draws much of its strength from a clear presentation of social and political tensions."   —*Times Literary Supplement* (London)

"Fast and exciting action."
—*Daily Telegraph* (London)

"The best L.A. earthquake scenes ever, the best private-detective-making-love-to-an-old-movie-star moments ever, the most-bearable private-detective-driving-a-beat-up-car scenes ever, the hands-down winner in the long-running 'Where is the next Raymond Chandler coming from?' sweepstakes—all these honors belong to ... John Shannon."   —*Chicago Tribune*

MORE MYSTERIES FROM THE
BERKLEY PUBLISHING GROUP...

CAT CALIBAN MYSTERIES: She was married for thirty-eight years. Raised three kids. Compared to that, tracking down killers is easy ...

by D. B. Borton

ONE FOR THE MONEY	TWO POINTS FOR MURDER
THREE IS A CROWD	FOUR ELEMENTS OF MURDER
FIVE ALARM FIRE	SIX FEET UNDER

ELENA JARVIS MYSTERIES: There are some pretty bizarre crimes deep in the heart of Texas—and a pretty gutsy police detective who rounds up the unusual suspects ...

by Nancy Herndon

ACID BATH	WIDOWS' WATCH
LETHAL STATUES	HUNTING GAME
TIME BOMBS	C.O.P. OUT
CASANOVA CRIMES	

FREDDIE O'NEAL, P.I., MYSTERIES: You can bet that this appealing Reno private investigator will get her man ... "A winner."—Linda Grant

by Catherine Dain

LAY IT ON THE LINE	SING A SONG OF DEATH
WALK A CROOKED MILE	LAMENT FOR A DEAD COWBOY
BET AGAINST THE HOUSE	THE LUCK OF THE DRAW
DEAD MAN'S HAND	

BENNI HARPER MYSTERIES: Meet Benni Harper—a quilter and folk-art expert with an eye for murderous designs ...

by Earlene Fowler

FOOL'S PUZZLE	MARINER'S COMPASS
KANSAS TROUBLES	SEVEN SISTERS
DOVE IN THE WINDOW	
IRISH CHAIN	
GOOSE IN THE POND	

HANNAH BARLOW MYSTERIES: For ex-cop and law student Hannah Barlow, justice isn't just a word in a textbook. Sometimes, it's a matter of life and death ...

by Carroll Lachnit

MURDER IN BRIEF	A BLESSED DEATH
AKIN TO DEATH	JANIE'S LAW

PEACHES DANN MYSTERIES: Peaches has never had a very good memory. But she's learned to cope with it over the years ... Fortunately, though, when it comes to murder, this absentminded amateur sleuth doesn't forgive and forget!

by Elizabeth Daniels Squire

WHO KILLED WHAT'S-HER-NAME?	WHOSE DEATH IS IT ANYWAY?
MEMORY CAN BE MURDER	WHERE THERE'S A WILL
IS THERE A DEAD MAN IN THE HOUSE?	FORGET ABOUT MURDER
REMEMBER THE ALIBI	

THE POISON SKY

JOHN SHANNON

BERKLEY PRIME CRIME, NEW YORK

THE POISON SKY

A Berkley Prime Crime Book / published by arrangement with the author

PRINTING HISTORY
Berkley Prime Crime mass-market edition / April 2000

All rights reserved.
Copyright © 2000 by John Shannon.
This book may not be reproduced in whole or in part,
by mimeograph or any other means, without permission.
For information address: The Berkley Publishing Group,
a division of Penguin Putnam Inc.,
375 Hudson Street, New York, New York 10014.

The Penguin Putnam Inc. World Wide Web site address is
http://www.penguinputnam.com

ISBN: 0-425-17424-7

Berkley Prime Crime Books are published
by The Berkley Publishing Group,
a division of Penguin Putnam Inc.,
375 Hudson Street, New York, New York 10014.
The name BERKLEY PRIME CRIME and the BERKLEY PRIME CRIME
design are trademarks belonging to Penguin Putnam Inc.

PRINTED IN THE UNITED STATES OF AMERICA

10 9 8 7 6 5 4 3 2 1

For Bob Coe

Thanks to Robert Stone for the crows on page 189,
and to David MacDougall for the lard.

"He would not satirize them as Hogarth or Daumier might, nor would he pity them. He would paint their fury with respect, appreciating its awful, anarchic power and aware that they had it in them to destroy civilization."

—NATHANAEL WEST

1

A HEROIC DIMENSION

THE SOURCE OF THE STOP-AND-GO SEEMED TO BE A BIG
dead Guernsey bull that lay against the center divider
with a flash red Mercedes accordioned up against it like
a matador who'd gone a little crazy. Neither looked like
they were going to make it to any more bullfights, and
he wondered what on earth the animal had been doing
on the northbound 405 just short of Mulholland Drive.

He was anxious to get past the jam-up because the
woman on the phone that morning had mentioned a
missing boy and offered actual, spendable money, which
he needed pretty bad. His child support was still touch
and go, and Kathy was threatening to cut off his visits
for good. It ate at something elemental in you when you
failed a daughter.

His old car coughed a couple of times as it fought its
way past the bull and then over the crest of the Sepulveda Pass. Down below he could see a thin blue smoke
settled around the taller buildings like the fumes off bat-
tery acid. Go Directly to the Valley, he thought—the
Big Penalty in a faddish board game of the 1970s called
Beverly Hills that had been loosely based on Monopoly.
This summer morning, however, he could still make out
the hills across the San Fernando Valley at Sylmar, and
that made it a very good day in the Valley.

Then he saw the real root of the problem: an immense
cattle truck was stove in and sideways across three lanes,

delaying the Big Penalty for all the northbound traffic. As he inched up to the truck, there was a terrible bellowing and a sudden ripple of the latticed metal siding.

Sometimes you just had to look away. Instead of thinking about the suffering animal inside, he entertained a fantasy of himself as Philip Marlowe in a sweat-stained homburg, driving his '38 Dodge over this very spot on the old Sepulveda Highway to answer a summons from some rich old man who spent his afternoons in a greenhouse behind a broad smooth lawn. He'd be asked to hunt down a wayward daughter, or take care of her gambling debts, and the butler would give him a check for a retainer. Jack Liffey had only had a client like that once. Usually his clients lived in stucco boxes, welshed on his fees, and the lawns ran to crabgrass.

Before long the traffic picked up and he barreled down to Victory and off into Van Nuys. The house was easy to find on a small cross street improbably named Sultanate Avenue. It was the damnedest-looking tract house he'd seen in a long time. The scalloped eaves of a gable extended across the stucco face of the house and then dipped some more, so it blocked half the entry alcove, just at waist level. It forced you to sashay to one side coming up the walk and a fridge would have had to go in the back door. There was simply no limit to the ludicrous things they had built in the early sixties.

A washing machine was running somewhere inside. Since it was ten in the morning he didn't expect a man, but a man answered. He was mid-fortyish, wore a black polo neck, and had tidy swept-back graying hair. A pipe was clenched in his teeth like an icon of fifties conventionality, and he carried a large paperback book.

"Mardesich?" Jack Liffey inquired.

The man frowned and rescued the pipe from his teeth but didn't seem inclined to answer.

"I'm Jack Liffey."

"Faye," the man hollered over his shoulder. "This whole situation is absolutely too reductive for me." He reverted to a kind of musing drawl, as if speaking to the pipe in his fist. "The boy . . . I just can't bear irreversible actions. Oh, come in, come in. I'm sure that's closer to the form of discourse you expected."

"On most of the inhabited planets," Jack Liffey said softly as the man walked away.

It took him a moment to figure out what he was looking at in the room, and then he still wasn't sure. He'd grown used to swimming against a certain current of the unusual in his life, but just now he was having a little trouble touching bottom. There were big white *X*s marked out on the carpet with tape of some kind, and scattered randomly through the rest of the room there were two coat trees, a metal Christmas tree stand, an upended milk crate, two wastebaskets, an upright vacuum, and a chest-high stack of books. It reminded him of a classroom he'd been in once where a naval historian had tried to mark out the Battle of Jutland. The man with the pipe had sidestepped away through the markers on a languid broken field run. There was also a heavy exhalation of Lysol in the air, as if someone had just made a stab at covering over something worse.

In a moment a heavyset woman hove into sight from a different direction.

"Mrs. Mardesich?"

She nodded gravely and waved the notebook she was carrying. "You Jack Liffey?"

"Uh-huh."

She glanced back thoughtfully the way the man had gone and then seemed to make a decision. "Let's go to Emily's. I'll buy you a cup of coffee. Can you drive?"

He felt like saying he'd been driving since he was sixteen, but he let it lie.

"C'mon. The world all makes sense, I promise." She put a confident hand on his shoulder and squeezed in a mannish way, like a football coach reassuring the new placekicker. "Call me Faye. This place must seem bughouse looking down from the outside."

"I try not to look down on people," he said.

"Well said, Jack. Can I call you Jack?"

"Oh, *hell* yes." He decided to go with the flow.

She laughed and gave him a one-arm hug. Out front, she squinted a bit at his beat-up '79 Concord as the passenger door fought against her tugs. "I see we're flush with success," she said.

"My Rolls is in the shop."

"Don't worry; if I'd wanted a big Beverly Hills detective, I'd have called one."

Jack Liffey wasn't even sure there were such things as big Beverly Hills detectives. He wasn't even a detective in any strict sense. He had blundered into his calling as a finder of missing children after his aerospace job had evaporated at the end of the 1980s. Finding missing kids didn't pay all that well, as callings go, but it was a genuine service to the world and it was better than frying hamburgers.

"Someone recommended you highly."

"Who's that?"

"I'd rather not say right yet."

Emily's was a busy coffee shop with garish blue-and-red plastic seats and a permanent aroma of chicken fat. He really only liked the darkest French roast he could get, but he let her order him a coffee and declined anything else. For herself, she ordered a Spanish omelette and Emily's West Virginia muffins with red-eye gravy.

She had addressed the airy diminutive waitress as Tinker Bell, and he couldn't figure out whether it was an endearment or an insult. Faye Mardesich seemed the kind of woman who would make up pet names for lots of things and make them stick.

"Our household must look pretty dysfunctional to you."

"I wouldn't know."

She stopped playing with the little stand-up plastic ad for strawberry waffles. "Milo lost his job at Lockheed five years ago. He was internally famous as the guy who'd designed the struts on the front landing gear of the L-1011. They were revolutionary and saved Lockheed a lot of money. All he knew in life was mechanical engineering. He went to the headhunters and the agencies and I helped him send out over two hundred resumes. Mostly they didn't even have the courtesy to reply. He got a couple of temp jobs with the old subcontractors he knew, but nobody's hiring aerospace fulltime, not around here. When it became pretty clear that the job blight wasn't temporary, he started taking it hard. It affected all of us. He'd been making the high seventies and now he felt like a bum. He drank and didn't come back some nights. He started yelling at Jimmy and he'd never even raised his voice to the boy before. Mostly he just withdrew. That was up to about a year ago, but, you know . . ." She considered a moment. "I think I preferred then, with all the melancholy introspection."

She ran down and he decided to let her go at her own pace. His eyes strayed to a haggard-looking woman who was making her way from table to table. She wore a green bandanna over her hair and carried a bundle in her arms. She seemed to be showing a card at each booth and he guessed it said something like *I Am Deaf Please Help.*

"I think I get the back story," Jack Liffey said finally, to save her the trouble. "I was a tiny morsel of the peace dividend myself. But why did you prefer the period with the melancholy introspection?"

She decided to carry on not answering for a while but it didn't make her uncomfortable. She was one of those people who always seem to be at ease with themselves, even when they fidget. It made him think she'd had a happy childhood in a big family.

Tinker Bell brought the food, curtsying as some kind of private joke, and Faye Mardesich tucked in hard. He sipped at the atrocious coffee that tasted like they'd melted plastic toys in the pot. Once she'd taken the edge off her prodigious hunger, she slowed down and waved a fork in the air as if beating time.

"Okay, I'm over the hump here. Milo's gone into a manic phase and it's like living with a Martian. He's teaching himself French critical theory." She laughed scornfully and shook her head. "He talks about structural change and reading texts and, oh yeah, ruptures in the historical process. I keep wondering if somebody makes trusses for history.

She chuckled at her own joke. "Don't get me wrong. I'm not rejecting the intellect. It just doesn't make any sense in his life. It all started after he got a job as a night security guard, which seemed to put him out of kilter with the rest of the world. He's an engineer at heart, for God's sake, not a critical theorist. He *loved* engineering." She toyed with another shovelful of the omelette but seemed to have lost interest.

"He used to talk with real enthusiasm about how much he liked being challenged to take some practical device and make it *work* and bringing all his knowledge of science and materials and *leverage* to bear on the problem and conquering it. And now he's reading French philosophers in his guard shack and writing essays on the autonomy of the critic and sending them out over the Internet. I'm all in favor of people trying to reinvent themselves, but this is a pathology."

She torqued herself around to scratch her back the way a man would, and the effort yanked open her blouse for a moment to show a black lace bra just barely containing an ample breast. She laughed at herself and buttoned up in a matter-of-fact way.

"I *am* a mess. I haven't even talked about Jimmy yet. Milo is just the context for the problem—" She waggled her eyebrows for an instant. "I'm beginning to sound like Milo. Let's set the *problematic* here," she said with a derisive flex of her lips. "Our son's run away from home. Jimmy is seventeen and I can't blame him for getting fed up, but he's not really seventeen, if you know what I mean. He's, maybe, *twelve*. He's so sweet it's eerie, he's unfailingly polite and helpful. He doesn't have a mean or rebellious bone in his body. Jimmy's just a big vulnerable kindly kid, trying to hang on to his merit badges, and anybody with an ounce of hurt in him out there can make a meal of the boy."

"When did he go?"

"Two weeks ago."

"You reported him missing?"

"Sure." She shrugged. "One runaway kid. They're not gonna mobilize the SWAT team."

"Where do you think he'd run?"

But the woman in the bandanna had finally made it to their table. She tipped her bundle forward to display an emaciated baby to Jack Liffey. He stared until he saw a flicker of movement in one tiny clutched hand, little more than a tremor. The woman set a card on the table, and a dried sprig of some herb. The card said, *Heather is Good Luck the world over. It is Traditional to warrant the Luck with a small Donation. The Romany have unforeseen Powers.* Heather didn't grow in Southern California, so it was probably just crabgrass. He had a folded dollar bill ready and he opened his fingers to offer it. Surprisingly, her dry hand clutched his wrist and turned his hand over.

She stared into his palm for a moment with spooky deep black eyes that had tiny specks in the pupils. Her voice came out as a croak, a word or two that he could not decipher. Then suddenly the dollar bill was gone and a flimsy slip of paper was in its place, like a fortune from a Chinese cookie. *You have a heroic dimension, but you will have to pass through much suffering.*

When he looked up she was moving away.

Faye Mardesich took the note in two fingers with curiosity and read it.

"It's for someone else," he said. "Where would Jimmy run to?" The dried weed was still on the table, and he picked it up and put it into the empty ashtray.

Faye Mardesich studied both sides of the paper, as if a more careful look might yield up her son's whereabouts, then she dropped it.

"Naturally I've checked his friends and their friends. I think they genuinely don't know. I didn't like to go into his room because I value privacy, but I had to. I found a couple of porn magazines." She shrugged. "That doesn't bother me. It was rawer than the stuff I saw his age, but the world is moving that way."

"Straight or gay?"

"Straight, except for some lesbian scenes. You guys all like to watch girl-girl stuff."

"When we're not chaining them up."

She let it go. "And I found this."

He knew what it was right away. The cover of the dog-eared pamphlet asked:

Is Your Soul Ready for the Next Stage in its Journey?

In each generation a few are within reach of the next Forward Thrust of evolution. Come in now for a simple and totally free appraisal of your spirit's readiness for The Leap.

It was from the Theodelphian Elect, and gave an address on Melrose. They used almost as many extra capitals as the gypsy woman.

"Do you know them?" Her voice sounded chastened.

"Oh, yes."

"Are they dangerous?"

He opened the tri-fold and saw the complex diagram he'd seen many times before, a kind of stepladder labeled *Soul's Work* that led upward from the core of the earth, through the *Breath of the Passions,* and then up through dozens of rungs with names like *Universal Vitality* and *Thinking 4,007 Times Faster Than Thought* and *Assuming the Voluntary Body,* steps whose meaning and internal logic had always escaped him. He knew that even the top step with all the yellow rays shooting out of it, a plateau called the *Germ of the Form,* was only the beginning of another ladder to another plateau. The whole course of metaphysical study led upward more or less as long as your money held out.

"Dangerous like the militias, no. This might not mean anything at all. They leave these everywhere. Do you have any reason to think he's mixed up with them?"

She rested her chin on her palm and for the first time he sensed a particle of vulnerability in her. "He's my son, Jack. I've had to pull him out of ponds since he was two. He's as bright as two dim bulbs but he's far too good-hearted and brave and headstrong for his own good. This stuff is perfectly calculated to suck him in. All you have to do is make Jimmy feel special, or maybe just *useful,* and he's yours."

It was best she didn't know too much at this stage, he thought. The Theodelphians weren't the strangest cult in L.A.—that distinction probably went to the Scientologists, who started you out with a kind of bland debased Freudianism and launched you quickly up through the technobabble of interplanetary wars. And the Elect weren't as old as the Rosicrucians or Madam Blavatsky, but they made up for whatever they might have lacked in ripeness or luster with the naked use of sex to draw adolescents into their orbit. That fact was what he was holding back from the boy's mother.

"I need to look over Jimmy's things."

She nodded. "Milo can't deal with any of this, but he's working swing today, from four to midnight. Come by this evening and we'll go through Jimmy's room."

As they stood up, she picked up the crabgrass from the ashtray and put it in a fold of Kleenex in her purse. "You never know."

In the car she gave him a check for a hundred dollars to get him started. It was more than he usually got. On the way back to her house they passed a barefoot man with a ragged straw hat like Van Gogh's. He was leading a big goat on a leash. They both watched the man for a while, but there was absolutely nothing sensible you could say about something like that.

She hesitated as she got out of the car in her driveway. "Jack, I've got to find my son, but in a larger sense I'm doing this to keep my spirits up. You know what I mean?"

"Lots of people are hurting," he said.

"The way I keep things from getting me is I keep moving."

HE went straight back over the hill to Chris Johnson's place in West Hollywood. That part of town was filled with hundreds of little boxy houses from the forties, most of which now had false fronts with outsized French Provincial details or overtall doors. Russian immigrants recently had begun moving into the area known as Boystown, and there had been a number of culture clashes with the gays and trendies who'd traditionally populated the place.

Chris Johnson's little box was still a little box, as unassuming as you could get, which was probably the idea.

"Dude, long time," he said with a kind of dry smirk.

"It's been about two weeks."

"Damn, I'm getting that disease . . . you know, the one that begins with *A*."

"Arteriosclerosis."

"That's it." He stepped aside to reveal the welter of electronics that filled his stucco box. "*Come,* as Commander Picard says."

"Who?"

"Don't shit me. You know *Star Trek*." Chris Johnson was tall and athletic looking and so fair you could just about see through him.

Jack Liffey swept a hand to indicate all the electronics. "I thought you were warned off this stuff."

"The conditions of my parole state that I may not possess a telephone or a modem. They do *not* say I can't have a computer."

"I need some research. A modem would have been essential." Jack Liffey looked for a place to sit and settled for a wooden stool. For some reason Chris Johnson had glued a lot of aluminum foil to the ceiling and the wrinkles made a mad glare of little multicolored lights.

"You got a cellular?" Chris Johnson asked.

"I think I must have left it in the Ferrari."

He laughed. "What do you need researched?"

"The Theodelphian Elect."

Chris Johnson made a big *O* of his mouth. "Dude, you know, if they even *think* you're investigating them, they come after your cojones with little plastic forks."

"So I've heard. My colleague Art Castro had a run-in with them once, trying to get a client's kid's money back. They swiped a sheet of his stationery and wrote a letter threatening to assassinate the president in *Art's own* handwriting. Really first-rate forgery. It took him a year to get out from under it."

A computer buzzed, a bit like a washing machine signaling that it was done. Chris Johnson sat down in front of it and typed for a few moments, then set it working again.

"You chicken?" Jack Liffey asked.

Chris Johnson grinned and got an electric screwdriver out of a toolbox, then brandished it with a whir in mid-air. He took the back off what looked like an old ham radio. "My parole officer checks this place out twice a week, on a random schedule, but he's so dumb the only way he recognizes a modem is he looks for the RS-12 jack. That's the little gizmo on the end of your phone cord. So you put a different plug on it and tell him it's a rapid data transductor." From inside the radio he took out a black box and a cellular phone.

"Who's the phone registered to?" Jack Liffey asked.

"You don't want to know, but the gentleman in question used to work for the Republican National Committee. Actually, I jiggered the code so it's a number Airtouch reserves for testing."

He plugged the equipment into the back of the biggest computer in the room and started to fiddle at the keyboard, then picked up a clipboard and scanned it for something. In a moment Jack Liffey heard a tiny voice talking from within the machine, "Nordstrom's lingerie department. Can I help you?" There was a buzz and then another dialing sound.

"It always helps to loop your calls through somebody's switchboard. These guys want to get cute and trace who's interested in them, let's see what damage they can do to all those red merry widows."

Jack Liffey knew Chris Johnson would be busy at the keyboard for a while and so he wandered around the room, trying to make sense of the things he saw. One big green screen in the corner was scrolling numbers as if it was working on something all by itself, and another was looping a piece of animation that showed a catlike being biting the head off a guitar over and over. On the wall, a hand-lettered sign said COLORLESS GREEN IDEAS SLEEP FURIOUSLY. Beside it there was a framed photo of Chris Johnson looking startled and leaning back in a chair as a slim stripper was advancing on him dangling a sequined bra. It wasn't very flattering and Jack Liffey wondered why it was on the wall. If nothing else, his girlfriend should have torn it up on sight. Dot Matrix had a legendary temper.

"That picture you're goggling at was from the last HoHoCon in Phoenix," Chris Johnson said. Nothing you did anywhere near him ever escaped his notice.

"HoHoCon?"

"It's the phone hackers' convention. It's held at an unannounced site every year. Don't you go to gumshoe conventions?"

Jack Liffey scoffed.

"I put it up to keep Dot on her toes. Hey, there's a

whole *lot* of stuff on these guys in here. What do you want?"

"Membership lists?"

He shook his head. "They won't have that on-line. They won't even have it on a computer that's accessible, if they're smart."

"How about stuff posted by their enemies. Ex-members' horror stories. Inside dope."

"You're gonna owe me a couple reams of paper. Come back in a while and take me to dinner." He winked. "Always remember the hacker's code—knowledge wants to be free."

"So do I but I always settle for a discount."

2

THE HOLY BOY ROAD

JUST NORTH OF HIS OFFICE, THE ROADWAY PASSED OVER the cement channel of Ballona Creek, where a trickle of industrial waste offered back a rainbow sheen in the noon sun. Santanas were due in a few days, and when those hot dry winds blew in off the Mojave, they would dry up the ooze as fast as it dribbled out the waste pipes of the little factories up the road. It was probably thinking about industrial waste that made him notice the battered old pickup truck, pied with primer and paint stains, that was parked just across the creek.

He lingered a bit on the bridge. Two men sat in the pickup, but he really only noticed the driver, who had bright red hair in a buzz cut. For just a moment the driver had braced a big pair of binoculars on the steering wheel. Jack Liffey had acquired an extra measure of caution after a run-in with a couple of minor heavies who'd worked for Vegas casino money. He was pretty sure he'd got himself clear, but he figured it never hurt you much to whistle when you passed a graveyard. His office was on the second floor of the mini-mall straight ahead, wedged between a CPA and a vacancy that had briefly been a clown-and-juggler service, and the red-head had looked straight at his office door.

There was no parking on the bridge, so he pulled out into the center lane and turned left, hoping they wouldn't notice him. Having crossed the creek, he had a long circuitous journey in order to get behind the pickup again. He began to wish that he carried a gun in the car, remembering Bogart popping open a secret hatch under his dashboard in some movie or other. He experienced a chill—a sense memory of the fear he'd experienced when the *real* heavies had been after him. On some of the worst days, he'd felt that something was *right there,* about to wallop into him, and he remembered actually bobbing a few inches to one side, though of course there was nothing.

This time he parked just before the bridge. The curb was red, but he couldn't do anything about that. The second man in the pickup was heavier and looked older, but that was all he could tell from behind. From time to time they exchanged a few words, and the passenger seemed to be drinking from a Styrofoam cup. Jack Liffey wrote down the license number. He wondered if they could be completely innocent, bird fanciers, business-license investigators, cops staking out a car parked in front of Dan Margolin's Coffee Bean, bill collectors after somebody who kept a blind box at Marlena's Mailboxes-R-Us downstairs from him, or party givers who were really desperate for a juggler. But his apprehension was the dark side of something that would keep him healthy and he had to trust it.

A motorcycle accelerated past like a scream of pain, and he walked back to the library and called the police and told them about two men in a pickup on Overland waving big black pistols at passersby. Then he went back to his car to wait. It wasn't long before a black-and-white came up fast in his mirror, flashing lights but no siren, followed by a second police car. They boxed in the pickup and two cops got out and approached with their pistols drawn. Jack Liffey was happy to see one of the cops was Quinn, a real hardnose he'd had a number of run-ins with. Let somebody else get rubbed in it. An amplified voice squawked over the PA from one of the patrol cars, and four empty hands poked out the windows of the truck. Then the men were out and facedown on the pavement without complaint, and he tried to get a better look at them. The redhead looked like a marine he'd drunk with at R&R on China Beach, but that had been so long ago the man would have been a lot older.

Things started going a little unusual then. The cops handed around an ID from the heavyset man and one of them laughed. They let the two men up and they all relaxed a little, but not as much as they would have if the ID had said they were feds. Quinn was waving his finger and having his say at the redhead, something he was prone to do, and the redhead glared back as if he was memorizing features to make sure he knew this asshole if he ever ran into him again. The redhead said something back and made a fist. There was a little more dick-waving like that on both sides, and the cops in the second car saluted in jest and drove off with that little burst of acceleration cops used to show you they were busy people and had important places to get to and didn't have to explain things to you, in any case.

Soon everyone was gone, leaving a hollow space in the street, and leaving Jack Liffey feeling very alone and vulnerable. It was something he had never got used to after saying good-bye to his comfortable cubicle job in aerospace and falling into whatever it was that he did now. This was a world where you were on your own and things like luck mattered a whole lot more than he liked.

Superstition kept him from going to the office right away, where he didn't have anything to do anyway. He bought some dog food at the 7-Eleven and drove to his condo, which was not far east on Jefferson. He wondered if he should start carrying a gun. It wasn't legal, but nobody else in the city seemed to let that stop them. He'd had a bad feeling all day, an itch just out of reach. He wondered if it was some kind of chemical imbalance in his brain, an oversupply of a neurotransmitter in the fear lobe.

He came around the walk into the alcove where his front door was and froze in place. Because of the Vegas wiseguys, he'd taken to kicking up a little crease in the welcome mat every morning when he left. Anyone stepping on it would flatten it out. The jute mat was dead flat now, and there was no Avon catalog on the doorknob, and no maid service business card stuck in the jamb. Somebody had been up to the door, maybe inside.

He put the bag of dog food down soundlessly and pressed his ear against the door. After a full minute of silence, he took a big breath and barked and growled for a little while. There was no answer, so Loco was either dead or playing with Marlena Cruz in the back room and feeling safe. He couldn't remember if she still had a key, but she was almost the only person Loco got along with. All in all, he figured there were two possibilities: he would run into a bullet from a hired killer or an emotional scene with a woman he'd never got straight with. Let fate choose, he thought.

Inside, there was a little yip and then Marlena's voice, "Jack? Zat you?"

"You bet."

She was sitting on the bedroom floor in an apron, the ghostly white Loco on one side of her and the old Sears vacuum on the other. Cleaning up for him was her way of saying hello and establishing something of a claim. He didn't like the way she did things for him without asking, but he didn't know how to mention it without feeling churlish. Something in it hurt him, made him feel exploitive and ungrateful.

"Me and Loco making friends again." She ruffled Loco's wiry coyote hair. He saw that she'd put on another few pounds but she still looked pretty good in it and her black hair was wound into a kind of bun that made her look like a flamenco dancer between sets.

"You're the only one he really likes," he told her. "He tolerates me because I feed him, but he knows a good woman when he sniffs one."

She beamed. "A good man's got to know a good woman, too."

"You bet," he said neutrally. He wasn't sure why he said something as dopey as that, but it seemed to put off dealing with any of the consequences right then. "If he's hungry, I've got some lamb here. He seems to have a species memory of running down sheep."

She relaxed, as if they were all friends again. "You looked in this dog's eyes? He's pretty spooky."

They were strange eyes all right, depthless and dull gray and fierce as steel. There was no pet in them at all, no urge to figure out who you were and what you wanted, just the basic outdoors urges working themselves out on their own hook.

"I always figure I'm part of the food chain to him," he said. "Long as I stay above him and bigger than him, I'm probably okay, but he doesn't get to sleep in the same room with me, I'll tell you that."

The dog's jaw hung open a bit as he looked back and forth, as if planning to eat one of them.

"Aw, he's just a cutie."

"Uh-huh, sure. You can look at it that way if you want."

She ruffled the hair under the dog's chin and Loco seemed to tolerate it. "You working today, *querido*?" she asked.

"Yeah, a runaway boy from a nice screwed-up middle-class family in the Valley. His mom thinks he's caught up in a cult." He shrugged. "He could be, or he could be hooking on Hollywood Boulevard."

She wasn't really interested. There was another agenda item stewing and he pretty much knew what it was.

"Do you ever feel that telling the truth is real important?" She was trembling a little with conflicting emotions. "You know, that it's like something that God demands so you stay a good person?"

"Mar, we've been together and then we've both been

with other people, and we ought to just be careful, is all. I like you, too, and you don't have to tell me any more about Quinn." He sat down and touched her hand briefly, just a tap. She was kindly and decent to a fault and he had liked the physical with her, too, loved to touch her and feel how it stiffened her and made her shiver. He could remember touching her in all the secret places, and he would have loved to do it again, but on the other side of the equation, she went to a screwball millenarian church every week and he hadn't been in any kind of church in forty years and she kept Chihuahuas that he wanted to cook up in the microwave and she watched soaps in the morning that made his teeth hurt and she admitted she was tempted to vote Republican because her abusive son-of-a-bitch dad had been a lifelong Democrat and because she owned a small business, and almost everything about the two of them was at cross-purposes. Still, he was lonely and wanted her and he knew it, and he had to be clear to himself about it. She let her warm puffy hand rest on his.

"Can I come over tonight?" she asked.

"I don't think it's the impossible dream."

DRIVING back to Chris Johnson's place in West Hollywood, he passed three young women, all with long blond hair and Nazi uniforms with the big black boots. They goosestepped along La Cienega in front of an outlet store. Suddenly they about-faced and headed back south, as if afraid of getting too close to the Jewish district up along Fairfax. There was probably no way on earth of figuring out what that was about, he thought.

Chris Johnson was looking pretty glum when he opened the door. "You look like your parole officer just dropped by," Jack Liffey said.

The young man didn't even give a snappy reply, just beckoned Jack Liffey in morosely and led him to the computer where he'd been researching the Theodelphian Elect and tapped the screen. Red text was slowly flash-

ing: MIND YOUR OWN BUSINESS THIS IS THE ONLY WARN-
ING YOU WILL BE GIVEN YOU ARE NOW OFF-LINE.

He handed Jack Liffey an inch-thick bundle of paper.
"I got this down before they struck. I underestimated
these guys, and that's for sure for sure. I'm not even
sure what clued them in to my nosing around, but I'm
lucky I keep that computer physically separate from my
other stuff. That machine is hosed, dude. I was running
every kind of antivirus software known to man and they
cut through it all like butter. Your generation just ga-
zumped mine. Maybe you old guys are meaner than we
thought."

"I thought you routed the call through some department store."

"I did a lot more than that, dude, and it's like none
of my protection was even *awake*. They just waltzed into
my computer and squashed it like a bug. That message
you see is the *only* remaining parcel of nonrandom data
on my hard disk. They trashed it all in the time it took
to blink, and that's not even physically possible. It takes
time to write over a six-gig hard disk. Don't ask me how
they did it. These guys are bad news, okay? Watch your
back."

Jack Liffey thought of the men watching his office,
but how could the Theodelphians have got onto him so
quickly?

"Sorry."

Chris Johnson shook his head. "Don't be. I always
told you I was the best. Man, sooner or later somebody
always walks up and shoots Wild Bill Hickok in the
head while he's holding aces and eights and I think we
just witnessed the new fast gun."

"You want to get even?"

He laughed ruefully and held up the flats of his hands.
"Talk to me later. I'm shell-shocked right now. Man, I
did think I was the best."

• • •

WHILE he was waiting for evening to drive up and see Faye Mardesich, he parked near the Theodelphian Elect headquarters on the unfashionable end of Melrose near Western. It was unmistakable—a whole-block agglomeration of what had been storefronts and three-story apartments lashed together by a coat of festive yellow paint over everything. He could see into a courtyard in the center of the block that was accessed through a triumphal entrance arch where a building had been demolished. Inside was an artificial lagoon and a pagoda. The place looked like a big toy city made of Legos.

He watched the bustle of coming and going past a marquee that said: "MY EYES ARE BEHOLDEN TO THE PROUD DELIGHTS LIFE IS OFFERING." —K.A. They were mostly young and most wore bright yellow short-sleeve tunics. He wondered if the yellow meant they had been elected or just nominated. The corner building on Melrose had a big well-lit Edward Hopper glass window, and a sign said it was the Reception Center, though nobody seemed to be going in there. Most of the traffic went under the arch past a guard shack. The kids going in seemed to be showing a card or badge, but the lion's share of the foot traffic was out, as if it was quitting time from the day's heavy metaphysical climb on the Big Ladder.

He looked over the papers Chris Johnson had given him, lots of tiny text and a mystico-muddle of graphs and drawings. *Region of the Second Permanent Retinal Image,* he read. He wondered if the leaders believed in their own cosmic mumbo jumbo or if it was all a big scam. But what he really needed to know was whether they kept new recruits squirreled away inside the Melrose complex, or if they were spirited off somewhere else, safe from the deprogrammers, some isolated ashram where the spirit coaches could dig their thumbs into all your emotional bruises.

He watched the kids for a bit because something seemed odd about them. They didn't migrate in groups like ordinary workmates or schoolmates, not even in twos or threes. Each one seemed to be utterly alone, and they went their separate ways at once, turning in different directions or spacing themselves out as they drifted away in these curiously emotionless gaits, not so much zombie-dead as simply preoccupied and uncomfortable. It was as if they'd been dropped there yesterday from Kansas and they were still unsure of what to do with themselves. Still, for all the oddity of the place, it didn't seem to represent the kind of cult that fried your computer and sent thugs to watch your office.

A bedraggled Latino family wheeling an infant in a shopping cart and trailing several other children made a slow procession past the complex. The father would work at day labor by loitering in front of the Home-Depot, Jack Liffey conjectured, and the mother would clean motel rooms. The cheerless family passed a dozen yellow kids without so much as a glance to or from, alternate realities inhabiting the same city without touching. Jack Liffey found he wanted to get out of the car and shout in one of the kids' faces, wake them up, introduce them to the migrant family, tell them a joke, make them read a book.

In his lap he read:

Level 2, Stage 5: Here the ego and the future Universal All-Soul come into conflict over the ego's wish to become fully present in its own life, but held back by the fear of lonely perception. Key: Door of true synapse speed. Wall structure: The Dark brick. Archetype: Dash runner. Physical body: All the animal traits of the region of soul-light. Modality: aural-oral repetition. Higher desires: Presence and dense touch. Lower desires: Breath. Elect guide: Socrates. Work goal: To take the first steps from the desire world to the Being World. Work tapes: Fulton Bell Lectures no. 321-329.

He read it a second time, but it didn't help much. He was haunted by the dull eyes of the kids, and he wondered if Theodelphia was onto anything at all—even idiots and con men caught on scraps of ideas. He knew from his own life, almost four years now of a kind of spiritual migrancy since his marriage and his old job had blown up in his face, that everyone lived in a kind of relationship to the catastrophe that could sweep over you at any moment, and all you could do about it was know where you stood facing the catastrophe, minute to minute, and if you tried to deny it and look away, it could swallow you up in such a paroxysm of grief and horror that nothing living would ever touch you again. So you pushed on with your life and did the best you could day to day, and in a poor light it passed for strength.

A boy was coming along the sidewalk toward the car and Jack Liffey rolled the window down. The boy was hardly twenty and his yellow tunic was permanently food-stained, as if it was the only one he had. A bad case of acne had left him scarred and shy. He glanced furtively at Jack Liffey watching him as he approached the old car.

"Don't drink the Kool-Aid," Jack Liffey said earnestly, and the boy glanced away and sped up half a step.

THIS time he drove into the Valley over Laurel Canyon. He thought he'd miss the worst of the commute traffic but a flatbed had apparently collided with a green Camaro convertible on one of the tighter curves and dumped three pianos onto the road. The drivers were shouting at each other over a shattered upright that was propping up a baby grand. Other cars had to eke past on the shoulders and a woman with long red hair was leaning far out of the mashed convertible and pounding away on the keyboard of the baby grand.

• • •

"**JIMMY'S** a California boy," she said, indicating the shelves built into the walls for sports equipment, a shorty surfboard, a bright blue snowboard, balls of various types, and an odd racket that he guessed was for something like lacrosse. He'd thought only rich kids at prep schools played lacrosse. For some reason, Faye Mardesich was wearing a baseball cap backward and when she had led him down the hall he read it: WHAT PART OF "BALL-BUSTING BITCH!" DON'T YOU UNDERSTAND?

The boy had the back room, on the far side of the house from his parents and away, too, from his dad's postmodern sanctum. They'd passed the father's den on the way and he'd glanced in at the piles and piles of books on the floor, each book dangling a limp tongue of a bookmark. As they'd contemplated the father's study, Faye Mardesich had remembered she was carrying a beer bottle for each of them, and she'd thrust one into his hand, but he'd managed to lose it along the way. It was too much trouble to explain that he didn't drink.

There was a CD player on a shelf of the boy's room and the usual CDs with the usual dark and riddling titles like Factory of Funk and Shrieking Death Angels. Jack Liffey's eye caught on one disc by a group called the Hot Bleeding Assholes. A lot had changed since his day and the Shirelles and Bell-Notes. His eye also caught on a black fielder's mitt, and he wondered when they'd started dying them black and why. It smelled right, though, that same oily animal aroma.

"He's not brainless, but he and his friends are afraid of being seen to know things, if you know what I mean." She held up a Game Boy player with something like contempt. "If I could only harness the hours he sat at the dinner table playing this beeping thing."

She took down a Van Nuys High School yearbook and thumbed through it while he poked at what passed for a desk. There was a laptop, but when he fired it up he couldn't find anything on it but games. A blue Post-it above the desk said *Marta Monday*. He put it in his pocket.

"Oh, man," Faye Mardesich said mournfully into the yearbook. "So much is the same, it really takes me back. We thought our problems were so gigantic back then. How were we supposed to know we were happy?"

"Are you happy now?"

She laughed softly. "I know I won't fall off the edge of the world if some handsome boy ignores me. I know pain goes away. I know things that I can do to entertain myself. That's as close to happy as anybody needs to get."

"Sounds okay to me," he said absently. He poked at a pile of discarded letters, shoved anyhow into a drawer, and pocketed a folded sheet of paper that was separate and caught his eye for some reason.

"Wish I could take that frame of reference back with me and do high school all over again," she said.

He pressed an ink stamp onto a scrap of paper. It was the number 88. The only thing he could think of was the metric caliber of a very fine antiaircraft cannon the Germans had made in World War II. He pocketed the 88, too.

"I know the boy I'd go after. That shy one, what was his name? Grant Ellis. He was always reading some book and staying off by himself. He seemed geeky to us then, but I'll bet he's a famous film director now, and he probably has a lot more interesting sex life than me, too."

"Maybe he's the kid who went up on the roof and started shooting the neighborhood dogs," Jack Liffey said. "Did Jimmy ever rebel or run away, cause you any trouble at all?"

She shook her head. "He was too *nice* ever to get mutinous. When Milo turned angry, Jimmy just got quiet and withdrawn around home." She waved one strong-looking arm, as if to erase that thought out of the air. "I don't mean Milo was Uncle Scrooge or anything. It just happened a few times, things getting to him. He'd snap out at me or Jimmy. I know it's hard being a man and not being able to provide."

No shit, he thought. Hard being anyone who couldn't take care of your loved ones. He noticed a book by the door and turned it over. It was Betty Friedan's *The Feminine Mystique*. "Do you think he's reading this?"

"Oh, that's mine. I must have left it the last time I was poking around in here. I'm in one of those consciousness groups, better late than never." There was a painful dependency in her tone that he noticed for the first time, under all that brusque assurance.

"Sure," he agreed.

"Here's his picture." She held the high-school annual flat and he leaned over to see a shock of hair like a question mark over the boy's forehead and a big grin, the kind of open smile that rarely made it past childhood. He was a handsome kid. She purposely pressed her shoulder against him, and he waited a moment before pulling away so he wouldn't seem skittish. A little flirtation he could always handle, but he began to wonder why he'd been hired and who had recommended him.

On the closet floor he found an old leg cast with a lot of names on it, a heap of sports shoes, and a box of old tape cassettes. He felt the shirt and pants pockets but found nothing.

"What's your next step?" she asked.

"I'll have to look it up in Chapter Three of *How to Be a Detective*."

"I saw that movie. Really, I'd like to know."

He shrugged. "Okay, you're paying. You're going to give me the names of some of his friends and classmates and I'm going to talk to them."

"Sounds good. Let's get started."

"Pardon me?"

"I'm coming along. Don't worry, I'll wait in the car if it'd cramp your style to have me listen while you're interviewing people." She seemed to be filling the door, as if he'd have to throw her a body block to get out of the room.

"Uh-uh. It doesn't work that way."

"Remember, I'm paying. Jack—can I call you Jack?"

"It's better than Veronica."

"I've been asleep for twenty years. You know what I mean? I quit college to support Milo through grad school. I took a class or two while Jimmy was growing up, but it wasn't the way I figured my life would go. I wanted it *all*, I wanted to *do* it, not just hear about it. The first week Jimmy was gone, this thing was giving me a serious case of the bads, but then I just told myself I wasn't going to let it go until it blesses me. Jimmy's not in that much danger, not really. He's probably just shacked up with one of those poor girls the Theodelphians use to get their hooks into their converts. See, that's what you were keeping from me, isn't it? I know who those creeps are. I can *use* this thing to help Jimmy and me both. I can feel it, it's a kick start for my life, and I'm going along with you for the ride. I pay, I come along—that's the rules." She set her fists on her hips and he found the determination made her strangely attractive in that way confidence always does.

"I think I ought to double the fee," he said. He didn't like it a bit, but he needed the money. "Did you have any strange phone calls today? Guys hanging around the house?"

"No, and you can't scare me off."

"The guys I'm thinking about will take care of scaring you all by themselves," he said.

She grinned. "Just think, if we run into bad guys, there's two of us, and we can play good-cop bad-cop."

"What the hell is a good cop?" he said.

In the car he opened the sheet of paper he'd palmed out of the boy's desk drawer. It was written in a scrawly boy's hand.

*The only people for me are the mad ones, the ones
who are mad to live, mad to talk, mad to be saved,
desirous of everything at the same time, the ones
who never yawn or say a commonplace thing, but
burn, burn, burn like fabulous yellow roman can-
dles exploding like spiders across the stars.*

It seemed familiar and he read it a second time before
he recognized it. Kerouac, talking about Neal Cassidy—
or Dean Moriarty—somewhere early in the book. He
was surprised kids still read *On the Road,* and even more
surprised that the boy would take the trouble to write
out the passage in his own hand.

He wondered if Jimmy Mardesich was embarked on
what Kerouac had called the Holy Boy Road. If he was,
his mother might not be able to get him back as easily
as she seemed to think. He'd be too busy burn, burn,
burning like a Roman candle or something.

3

TOO MUCH BELIEF

PERRY MUTH SAT ON THE FRONT EDGE OF THE SOFA THE
way big guys did when they pretty much wanted to be
somewhere else. His bulk cut deeply into the gold pillows. "Mom, *please.*"

The thin woman hovered in the doorway holding a
big flour-dusted wooden spoon like a scepter, rapping it
absently on a knuckle to give off little white puffs. She
looked like a goddess setting up to make some decision
that would alter worlds. "We don't have any secrets in
this family," she said imperiously.

Oh, yes we do, the boy's eyes said. He was handsome
in a wholesome-looking all-American way, with blue-
green eyes and a square jaw, and he wore a jacket with
white leather sleeves and a big VN patch on it. Jack
Liffey was glad to see they still had letterman jackets,
though he wasn't quite sure why. He'd never had
enough of a stake in the way things were back that far
to want very hard for them to stay the same.

"If you could just tell me the last time you saw
Jimmy."

Things had gone strange from the first, with Faye
Mardesich striding up to the front door with him, blinking as the porch light came on and introducing him to
the family, and then offering no rationale at all for her
retreat to the car.

"Practice last Thursday, after school. He's offense and

I'm defense, and guys from the two squads don't usually hang together, but Jimmy and me did. You know, offensive players are your uptight kind of guys. They always want to keep things neat and all in order, and we're a lot more hang-loose." He grinned. "We like to bust things up. That's what defense is all about, messing up the neat lineups and things. Anyway, right after practice Jimmy told me he and his girl had a fight and he was going over to NoHo to see her and straighten it out."

"What's Noho?"

"Would you like some juice, Mr. Liffey? As a good Mormon family, we can't offer you anything stronger."

She hadn't budged and didn't really seem to be offering him anything to drink. Probably it was just her oblique way of trying to nose out if he was a good Mormon, too, or a good anything. He was beginning to see why the boy liked to bust things up.

"No thanks."

"NoHo's over in North Hollywood. They tried to make this arty area, you know like SoHo or whatever in New York. Most of it's pretty lame but there's some places you can go."

"Where would Jimmy go?"

"Jill hangs at a girls' coffeehouse called the Broom Closet."

"What's Jill's last name?"

"Annunziata."

"Was anything bothering Jimmy in the last few weeks?"

The boy thought about it for a while, visibly torn between talking and not talking. Jack Liffey made a mental note to find him again when Mom was absent. "I think it was pretty hard to miss that he and Jill were going off on different paths."

"What paths were those?"

He was like a dog out at the end of a taut chain, but still a few inches from the bone. "I'm not sure."

The mother stirred again. "You haven't gone drinking with Jimmy Mardesich, have you?"

"No." A tiny thrill of rebellion seemed to seize the boy, wholly against his will. "Drinking isn't the worst thing in the world, Mother. If Charlie Manson's family was LDS, you'd probably worry about him poisoning his body with stimulants."

She came a step into the small living room, but apparently decided this wasn't the time for a real showdown. "Stimulants and disobedience may have been the start of all that evil behavior, how do we know? You have to be respectful of your body."

"Yes, ma'am."

"Does this mean anything to you?" Jack Liffey showed him the paper with the number 88 on it.

A cloud crossed the boy's face. He threatened rain but couldn't let it happen. "Huh-uh."

"Who's Marta?"

"She's a friend of Jill's."

"Why do you think Jimmy would have a note to call her or see her?"

He shrugged his big defensive lineman's shoulders. "Maybe he was trying to get her to talk to Jill for him."

"Do you think Jill would be at the Broom Closet tonight?"

"Sure, probably. It's over on Lankersheim. I can show you."

"No, sir," his mother said emphatically. "You have homework to do here, young man."

The boy thought about it for a moment before succumbing. Jack Liffey could see that the power arrangements in this family were due for a big change soon. He was amazed the mother couldn't see it, too, and opt for a small mid-course adjustment before it was too late. Perry Muth looked like a good kid, but you could never tell where an adolescent would spin off the merry-go-round if he was driven to take the leap. Maybe this was the one who'd spin up into city hall tower and start shooting the clerks. He was the nicest boy, the neighbors all said.

"I want to thank you for talking to me." He left one of his cards, printed up by Marlena a year earlier in a burst of optimism about his business. Outside Faye was standing on the far side of his car, smoking a skinny pastel cigarette. It gave him a pang. He dreamed now and again that he'd started smoking again, which filled the dream with waves of guilt and humiliation.

"I didn't know you smoked."

"I gave up years ago, but all this has brought it back." She grinned. "It's like meeting up with an old lover for a forbidden fling. What did you learn?"

"That kids get pissed off if you don't treat them with respect."

"You just now learned that?"

"Everything gets harder to remember."

FAYE directed him east along Magnolia and they passed a small knot of picketers in front of what looked like a warehouse, strutting in and out of the yellow funnels of the streetlights. The signs said things like PORNOGRAPHY EXPLOITS WOMEN and THE BODY IS THE TEMPLE OF YOUR SPIRIT, distant echoes of Perry Muth's mother. One tall sign carried aloft by a minister pointed the wrong way to read. But Jack Liffey's eye was drawn to a woman in a flesh-colored body stocking with black lingerie over it. She carried a sign that said FUCK ME—I'M A SLUT. A more matronly woman beside her carried a pink plastic dildo the size of a fire hydrant. He couldn't quite work out the point of view of the demonstrators, but he did know this area was called Porn Alley, the center of the blue film industry for the whole country.

"Land sakes," Faye said as they passed.

"You can say that again."

"Land sakes." She laughed. "Sorry, I couldn't resist. Every once in a while you get bushwhacked by the peculiar in this old town."

"My daughter and I trade examples we find of L.A. oddity. It's a sort of game."

"How old's your daughter?"

"Thirteen in a month. She lives with her mom but I see her as much as I can."

"I hope she turns out okay for you. I never used to worry about Jimmy going bad. I worried about him feeling inadequate because he tried so hard and just couldn't get As, but he didn't have a single nutty gene anywhere in his DNA." There was a moment of quiet. "Now I'm worrying a bit."

"I know what you mean. There's just too much *random* in the world."

"You hit the nail right on the head."

Magnolia was one of those commercial wastelands that festered out along the big L.A. thoroughfares, constantly in nondescript transition from something to something else. Atlas World Famous Sausages was next door to Gurjian Rug Cleaners, and then Mr. Radiator/Señor Radiadores, Greenglow Hydroponic Vegetables, Abbarotes Tijuanas, the Great Wall Bar with the Institute of Paralegal and Metaphysics upstairs, Cash for Your Car bedecked with colored pennants and big dollar bills, Golden Touch Fire and Motoring Advice, a weedy lot with a big billboard that said STILL GUILTY, and then a welter of color called Almost Humanoid Pottery. When he drove past a liquor store, prosaically named Art's Liquor, it was a mercy.

"Random," she said, "is what's preying on me. Random killers and random muggers and random this and that."

They passed the Bahia Caporales, Joey's Tattoos and Truck Lettering, a little theater doing Neil Simon's *Chapter Two,* and a fern bar called Molly's Toucan Play That Game. Just random places.

THIS time she was coming in, too, but separately, and after she'd agreed to give him a ten-minute head start.

The Broom Closet was a coffeehouse and bookstore that exuded the New Age through every pore, like righteous indignation. He slid in past a skinny dark woman with green hair browsing the bookshelves at the door who excused herself and duckwalked out of his way rather than be touched. Just inside was a big sign that said AN YE HARM NONE, DO WHAT YE WILL. The walls were lavender where they weren't covered with wavery watercolors of women blessing someone just out of frame. Display cases of trinkets sat around for browsers, but no one was browsing. A dozen women chatted away at round tables, mostly in long dresses with a lot of jewelry. The woman at the coffee counter thought about it for a moment before pointing out Jill Annunziata, who was sitting with two older women sipping what was undoubtedly bat-wing tea.

She had Big Hair, jet-black and shiny and plumped out to the sides as if hit by sheet lightning, and her face was so regular and sharp-featured and beautiful it hurt your eyes. She wore turquoise on an overlarge plaque suspended around her neck and on every finger, and she had a calm about her that seemed to infect the other two women, who banked a little this way and that as she talked to them. She saw him coming across the room and took them all to silence with some gesture so small he couldn't make it out. A New Age noise began to wail softly from a sound system, like a sinus being rasped away.

"You're looking for Jimmy," she pronounced, before he could introduce himself.

Of course, he thought, what else would a fiftyish male be doing there? But he could see she liked to play at omniscience. "Am I going to bark like a dog when you snap your fingers?" he said.

She waited a long time, on the edge of a smile. "We don't play tricks like that," she said equably after he had been made to wait a suitable stretch. "Please sit down."

"But we could, couldn't we?"

Jill Annunziata dismissed the other two, but so politely and so subtly that they seemed happy to leave.

"Everything you think you know about Wicca, what you call witchcraft, is wrong."

"I think it's a way of insulating yourself from misogamy and male authoritarianism and also staying well away from the fixation on guilt that informs most Christian faiths."

She did smile, and he almost had to look away. "Well, maybe not *everything*. But you're still on the other side."

"My insolence is just a bad habit. I don't really make fun of anyone's faith to their face."

"And in private?"

"In private I never stop laughing," he said.

Her face had returned to its neutral gaze. Her eyes looked amused, but the rest of her wasn't ready to sign on.

"Just imagine a God who wants a lot of people to troop into a big room and sing His praises for hours on end," he said. "Would *you* want that? I can't imagine a God who's that much more vain than I am."

She laughed easily and a waitress, or acolyte, brought strong black coffee, which was just what he wanted without actually ordering it. Of course.

"The word *wicca* is really the same as the common English word *witch* and it traces to an Indo-European root that means to bend or change. We try to bend the sad and cruel around us. In general, we're life-affirming. We try to stay in touch with the divinity that exists all around us in nature and science, in wind and mountains and bodies of water, and some of us believe we can change our own consciousness by using ritual and our own willpower plus herbs and a positive frame of mind. If we align ourselves with the most likely paths people's lives may take, we may even be able to influence others or alter events. We believe that whatever you do comes back to you threefold, so we wouldn't want to do anything dark or angry. No one I know believes in anything like a being such as Satan. Does that ease your mind?"

"My mind is just fine." He sipped the coffee. It was
dark, burned, and strong, and he liked it. The women at
the next table were slowly laying out tarot cards and
overdoing their responses. They were too emotional, too
underlined, outsized. That's what a man would think, he
thought.

"Are you a policeman?"

"I'm just a poor agnostic who looks for missing children."

"You're a cult deprogrammer."

"Not that either. I've never made anyone go anywhere
against their will. Jimmy's mother asked me to try to
find him and find out if he's okay, that's all. Can you
tell me where he went?"

"Are you asking if I *know* it, as you mean knowledge,
or if I can divine it?"

"I'll settle for what you have. I'm not finicky about
epistemology."

From somewhere she had brought out a small glass
vial of amber-colored liquid and she toyed with it absently with one manicured hand. Her filmy dress rippled
with every move.

"I don't know where he is, but he's all right. He's a
high-minded person."

"Did you have a fight when you last saw him?"

It was the first frown he'd seen on her face and the
effect was startling, giving him a sudden heartache, as
if his big clumsy paw had bruised something helpless.

"He was upset because he wanted to test the waters
in my covenant for himself. I had to tell him he wasn't
really ready. He wasn't. He was full of confusion and
anger at his father, amongst other things."

"Other things?"

She shrugged.

"He didn't threaten anything or say where he was going?"

In the corner of his eye he saw Faye come in and

browse the magazines. The stretchy top that she wore looked as out of place as a zebra on Wilshire Boulevard.

Jill Annunziata sighed. "He said he would show me he was ready. I honestly don't know what he meant. I don't read minds. My beliefs may seem quaint to you, Mister . . ."

"Jack Liffey."

"Mr. Jack Liffey, but I don't engage in trickery. In what we call the Burning Time, they killed tens of thousands of decent women just like me for trying to worship and heal in their own way. We're just thankful that Pat Robertson and the pope no longer have that kind of power."

He saw Faye drift to the coffee counter and begin talking to the woman there.

He showed Jill Annunziata the "88." "Do you know what this is?"

She grimaced. "If it's his, it's only a joke."

"But you know what it is."

He could tell that she really didn't want to say, but she seemed to decide it would be worse not to. "*H* is the eighth letter of the alphabet. The '88' stands for 'Heil Hitler.' There's a handful of skinheads at school who bought ink stamps like that and went around stamping things. They're just sad, unloved boys. Jimmy isn't like that and he had nothing to do with them. If anything, he probably took it away from someone."

"Would I find Marta here?"

"Marta Rodriguez?"

He didn't reply.

"No, you wouldn't."

"Is there some coffeehouse that specializes in her religion?"

Her smile threatened to return. "Quite a few of them. She's Catholic." She got out an ordinary address book and gave him Marta's phone number. Across the room Faye Mardesich was in animated conversation with the two women who had been sitting with Jill. The wailing music broke off and a hypnotic drumming started up.

Jill Annunziata leaned across the table without warning and dragged her forefinger lightly across his forehead to leave a trail of musky scent from her vial.

"I hope that doesn't turn me into a frog."

This time the smile broke through the clouds. "It's musk and rose and cherry. They're all oils that relate to love. You will look more warmly on every woman you see tonight, and if you are open to it, you will fall in love and marry one of them."

"I predict that a girl who looks like you is going to get in a lot of trouble rubbing love potion on men my age."

"Blessed be."

HE waited outside on Lankersheim, watching the sporadic traffic. All of a sudden he noticed a sooty homeless man up the street who stood with his feet set wide in a planter in front of a dentist's office. His craggy face was so filthy he looked like he'd just ridden a tramcar out of a coal mine, and he was hurling blades of ice plant torn from the planter at the passing cars. Now and again a driver stopped and got out and glared, but saw the tattered clothes and dirt-encrusted hands and decided there was nothing to be gained by picking a fight. Jack Liffey eased his way up the block to talk to the man.

"What's up, man?"

"I testify there is nothing anyone can do against me in the flesh!"

"Is somebody trying to hurt you?"

"I set myself against them all, every one! They can't harm me!"

"They'll harm you, old man, if you keep throwing things."

He hurled another stalk, but it skimmed harmlessly across the pavement ahead of a Toyota four-wheeler.

"Can you make a finger?" Jack Liffey asked, and he

demonstrated, thrusting his middle finger angrily at the Toyota.

The old man watched him, fascinated.

"Come on, *curse* them. You're all *bastards*!"

The old man worked one hand into the proper gesture with his other hand, tugging the fingers into position one by one as if he had arthritis. He kept glancing at Jack Liffey as a model.

"Bastards!" Jack Liffey shouted at an MTA bus that rumbled past.

The old man took up the shout, too. "Bastards! Make your plans for my internal organs, will you! Take me to hospital, gang up on me! *Bastards*!"

"You can't touch us! You're all swine!"

"Swine! Swine!" the old man picked up.

A woman in a Volvo looked at the two men gesturing wildly at her car and quickly looked away as she accelerated.

Jack Liffey walked back to his car with a smile of satisfaction. He sat on the front fender to wait for Faye as the old man carried on whooping and gesturing at the traffic. The night was warm and airless and Jack Liffey smelled musk and fruit on the air, then realized it was steaming off his own forehead. He wiped a sleeve across the perfume brand. Luckily it wasn't a homeless *woman* in the planter, he thought. He'd have had to marry her.

Faye Mardesich finally came out carrying a paperback book. She heard the commotion and watched the old man cursing and waving his middle fingers at the street.

"I taught him that," Jack Liffey said equably.

She caught a whiff of something and leaned closer to him, sniffing the air. "You smell like condensed sex. Just add hot water."

He rubbed again. "It'll do until the real thing comes along. What have you bought?"

They got into the car and shut out the old man's howling. Jack Liffey glanced at the title of the book she held.

Craft and Rite, a misty drawing of Stonehenge on the cover.

She scowled. "I thought it might tell me something about them, but it probably won't. Do you ever feel there's too much belief in the air? It's like a big toxic spill of wishes and notions. The bottom falls out of Pandora's box and everybody's grabbed onto something, just whatever fell nearby, and everybody's waving these notions at each other like that old wino until you can't hear yourself think."

"We've probably had enough detecting for one night," he said, and he U-turned back up Lankersheim. He waved at the old man as he passed. The old man gave him the finger with both hands.

4

IF YOU LIVED HERE, YOU'D BE HOME NOW

IT WAS AFTER MIDNIGHT, AND AS USUAL A FEW KIDS WERE still hanging out in the courtyard, sitting on the retaining walls and laughing languidly in the blood-warm night as one of them bounced a basketball. The air was so heavy even the feathery bottlebrushes behind them were motionless. He'd seen most of these kids around but he didn't know any of them by name.

" 'S up," one of them offered as he passed, a rare tribute to an old white guy.

"Not much," he said. He could have come up with a swifter reply, but it might have been seen as getting competitive and there was no percentage in that.

"A couple a your homies was in to visit, cuz."

He stopped. "You mean into my house?"

"Uh-huh. Your Mexican lady let them in."

His blood froze. "When was this?"

"Couple hours, it didn't look like nothing."

"Did one of them have red hair?"

"Ye-eah. Like a real enough jarhead."

"Thanks."

Jack Liffey slipped into his alcove and listened. No dog, no radio, just the steady *thut-thut* of the basketball behind him and a car alarm cycling through its warnings far away. He thought of going back to ask if any of the boys was packing, but there wasn't much chance they'd own up to it.

He stared glumly at his front door. This was the second time this week he'd come home on something unexpected, and the odds were bound to get him sooner or later. Once again he noted that it was easier to keep your routine and risk death than make a scene. He knew perfectly well you had to live with the results when things didn't go right, that was the deal.

He let himself in and immediately heard a scrabbling from the back, like a playing card in the spokes. A light was on in the bedroom.

"Mar," he called.

The bike speeded up and became erratic, dog claws on a door.

"Shut up, Loco, I'll get to you."

For some reason, his Mennen Speed Stick lay on the floor of the hallway with its plastic cap off and crushed underfoot.

"Mar!" he called again.

The claws grew frantic on the closed bathroom door as he eased down the hall toward where the light was on. He pushed the door open slowly to see Marlena on the floor with her back against the bed, her wrists handcuffed awkwardly beside her to the bed frame. She was gagged with silver duct tape and what looked like a wad of his favorite blue shirt. There was shock in her eyes and something was wrong with her complexion.

The instant he pulled off the gag, an exhaled sob set her heaving and bucking and made whatever she was trying to say incomprehensible. He clasped her and held on through the worst of the ride, wriggling himself around to find a comfortable position.

"Shhh, shhh, Marlena. It's okay now. I'm here. Shh."

He hadn't checked the living room or the closets but she wasn't behaving like someone with assailants still in the house. He was overwhelmed by a sicky-sweet smell and then he saw they had swabbed his deodorant all over her face. When he pulled back a little, he smelled cigarette smoke and ash, too, and he saw someone had smoked one of the cigarettes that he left lying around and stubbed it out into the carpet. He hadn't touched tobacco for years, but he left cigarettes around because he enjoyed the ascetic buzz he got out of beating the temptation day after day.

"Jack, it was *horrible*! They said they were friends. I opened up for them." He wiped gently at her face with the shirt that had been used to gag her. Little flakes and chunks from the Speed Stick clung to her cheeks.

"It's okay. They're gone."

"How did you make them so *mad*?" she asked, and there was an undertow of blame, as if he'd purposely set them on her.

"I don't know."

"They said you do," she complained. "They said to leave it alone."

They always say that, he thought. "I don't know who they were, Mar. Really. Did they say anything else?"

"Only a foreign name, Ethel something I think. The one with red hair said it to the other one."

"Did they hurt you?"

She nodded, then shook her head as if overcome by the strictest of scruples. "It was more like making fun of me."

"Why did they use the deodorant?"

"I don't know. They pushed it against me hard. They joked about my breasts and kept asking if they were real or chemicals but they didn't do nothing to me but touch."

"I'll be right back," he said. "We've got to get those cuffs off."

He kept his tools in a storage closet off his patio. He unlocked the door and dug around in the mess until he came up with a big red bolt cutter with three-foot arms. It made short work of padlocks and would probably work on the handcuffs, though he'd noticed they were a good pair of Peerless, the kind the police used.

Loco was still scratching away when he came back.

The inside of the bathroom door would be a mess, he thought, but dogs had to wait. That was just the way it was. He didn't have time to deal with the displaced aggression that opening the door would unleash.

"Lean forward, Mar."

One powerful bite of the bolt cutter severed the three-link chain between the cuffs, and she brought her arms around front and slumped to one side.

"Let's see a wrist."

It was a good-quality stainless steel and wouldn't give up without a fight. They'd snugged it tight and he was a bit worried the loop might deform and cut her when it broke.

"I'm scared."

He picked a point of attack and rotated the cuff so the hinge point was away from her wrist artery. Resting one arm of the bolt cutter on the floor, he put all his weight on the other arm and suddenly the tempered jaws bit through the cuff with an audible *clack* and the metal fell away. She wasn't as lucky on the second one and ended up with a blood blister where a bit of skin was pinched.

She fell against him to hug his neck. "I want you to know they didn't spoil me."

"Mar—"

"No. They didn't, they just touched me."

"Mar, nobody can *spoil* anybody. If one of those jerks picked up . . ." He looked around and saw a Wallace Stegner on his night table. "Say that book. It's a good book. If he sat there and read it, it wouldn't *spoil* the book. I'd still like it."

"I'm not a book. I know how men think. My father sent me away when a guy spoiled me the first time."

"I know that story, but you don't begin to know how I think." And he didn't really want to deal with her sad story just then. Her father was a poor disoriented immigrant who'd grown up in a Sonoran village and couldn't really handle a world that was so much more complicated than his own father's farm, and he had driven her out of the family bungalow in Baldwin Park at fifteen and straight back to the biker who'd already taken what he could get, and then the biker had passed her around to his friends, and she'd learned to live with a particularly gruesome form of self-loathing until a cousin had taken her in and started restoring her to the human race. Jack Liffey took her face in both his hands. "What you have inside you can't ever be spoiled. That's the absolute truth."

She took his hand and placed it against her breast.

"Do you still want me?"

"Yes, of course I do."

"Come to my house tonight. I can't stay here."

He wasn't really in the mood, but he could see it was going to happen, whatever he wanted, so he worked up enough enthusiasm to kiss her, and she kissed back hungrily.

"As soon as we feed Loco."

"**WHAT** you laughing at?"

He pointed. He'd burst out laughing the moment he read it, lit by the orange street lamp at the corner. Neat sans serif lettering on the back of the bench spelled out IF YOU LIVED HERE YOU'D BE HOME NOW. He didn't know whether it was political commentary on the homeless by one of the city's guerrilla artists, or just a teasing ad ploy for something incongruous, like the billboards an L.A. magazine had once put up hawking drive-through high colonics. A lot of people had taken them seriously, trying to figure how it was done.

"I don't understand." She whisked her lap, as if she'd spilled ashes on her skirt.

"It's just the absurdity, I guess."

"You can't live on a bus bench," she complained.

People try, he thought. "No, you can't, you're right." He liked her quite a lot most of the time, but their worlds didn't overlap by much and that made it hard sometimes. "How's your wrist?"

"It hurts." She was aggrieved for some reason, and it made him feel helplessly insensitive.

HE walked gingerly, trying not to bump into a dog of some kind, the big flocked red ones on the floor from TJ, little porcelain poodles on the Danish Modern coffee table, plastic head-bobbing toys meant for the car window, stuffed-rag dalmatians, and a set of handblown glass Afghans like the ones you saw made at the crafts fair. Marlena liked dogs. There was even a real one, of sorts, a mewling Mexican hairless named Fidel. There had been three, but Raul had got distemper because his shots hadn't taken for some reason and Che had been run over by a Sparkletts truck.

Jack Liffey was happy he was wearing black shoes. The randy little Fidel invariably tried to mount his brown shoes.

"Would you get yourself some ginger ale, Jackito. I got to get ready some."

"Hi, there, Comrade," he said to Fidel, who was panting a mile a minute and eyeing his shoes, apparently unconvinced of their color. The dog yipped once and backed off all of a sudden, probably getting a whiff of Loco. The minute Marlena left the room, the dog went up to her sofa, lifted a leg, and sprayed it with a few drops, then fixed Jack Liffey with a stare, as if daring him to rat. "Whoa, little fella. Looks like you and I have something in common." It was a point of honor in his life to challenge only what could hurt him, and he could see a bit of that ethos in the tiny canine, too, and he liked the dog a lot better for it.

"Never forget that dog is god spelled backward," he said equably.

He bent to pet the dog, but Fidel yipped once and hurried off. Jack Liffey found a big ginger ale in the fridge and some ice and poured one for her, too. A memory of exquisite lovemaking was beginning to work on him. She still carried a lot of guilt about her sexuality, and she'd usually slam one foot all the way down on the gas and keep the other hard on the brake, and that made it all spectacular, somehow.

He leafed through a big picture book on dogs on the coffee table and learned that two dogs with well-defined territories would exhibit what was called "agonistic behavior" when they met on their boundaries. They'd turn their flanks to one another, offering neither to fight nor flee, a kind of posture of armed truce that entailed the least likelihood of attack. He wondered if it was possible for him to work out some kind of agonistic deal with fate. He'd like to approach the front door of his condo without worrying who had been there, or was still there, and once in a while he'd like to pass a dark doorway without feeling compelled to shout a challenge into the darkness.

She came in wearing mesh nylons, a black garter belt, some kind of complex semitransparent merry widow arrangement on top, and nothing else. "You like me?"

"Oh, yes," he said. It was all so earnest and calculated that he had a little trouble not being amused.

"Is this equipment all new?"

"I been keeping it for you. It's not for nobody else."

Luckily his tenderness took over and he started getting aroused as she cupped the underside of her breasts.

"You want me to do a strip for you? I do anything you want for you, Jackito."

"That's very sweet," he said. He felt stupid and confused and a little alarmed by her intensity, but they were both grown-ups, and if he didn't feel completely and overwhelmingly in love, she wasn't asking him for that. There it is, he thought—he could confront a scruple and dispose of it as decisively as anyone.

"I guess I'd better change my brand of deodorant," he said. He sat up on the edge of the four-poster bed and pulled on a T-shirt, but he could see she wasn't ready for jokes about what had happened to her. He felt a need to shift gears. He wanted to shake the feeling that he had just taken advantage of a woman he didn't quite love enough, at least in the big scheme of things. But you never got to live in the big scheme of things, he thought. You lived in the right now, and the right now was always full of adjustments, and properly adjusted, he did like Marlena quite a lot.

He touched her cheek and she pressed into his palm.

"You said they used a name like Ethel."

"Uh-huh. It was strange, maybe it wasn't a name."

"Would you remember if you heard it again?"

"I don't think so."

"Maybe Ethel Somebody is the Aimee Semple McPherson of her day. She's founded one of these new religions that we're all drowning in," he said, and saying it changed something, left him feeling as if he was falling through a crust into a different place and being forced to notice the difference.

"They scared me."

"I don't know what it was all about, Mar."

HE parked up the road from the big yellow toyland of the Theodelphian Elect and watched a guy in cowboy black, like Johnny Cash or Roy Orbison, including the ten-gallon hat, walking along Melrose digging coins out of the fringed leather pouch at his waist and feeding the parking meters. Meter after meter he went, like Millet's Sower, seeding each one with a little pivot at the waist, a poke with a quarter, a twist of the knob, and then on to the next. Jack Liffey had heard of him, Johnny Meterman, bane of the parking enforcement corporation, but he'd always thought he was a myth. Go go go, he rooted. It made perfect sense, and it was one of the few vocations he'd ever seen that did.

"You wanted to be dealt in," he said to Faye Mardesich. "All you have to do is go in the reception center and tell them you're lost and you want to be found. You can play lost, can't you?"

She started laughing, stepped it up a pitch, and then had a little trouble climbing off. "How little you know, tough guy."

"You think I'm a tough guy?"

"Ooo-la-la. Don't disabuse me, all right? I need that strength. Jack, I *am* lost. It's just that other women my age go bats and don't even know it's happening until some bartender shakes them awake at two A.M. You know what it means to be supported and have nothing of your own? I am the original soccer mom, and now Jimmy doesn't even need me. I didn't used to be stupid, I used to think I was smarter than Milo, but your brain goes to mush if you don't use it."

She looked at her hands for a bit. He didn't really want to hear this, but she was paying.

"One by one, all the things you're supposed to get comfort from fail you. It's like being in a peewee-league version of Chekhov. Everybody's unhappy and nobody gets what they want and nobody knows what's going on."

"Nobody ever gets just what they want, Faye."

"Yeah, I know. Some people do okay settling for third or fourth best. Maybe that's all wisdom is."

A yellow Cadillac pulled up and turned in, its bow wave opening a channel among the kids in the yellow cadet suits who were flowing into the courtyard of the Theodelphian compound. The windows were smoked.

"You know what starts getting you, Mr. Tough Guy? It's when the box boys at the supermarket don't even look at you anymore. You're not even worth a mental undressing."

She seemed plenty tough and self-possessed to him.

"So, yeah, I can play like I'm lost."

"I'm convinced. If you turn out to want to stay in that place until light rays come out of your eyes, just give me a sign and I'll stay out of it."

She snorted. "The day I believe in crap like that you can tie my tail to the old oak tree."

The marquee had changed and now said: "THE SCI-
ENCE OF THE THIRD HEAVEN BEGINS WHERE MATERIAL
SCIENCE LEAVES OFF." —DL. He wondered if they
changed the sign every day, and then he wondered what
had gone wrong with the first two heavens.

"There's a coffee shop up on Santa Monica. Wingo's.
I'll meet you there at noon. That ought to give you time
to find out what they do with new initiates."

"Are you going in, too?"

"You could say that."

HE watched Faye Mardesich storm away from the car
with a fierce sense of mission, and he wondered how on
earth she was going to convince anyone she was a helpless waif. But that was her problem. He was going inside
the compound, too, and that was going to be *their* problem. Handcuffing Marlena to his bed—the thought put
him into a slow cold fury and he knew he wouldn't let
up now until he'd evened the score.

He opened the trunk and got out a greasy jumpsuit
that he used whenever he had to lean over the engine
and wiggle wires until it started. He contorted himself
around in the front seat to put it on and cinch it up over
his street clothes. The painters working on the front of
a 99-Cent store up the street had gone on coffee break
somewhere and he picked up their stepladder and carried
it toward the yellow compound.

A young Latino in the guard shack eyed him as he
turned in.

Jack Liffey nodded. "The big guy needs his frammis
fixed."

The guard shrugged back and Jack Liffey joined a
couple of yellow cadets heading for the big lagoon in
the middle of the compound.

"You gotta keep incarnating until you feel the burn,"
one of them said.

"Yeah, I guess that's the signification."

Verily, Jack Liffey thought. If you lived here, you'd
be home now.

5

ROOM 101

HE PICKED OUT AN INNOCENT-LOOKING GIRL IN THE HALL-
way. "Hey, where's the big guy's office?"

"You mean Hedrick?" Her eyes went wide, like a
young deer in the headlights.

"Uh-huh."

"He's on band three."

"I don't know my way. Show me."

She peeked at her wristwatch as a bell rang and other
cadets streamed past—the place reminding him more
and more of a junior high school. "I only got five
minutes before my level-ten impression."

She had a round unformed face and pouty lips, and
reluctantly she beckoned and led him up a dank stairwell
where he had to maneuver the ladder around the turns.
A paint can would have been a lot more convenient
prop.

"Been here long?"

"A couple months."

"You know my pal Jimmy M?"

"I only know the girls. I'm not past the Archetype of
Forms yet."

"Oh, sure."

"It's just up to the top and to the right. I got to go."
She slid past him and fled down the stairwell.

"Have a nice day," he called. At the top, he poked
into a room filled with people sitting at tables with head-

phones on. Now and again one of them pushed a button on a console. If they'd been talking back he'd have figured it was a language lab, but there was no provision for talking back.

"Have a nice day," he said again, but no one looked up.

There was a big alcove off the end of the hall with a couple of ordinary-looking secretaries typing away. He cocked his head at the door between them. "That Hedrick's?"

An olive-skinned secretary nodded. "That haircut doesn't suit you," she said.

"I can't afford haircuts," he said. "You must be a worrier."

"I am. Are we repainting? Goodman didn't tell me."

"It must have slipped his mind." He shouldered open the door and walked straight into an office the size of a retail store with a half-dozen windows to the outside. The only furniture was gaudy pillows arranged in little shoals here and there, like the conversation pits they'd inflicted on upscale suburban homes in the sixties. One little clique of pillows was occupied by a large bald man in a bright yellow robe surrounded by telephones and laptop computers with their screens up. He looked up as Jack Liffey set the stepladder down, a man in his late forties with every bit of hair shaved off him, even the eyebrows.

The secretary had come in behind. "Mr. Hedrick, are we painting?"

Hedrick held up a palm and something about the gesture dismissed her. She backed out and shut the door. The light glistened off the top of the man's shaved head.

"The only sin is ignorance," the man said evenly. He had a smile that was probably meant to be beatific, but Jack Liffey saw it as smug, the kind of look you put on when you knew you were holding way more than enough aces. His voice had a weird baritone edge to it that did not sound quite natural. "All sorrow, suffering, and pain are traceable to ignorance of how to act."

It was offered like a formula greeting, and he guessed it was a small test of how you would react. "Except toothache," Jack Liffey said. "Knowing how to bite doesn't really help very much."

The smile broadened slightly. "You're not a painter, are you?"

"No."

"Have a seat. Please. You may wish me harm but you will find that only those who wish to be harmed can be."

He wasn't there to argue or he might have mentioned six million or so Jews who probably hadn't wished to be harmed. Jack Liffey wondered what the man knew, or thought he knew, about his interloper. He sat as best he could, wincing at his stiffness. He folded his legs under and found himself sideways a bit, resting a hand on a small pillow.

Hedrick held a palm in front of his face parallel to the ground as if describing the height of an elf. His hand was rock steady. "I could do that for a week," he said.

"Good for you."

"The first time I taught myself stillness it was for long-range reconnaissance patrols. In I Corps."

"Marines," Jack Liffey said. *"Fuck that."*

"You were there, too, but you weren't a marine."

"Just a lowly E-4 technician in the draft army."

The man set the palm flat on the ground in front of him and leaned gradually over it and kept going until his legs were straight out behind him and his neck was extended and his elbow formed a lever that held him up so that only the single palm touched the ground. There was only the slightest trembling. The one-hand gymnastic stand was impressive in such a big man, probably impressive in anyone.

"Nine-point-nine," Jack Liffey said. "Performance *and* degree of difficulty." Somewhere deep in the building people were chanting.

"Even during life in the dense body, we are in contact

with the invisible world at every moment of our existence." There was no strain apparent in his voice. "In
fact, the invisible is the real and permanent world."

"Goodman Hedrick," Jack Liffey tested the name, as
if a careful enunciation would reveal a new meaning.
"That sounds like the name of somebody in charge of
the Salem witch trials."

The man righted himself slowly and breathed deeply
a few times. The only flaw in the picture came from a
tiny film of perspiration at his temple. He patted at it
with a small pillow. "Goodman Hedrick was the name
of one of the early Theodelphian Elect. According to
our incomplete records, he lived in the second half of
the eighteenth century. He discarded his mind envelope
and I took it up two hundred years later to encapsulate
my vital persons."

Now Jack Liffey recognized him. It was the context
that had thrown him, but the shiny handsome bald face
was unmistakable. He had read the man up in a Sunday
magazine years ago, one of a long line of Westerners
who'd passed through the flame of Indian culture and
come out thinking he was an avatar of something or
other and then come home to gather a cult around him.
"You're Baba Ambu," Jack Liffey said, "and you had a
big ashram up in the hills above Malibu."

"And I am Tom Clayton, mendicant in Asia. I wandered from one end of India to another, seeking escape
from the shame of the things that I had done and seen
done or just let pass without stopping them. Before that
I was Captain Tom L. Clayton, U.S. Marine Corps, assassin. It is possible for each existence to subsume and
transcend all the previous ones. Just as your life has
changed dramatically, has it not?"

"Yeah, it's changed. I just don't think of it as a steady
march up to Glory."

"It may take longer than you think to work out which
way is upward. Maybe more than one lifetime."

Jack Liffey kept his ear tuned for even a hint of irony,

but couldn't catch any. The man's eyes were boring into him, and he saw it as the old Special Forces challenge, what they called Mad Dog. The first to look away was weak, a pussy.

"Uh-huh, God's secret plan. I'm surprised you consider this Theodelphian thing a cosmic step up from the ashram."

There was a flicker of annoyance, and Jack Liffey wondered if he was getting to him at last. He'd been there twenty minutes and the man hadn't even asked who he was. He was happy to go with it and pick up what he could, but the back of his neck prickled from time to time and he expected the thugs to come through the door at any moment.

"There are only three Paths—the Path of Love, the Path of Works and the Path of Knowledge. I discovered that the East generally offers a full spiritual tuition along only two of the three, and the Theodelphian Elect offer a perfect balance. When you see the truth you have to act, even if it means giving up something you have built up carefully and cherish. I've never been slow to accept a challenge. I found I was offered a chance to take a small step upward in human evolution and help others do the same."

A part of the man seemed to go onto autopilot as another part was working out something else. Perhaps he was just counting down to the arrival of the troops.

"Is your spirit reaching that same point, do you think?" Hedrick asked. He glanced at the ladder, as if seeing it for the first time.

"I came to ask about Jimmy Mardesich, one of your disciples. You can get rid of me right away by telling me where he is."

The atmosphere shifted suddenly toward winter. "Did you try to access our computers?"

"Would it matter?"

"We don't allow that. Now I see who you are. I let you stay because I believe in the Eternal Law of Accident. I knew you were planning something, you may even have thought you were an enemy of the Elect, but I could also see that you were in great spiritual crisis. Perhaps the Eternal Law had brought us another sublime soul." He almost stopped, but finally decided to offer a further pearl. "The first few steps are really very beneficial for your earthbound shell, and not all that difficult. Before you begin the steeper part of the climb, we fix open wounds like yours and then you are much stronger at the wounded place."

"Just tell me where Jimmy is. If he wants to stay, that's fine."

"I offer you much more," he said, opening his hands in an expansive gesture. "But men like you are always tempted by less. Under no circumstances do we discuss the spiritual progress of any of our souls, or even who is amongst us." A terrible lassitude had come into his voice. "You may go. Don't make me spring the trapdoor."

Jack Liffey glanced at the floor quickly. He had a vision of sliding down a chute into the basement like a gigantic Looney Tune. The floor looked okay.

"It's not literal."

"Your strong-arm pal from the marines, the guy with the red hair, he's literal enough. Keep him away from me."

"I don't know what you're talking about."

"I think you do."

Jack Liffey got up and shouldered the ladder. "You could have got rid of me easy. Now I'll keep a picture of you over my desk, like Montgomery did with Rommel."

"The picture was irrelevant." Goodman Hedrick's mouth worked around the words as if they were something repellent. "Montgomery had more tanks."

The secretary jumped up to hold the door open as he carried the ladder out. "Many worthy lives," she said to him.

He didn't know whether it was a greeting or a prediction or an offer.

"Rain never falls up," he replied, and he guessed she watched him all the way to the stairhead.

He left the ladder in the courtyard, beside the placid lagoon, where a few ducks swam in sluggish circles, and slipped quickly out of the overalls. Outside, up the street, he saw an angry conference of squat brown Latinos in paint-spattered clothing. He walked calmly up to the buzzing circle and pointed the way he had come.

"*Compañeros,* I saw a guy take your ladder inside there. *La escalera.*"

"*Gracias.*"

There wasn't a manual laborer in the city who spoke much English. If the Republicans succeeded in sealing the borders, he thought, everything in the built environment would crumble away inside of a generation. The painters went off in an angry clump, nobody even glancing twice at the painty jumpsuit crushed up in his hand.

He drove up a side street as the sun was turning fierce and he felt the hackles on his neck prickling. Dry santanas were coming, the hot winds that blew west and south off the Mojave down all the mountain canyons and propelled the smog back into the city from Riverside and Pomona. If they blew for two days straight, they'd push the evil brown cloud right out to sea, where it would hover off the coast like bad luck, poisoning the whales, until the wind dropped enough to let it back in.

He came to a halt at a red light next to an old man wearing an old-fashioned sandwich board that said TENDONS OUT OF BALANCE $=$ BLOCKED BIOENERGY, and a lot of fine print. The man caught his eye. He had a stringy white beard like Uncle Ho and didn't look all too clean.

"Frogs," the man declared, quite distinctly, right to him.

"Are you sure?"

"Frogs!" His neck pumped with a fierce certainty. "*They* know."

The light changed and Jack Liffey nodded back as he drove away. He wondered what frogs knew, but since the sign had been about tendons, frogs seemed a pretty good candidate. He flexed his arms a bit, just to make sure the tendons were working.

It was still early for the lunch crowd and he waited in a green plastic booth at Wingo's and ordered another bad coffee. It made him uneasy that a guy like Goodman Hedrick had jumped to the conclusion that he was in spiritual crisis and that he needed fixing. He wondered if he was broadcasting a subliminal distress signal. If it was true, he'd have to do something about it. L.A. was too full of predators to let that go on.

But everybody these days had an extra helping or two of distress, he thought. He was broke, and he missed his daughter, and once in a while he even got nostalgic for his nice secure aerospace job and his suburban house and the big garage-workshop with his radial arm saw and drill press, now parked at a friend's, and even the little slobbering friendly cocker spaniel instead of the permanently pissed-off half coyote he'd acquired. But he knew he could shove the regrets down inside himself and hold them there out of the way, along with all the other stuff that he'd dropped overboard or screwed up or never quite got right. Stuff came and went and you just had to let it go.

He sipped at the coffee and made a face. There was one thing he'd never quite locked down, if he let himself think about it. It was Hedrick talking about his time in Vietnam that reminded him. For a few years in the early seventies, just back from the war and wandering around in a bit of a druggy haze, he'd fallen in with some angry vets and they'd dragged him along to meetings of the Vietnam Veterans Against the War. They'd really pumped themselves up with the possibilities of changing things, the war, then racism, sexism, capitalism, lots of things. He'd got a real charge out of it for a couple of years, until one day during a march on the Federal Building on Wilshire everything had suddenly turned pointless on him, just like that, and he'd been clobbered by the realization that he wasn't really part of some vast social movement that was going to carry them all toward a worthy goal.

What he'd seen in one disturbing moment was the fact that life pretty much chugged along on its own, and things strayed here and there without much purpose at all. You did your best with what you had, but there was no guarantee it would ever mean much. He'd rocked back on his feet at the time, hit by a genuine wave of nausea. It wasn't really belief in anything specific that had fled as much as the capacity for belief. And before very long he found there wasn't even a seam where it had been. Whatever it was had been torn out of the continuum of his life and the gap had clanged shut, and all he'd been left was a vague sense of deprivation, a feeling on late nights that something ought to be different. Too, he wished he had back his Good Conduct Medal that he'd tossed over the fence at the VA.

There was a plus side to it all, though. In the years since that queasy revelation he'd grown used to the kind of randomness of things that plagued Faye. That kept him from thinking he had it all figured out. He didn't much like people who thought they had it all figured out, which was probably what irked him about the big bald guru.

"Refill?" The waitress had a vertical scar on her cheek, as if a rotten boyfriend had cut her for some reason. She carried a round glass pot in each hand, one with a brown neck and one orange.

"Thanks, regular. You a vegetarian?" he asked.

"Huh-uh. Do I look like it or something?"

"Everybody seems to be something these days."

"I've started doing a little past-life research," she admitted. "My roomie said she found out she used to be a Nabatean princess."

"Far out," he said. They never found out they'd been serfs or cabdrivers, or night soil workers, he thought.

"Maybe I'll be something nice."

"Good luck," he offered as she wandered away. If everybody got their deepest wishes about life, he thought, things would probably be even worse than they were.

People were arriving in clumps and the place began filling up. Just after noon, Faye Mardesich wandered in carrying a string bag full of pamphlets and books. She looked the place over for a minute before finding him and he had the distinct impression she would have burst into tears if she'd had to look around *one more instant*.

"Oh, Jack," she started, and ran down. She sat heavily.

"Let's get you some coffee. You look thwacked." He held his cup overhead, and a different waitress brought a pot for Faye.

"Give us a couple minutes," he said.

"Sure thing."

"Oh, Jack," she tried again after the waitress left. "I couldn't just mark time in there. I had to pretend to take it all seriously so they'd take me seriously. They really know how to work on you and your disappointments." One tear made its way down her cheek and she flicked it free with the tip of a finger. "Man, they know how."

"It's their stock-in-trade."

He handed her his napkin and she dabbed at her eye. "Whew. Wasn't there something in *1984* about authoritarians using your one real terror against you?"

"They called it Room 101, I think. Whatever it was you really hated and feared, they kept it waiting for you in Room 101."

"Well, these creeps took me to 101. But not my fears. My big *disappointments* in myself. When I came in reception, I could see a girl with long blond braids weeping. They led her out of one of the cubicles, where they took me. I should have left right then."

She sipped at the coffee pensively.

"Did you find out anything useful?"

"In due course," she snapped. She looked at him, as if seeing him for the first time. "You're an impatient man by nature, aren't you?"

"Sure."

"Well, keep your shirt on. Are my eyes red?"

"Nothing that would get you thrown out of an AA meeting."

An old couple nearby had fallen silent and were trying to listen in. The woman tapped her husband on the arm and nodded in their direction, her chin fixed in a kind of righteous indignation. He wondered what they thought they were overhearing.

"They set you down and a guy asks you a lot of questions about your life and doesn't respond at all when you answer. He just takes notes. Then about forty-five minutes into it, he says he has to enter the information into their supercomputer, and he leaves for all of about a minute and a half. Then he comes back with a new clipboard and says there's a good chance your soul's a worthy one, ready for the climb, and it's worth doing a few more tests." The waitress was heading back and he waved her off.

"Then two of them, a new man and a woman, come and take you into another room, where they strap you into a kind of lie detector. There's this accordion hose around your chest and blood pressure cuffs on your arms. They say it's a way of focusing on the soul's truth, not just the mind's truth. Before they start in, they have you breathe deeply for a minute or two, and I got a bit woozy. Then the questions. They start slow but before long they're going at you good. 'Tell us your greatest moment of shame.' 'Was there a time you thought you betrayed someone you loved?' "

The old woman nearby swiveled a full head of gray

whipped-cream curls to meet his eyes. She seemed disapproving, and he wondered if she was a Theodelphian acolyte, but that was just too paranoid.

"Then they start tearing you down. Just a few suggestions, some reminders of little things you've revealed to them. All the friendliness is gone from their voices and it really hurts. This goes on for a while until you're a bit weepy and then they skedaddle. They just leave you alone to think about it. That was the strangest thing, Jack. I knew what they were doing to me, or at least I knew they were messing with my head, but when they left me alone . . ." She shook her head, as if to clear it. "It was the worst sense of abandonment I've ever felt. I would have done almost anything to get those two creeps back in there to talk to me and be friendly again."

"The heavy breathing is probably the key," Jack Liffey said. "About half the religions in the world use hyperventilation to change your mental state. They make you dance, or whirl around, or chant, or belt out psalms. That gets you suggestible and then they offer you a revelation or a vision or a demand for money. These guys weren't the first to figure out what extra oxygen in the blood does to you."

"It damn well works." She handed him a small card that said *The Rising Course of Human Evolution Study Center, Ojai.* "I'm sublime, *okay.* I'm the cat's pajamas. I *graduated* or whatever it was. That's where I'm supposed to go one day. Something about a ladder."

"Good work." He chuckled. "But *I* had the ladder. By the way, what was in Room 101?"

"I don't know you well enough."

The old couple got their check and the woman glared at him as they walked past.

"It was just child pornography," Jack Liffey said to her.

6

THE PASSIONATE LIFE

NORMALLY HE WOULD HAVE SLEPT RIGHT THROUGH THE phone, but Loco took the ringing as an excuse to hurl his muscular body against the bedroom door, and Jack Liffey woke up quick—a perfectly ordinary dream about not being able to find his parked car in a confusing city suddenly invaded by men with big guns and red marine haircuts. As long as he'd jangled himself awake, he went out to the living room and picked up the phone just as the machine kicked in.

"Jack Liffey can't come to the phone right now. Please leave your name and number . . ."

"Shit. Hold it." Loco got between his legs, trying to trip him up, as he fumbled the plug out of the wall. One day he'd make a fortune designing an answering machine that did what people wanted it to do.

"Okay."

"Jack, this is Faye." She sounded distraught and he glanced at the digital clock on his VCR. It said 3:25. It was a moment before those numbers made sense to him: *A.M.* "Milo's in the hospital. Some sort of industrial accident while he was doing his rounds at the plant. I'm sorry to ask, but could you come out here?"

Why me? he thought. But she was his only paying client. "Where's here?"

"I'll be at St. Agnes. He's on a respirator in the ER."

He left dry food for Loco and grabbed some coffee

at a twenty-four-hour gas station. It was still warm and breezy. He couldn't remember another time he'd been on the road at four A.M. and it was astonishing how many cars there were, going to work, or going home, or just going, one cheerless moon face per vehicle.

On the way to the freeway he saw a big square bed of ivy in front of a mini-mall where a group of bleary-looking kids were bump-grinding Hula Hoops frantically to a couple of boom boxes. It looked like a scene from *Laugh-in*. When he got closer a skinny girl looked up with a smirk, as if inviting him to share in the joke. He grinned back and gave them a little Groucho multiple elevation of the eyebrows and toasted them with the Styrofoam coffee cup before driving off. It was a city that didn't always offer a reason, and that was okay if you weren't feeling pressured.

The freeway was very fast and polite, full of people who were used to the hour and to one another like a secret fraternity, the Lodge of Night Drivers. He felt a peculiar kind of woozy ease settle onto him as he drove over the pass, as if he'd been out of sync with things for a long time and now he was dropping into the groove. It was a dope kind of feeling, probably something to do with dream deprivation.

The main hospital building was tall and modern and nondescript and could have been anything. A lit red sign pointed toward the emergency driveway, where two heavyset women in white coats were hauling a folding gurney out of an ambulance.

A signboard by the main door nearby announced a lecture series by Raju Iyer: IDENTITY TODAY: ELEVEN WAYS OF BEING YOURSELF. Jack Liffey smiled as he walked past: he'd always figured the one was enough.

Faye was sitting on a long bench in a hallway outside the ER. She'd been crying, but there was something else in her manner that he couldn't quite work out. Her eyes were puffy and he found being a little out of kilter suited her. She tried so hard to be tough and solid most of the time that she didn't leave you much to get hold of.

"Thanks for coming, Jack."

"How's Milo?"

"He'll make it but he won't be smoking his pipe for a while. He won't be talking, either. They've got him intubated. I had it once and it really messes up your throat."

He sat beside her and she relaxed visibly and set aside the old *People* she hadn't been reading.

"I'm glad you came." She seemed about to say something but ran down.

"Do you know what happened?"

She blanched when a piercing scream skirled out of the ER and banged around in the hallway a bit. A man in sweats burst out through the double door and then stood with his face to the wall. Beside him was a poster for Allergy Awareness with a big shaky-looking cartoon man sneezing.

"He was temporarily on graveyard shift up at Green-World Chemicals. There's two guards, but only a skeleton crew of workers on grave. Apparently some chemical processes have to go on twenty-four hours a day and they can't shut the whole place down. The guards take turns with one roving and one staying at the gate. Milo was roving, inspecting one of the areas that was as good as shut down for the night and he didn't come back on time. The other guard found him unconscious between two buildings, where there was a terrible smell in the air. He said it was like old gym socks, but he's not a chemist. There's a hazmat team from the fire department out there now trying to find out what it was."

A woman leaned out the double doors and called to the man in sweats, "Elden, don't you dare!"

"It's just the same old hustle."

"I know, baby."

He turned around wearily and went back inside, chugging a little with his fists like a man warming up to dance.

"Something else is bugging you," Jack Liffey said.

"Does it show?"

"Only when you laugh."

She handed him a folded sheet of paper she'd been keeping in the *People*. Childish capitals were scrawled across the paper: SEE WHAT HAPPENS!

"If I worked out the time right, this was stuck under our front door about a half hour after the accident. It takes about fifteen minutes to drive to our place from GreenWorld."

He looked close, turned it over, sniffed the paper, held it up to the light to look for watermarks and secret ink, and in the end didn't know any more than when he first glanced at it. The writer made his capital *E*s like backward "3s," and the *W* was a "3" on its back. The way things were going, he thought, with witchcraft and Theodelphians and God-knows-what in the air, he could start looking for a crazed numerologist.

"It scares me," she said.

"Um-hmm." He handed it back. He just couldn't tie it to the balding guru in the office full of pillows. It was overkill, even if Hedrick/Baba Ambu was still pissed off. It was way overboard for somebody trying to locate one new acolyte.

She turned the threat over in her palm a few times. "I'd like to give this back in spades," she said angrily. "To wherever it emanates from."

"It doesn't emanate, Faye. It was delivered very pointedly. Whatever they're up to, you can count on them being meaner than you and me. Give it to the police."

"Maybe. I feel so heavy and stupid. Milo's sedated in there and I just can't sit in this horrible corridor the rest of the night, but I'm scared to go home. Can I stay at your place, Jack?"

He thought of his apartment. There was probably a good strong aroma of Marlena on the bed and the sofa, too, after the last time they'd thrashed their way about

the place in heat. And the condo was a real mess anyway. "It's too small really."

"Would you stay at my place, then? Just till the sun
comes up."

"I've got to pick up my daughter in the morning. But
I'll watch over you until you can get a friend in."

HER home was a whole lot tidier than when he'd last
seen it, as if she'd set out to normalize things. The tape
was off the rug and all the items set around as markers
were gone. There was a gold Navaho rug that he hadn't
been able to see before and a giant coffee-table book
about the ballet and a coffee table for it to sit on. A
magazine rack held *Harper's,* the *Atlantic Monthly,* and
The New York Review of Books, as if somebody were in
practice to be a junior-college English instructor.

She got herself a stiff drink and he refused the same.
He leaned back on the sofa and closed his eyes. Three
hours' sleep. It was not going to be a very pleasant father's day with Maeve.

She put on Judy Collins softly, which was a little too
soothing, and he jolted once, one of those little presleep
spasms of nervous energy, like the top of you dropping
through to the bottom.

"Sure you won't have a drink?" He felt the sofa give
and eventually opened his eyes to see her at the far end
clutching a big brown photo album.

"I don't drink."

"You have trouble with it?"

"Not the way you mean. My life's going through an
abstemious phase."

"Does that mean temperate?"

"Uh-huh. Do you have any idea who'd be threatening
you or your husband?"

"I'm president of the Friends of the Library. Maybe
somebody got mad at a big overdue fine."

The joke seemed so out of character, or out of the
moment, that he rolled his neck to look at her taking a

big swig. "Sorry," she said. "This kind of thing is so far outside my experience, I can't even guess. You said the Theodelphians can be vicious."

"Can you see them sneaking up on your husband and loosing poison gas on him? I can't."

"That religious freak in Japan set off nerve gas in the subway, didn't he?"

"I guess anything is possible. But we ought to start with the plausible. Do you know what your husband's really up to? I can't believe an aerospace engineer is adrift in French critical theory."

"You're welcome to look in his study, Jack." She was quiet a moment and he nearly fell asleep again. Maybe he did. "How come your life took its abstemious turn?"

"Probably just vanity," he mumbled.

"How do you mean?" She finished off her drink and looked like she wanted more.

If he hadn't been so drowsy, he probably would have fobbed her off and left it. "The first real thing you learn when you hit middle age is that things might just not work out for you. It's a shock. Then they actually *don't* work out. At that point you start thinking about mortality, you're part of the human condition after all, not some exceptional case. Death is really waiting up the road for you. I get that feeling on every long car trip now." He wondered what on earth he was yammering about, but he was too weary to listen closely to himself. "When you get in that state, every car coming toward you is a danger. Your kitchen knives are too sharp. The airliner overhead might fall on you. You get the feeling you've been surrounded all your life by deadly stuff that's been watching you with a kind of testy patience, and all you've got left to keep that stuff at bay is doing your job the best you can, trying to measure up. So you clean up your act." He broke off, feeling foolish.

"Wow," she said. "You have one *demanding* guardian angel."

"That must be it."

She went to the kitchen and got herself another drink. From the depth of color, he wondered if it was straight booze.

"I think I know you well enough now." She opened the big photo album and slid it toward him on the coffee table. It was an old-style album, musty smelling, with the items held in place by little stick-on corners. He saw a hokey posed photograph of a line of a little girls in tights doing their best to take up some ballet posture on one raised toe as they clung to the barre in front of a mirror wall. PITIKOVSKY DANCE STUDIO, MARCH 1962 was picked out with stick-on white letters on a changcable board propped against the wall. The camera was at enough of an angle so it didn't show itself in the wall of glass. One little girl, smaller and skinnier than the others, had her face circled in red ink and a mashed string of red yarn ran off the photo to the caption, *Faye Trani, age 9.*

The next page was a clipping from a local newspaper about a junior ballet performance. Faye's name was circled halfway down the story. There was another dance-studio portrait, then a sole portrait of the little girl in a tutu in front of a painted backdrop of a Swiss mountain. The book of memorabilia went on like that, except Faye's name started featuring in the headlines, and the groups of girls that seemed to be flocking here and there like quail became centered on her. There were a lot of pink ribbons clipped off ballet slippers, mash notes from people praising her work, an amateur photograph of her on stage taken from the audience, then, all by itself, a letter offering her an apprenticeship with the Western Metropolitan Ballet Theater.

"I lived dance," she said. "The way moving your body with grace can make you feel. It's more satisfying than an orgasm."

"And all that applause."

"That doesn't hurt, but the real reasons are inside yourself. Feeling the movements. Hitting exactly the right pitch, I mean *exactly,* like an archer splitting the previous arrow." She made a small clutching gesture with two fists like a golfer who'd just nailed a long putt.

"I know the punch line is coming," he said, "but this time I'll keep my shirt on."

She acknowledged his patience with a little nod. "I would never have been the prima ballerina in New York, but maybe in a regional ballet. I was *very* good and it's enough to excel. That's what I grew up wanting. I wanted to excel. That's vanity, Jack."

"Maybe not, if you're good."

She went on as if he hadn't spoken. "I was sixteen. It started as a little crack in a bone called the navicular, up in the arch of my left foot. The ligaments of your foot are so strong that sometimes, under a sharp stress, the bones will break before the ligaments even strain. I felt something and I iced it, but of course that didn't help. Then I danced on it. The pain was excruciating. I guess they call it playing hurt in football, but it's really stupid. Three operations later they told me I should never go up on pointe again or I'd end up crippled. For a long time after, even when something that important to you is gone, it's still all you have. I even considered going to Vegas as a chorine." She shook her head. "I married Milo and let my body go. That's what those little Theodelphian bastards found out about me by banging on my religious reflexes. I didn't even know it still hurt so bad, but they hurt me with it."

All of a sudden he realized she was sitting right next to him, and she turned one more page to display an X ray of a foot. She tugged it out of the corners and held it against the light to show him a hairline crack. "God, I hate that little white line. Nothing has ever been right since." Her voice was slurring, and she rested her head against his shoulder. "Just substitutes. You wonder if it's God's vengeance for being so vain, for wanting the passion so badly."

"Accidents don't have meanings," he said.

"I know. All that stuff you saw in this room, I was just trying to work out some choreography I remembered." She shrugged and rubbed her head against him. She caught up his forearm and held it for a moment, then pulled his arm around her shoulders, like teens at the drive-in. "Things haven't been working between Milo and me for over a year, Jack," she said, and then she was asleep and snoring softly.

He was relieved because her story made him like her a lot more than he had at first, but he couldn't have let things slide any further. He lowered her so her head settled against his leg and then leaned back himself. He was so weary he couldn't hold his eyes open. Some bodyguard he'd make, he thought, when the redhead came in through the window.

He woke with a start, a cramp seizing his leg. He was alone on the sofa, and light streamed in through gauze curtains. Soft classical music was playing, and like an apparition, Faye suddenly danced across his vision wearing tights and a black turtleneck. She was very graceful. She kicked, spun, and performed some fluid gesture with her arms, then disappeared again.

"It's a wonder you didn't take advantage of such a vulnerable creature last night."

"Who says I didn't?" he said, now that it was safe.

She laughed, somewhere out of sight, and came right back with a mug of black coffee for him. It smelled heavenly.

"I think I kind of made a fool of myself."

"Not with me, you didn't."

"Oh, yes, I did." She sipped from her own coffee mug, tucking one leg in and extending it repeatedly, as if testing her memory of the movement. "You never forget how to do it," she said, and smiled. "If you're going to be abstemious, you ought to deny yourself caffeine, too."

"Everything has its limits, even moderation."

"I used to think people either chose the passionate life

or they chickened out and gave up to get calm and security. But they're both choices. Whichever way you choose, you lose the other."

"It's probably possible to lose both," he said. He had to get home and shower and change before he picked up Maeve. "I'd like a quick look in Milo's study."

"Help yourself."

A kind of tension developed inside him as the day took on reality. Beside Milo's desk there was a three-foot-high stack of books resting on the floor, each with a number of paper bookmarks. Barthes, Derrida, Baudrillard, Deleuze, plus a lot of names he didn't recognize. There were small slips of notepaper scattered across the desk. He picked up a few at random:

> *Spectacle is a degree of accumulation beyond the physical. It is money only looked at.*
> *Commotion is the result of the cultural exhaustion of a people.*
> *There are already too many ideas—and rhetorical excess is used to squeeze out one essence, any essence.*

Yes, indeed, Milo did seem to be thrashing around in critical theory. There was a yellow Post-it stuck to the computer screen, the message a bit different from the other notes: *Against so many lives, I don't matter a damn.*

He fumbled around until he got the computer and the modem turned on. He knew enough about personal computers to sign the machine onto the Internet, but as he'd expected, he couldn't get into Milo's E-mail without a password. He left it running.

There were a few computer books on a shelf behind the computer, a lot of printouts of philosophical monographs that looked as impenetrable as the notes, a photograph of Yosemite with Faye and a young boy standing in front of Bridal Veil Falls, and a couple of handmade ceramic pots.

He hunted Faye down. She was still tucking and un-tucking her left leg and staring dreamily out the kitchen window.

"I'll call you later."

"Thanks for looking after me, Jack." She seemed about to make another confession.

"I've got to run. I turned on Milo's computer. Don't turn it off until tonight."

That intrigued her and broke her concentration so she stumbled.

7

FULL COMBAT GRAMMAR

IT WASN'T THE USUAL BOYFRIEND HE SAW PEERING OUT THE
window to make sure Maeve got into a nice safe car.
The man had a scrubby little caterpillar mustache and
beady eyes, like Neville Chamberlain stepping off the
plane from Munich. So Kathy had dumped the English
teacher, he thought. He was happy to see that her love
life wasn't working out much better than his.

Maeve came gaily down through the bougainvillea
swinging the little checkered suitcase that looked like
something an Eastern European refugee would carry.
Her limbs were still as gangly as when he'd seen her
last two months back—it had taken Kathy that long to
relent on the visits—but Maeve looked like she was
starting to get breasts, and he figured that was something
he'd better not tease about.

"Daddy!" She pecked his cheek and he took the suitcase from her. It was as if they'd only been apart a day.

"Hi, sweetie. Wouldn't you like something a little
more stylish than this?" He put it into the trunk carefully, trying to keep it away from various grease-stained
car parts.

She shrugged graciously. "I know you don't have a
lot of money."

He laughed. "That's like calling the bubonic plague a
little chest rash, but we might be able to work something
out. I've got a couple of clients."

"A couple?"

"Okay, one," he admitted. "But she's paying. Who's he?"

She knew who he meant but she didn't really want to talk about it.

"So the English teacher went and got his verbs all parsed? What's this one do? Install carpets? Hit man?"

"Dan sells real estate."

"Oh, *Je*sus."

"Don't be bigoted."

"*Bigoted.* We're getting a vocabulary."

"Pooh. Dan's a nice guy."

Jack Liffey put on an odd strangled voice. "I can't be selling da house today. Da voices tell me it is time to clean all da guns."

She started giggling and climbed in. "I know he looks strange, but he's not weird, *really*. You're weird, you know, and I've got something else weird for you. I've got to know one thing first." They saved up the oddities for one another like jewels—and it was a regular battle to one-up the opponent with the strangest. "You still touchy about earthquakes?"

He wrinkled up his forehead. An aftershock of the last big quake had caught him in a collapsing house trying to rescue a client and given him a skull fracture. He'd been in a coma for a while and it had been touch and go, and the hair was still growing back where they'd put a metal plate in. He'd never go into an airport again without setting off all the alarms.

"Touchy's not in my vocabulary, honey."

"Good. Turn left up on Artesia. You'll never beat this one."

There was a last disturbance of the front curtain as he drove off; he guessed it was Kathy this time. Okay, sure, he was still driving that 1979 AMC Concord with one primer fender.

"You look tired, Daddy."

"I was up early beating up bad guys to defend my client's honor."

She clung to his arm and rested her head against him. "I wouldn't have it any other way." And he felt such a wave of love for her that he had to slow down for a bit.

THE road ended in a forest of parking meters fronting the beach. The last shops near the beachfront were pretty much what you'd expect—a seafood café, a bar, a liquor store, and a swimsuit bazaar with all the bright little hankies of cloth hanging limp from racks.

"It's over there on the side of Jeannie's."

He parked and followed her to the tiny shingled café where a sign hawked cappuccino, burgers, and menudo. She skipped ahead a bit in the sun and it took her age back a notch or two. It was going to be a scorcher, he thought. He'd only been out of the car a minute and his hair already felt like hot wires burning his scalp.

She went along a little concrete alleyway and made a grand flourish to end up pointing with both hands at something on the wall of the café. When he caught up he saw it was a plaque, cast in some sort of bronze-colored metal that wasn't doing so bad at resisting the salt air. He had to stoop a bit to read it.

NEAR THIS SPOT ON MAY 7, 1972, AN EIGHT-FOOT ACUPUNCTURE NEEDLE WAS INSERTED INTO THE EARTH TO CONTACT THE SOUTHERN ENERGY CONVERGENCE OF THE REGION'S LATERAL TORSION MERIDIAN AND PREVENT ANY FURTHER EARTHQUAKES. ACUPUNCTURE NEEDLES WERE INSERTED SIMULTANEOUSLY AT GRIFFITH OBSERVATORY AND THE BED OF THE LOS ANGELES RIVER AT HOLLYDALE PARK NEAR LYNWOOD. HERMOSA TEAM: THOM BREEDSDALE, MARIANNE STONE, JACK LIVEY, PICO RAMOS. ACUQUAKE '72 PROJECT. POSSUNT QUIA POSSE VIDENTUR.

Neither of them spoke for a moment, then Maeve pointed at the name Jack Livey. "Is that just misspelled?"

"Yeah, it was me. Sure. I always keep an eight-foot acupuncture needle handy. Too bad it didn't work."

She seemed a little hurt by his lack of reaction. "What's the Latin?"

"They can . . . that . . . can. Ah, those who think they can, can. Something like that." He tried to imagine four hippies standing there with a big steel needle, surrounded by a crowd of cheering drugheads in bell-bottoms and 1972 granny glasses. It wasn't that hard, but he glanced at the plaque again and its permanence gave him second thoughts about the scene. It had been an art happening. His mental picture of the geo-acupuncturists aged and hardened. They had beards, wore black, offered cocky declarations, and wrote up their reflections in a journal later. He saw them passing around champagne like a gallery opening.

"It's pretty good."

But that wasn't adequate. She frowned. "I knew you'd be freaked out by earthquakes."

"No, honey. It's weird, all right. It's just it all seems . . . so *studied*. There's too many layers of irony here. My idea of oddities is a bit more innocently goofy. But I'll give you a full point, two points." He offered his crooked elbow to take her back to the car. "Are *you* touchy about geeks?"

"Computer geeks?"

"That's the ticket."

"I'm not *bigoted*."

He smiled. "Good. We have to drop by a little company called PropellorHeads that's chockablock with them."

"PropellorHeads! They made Night Dogs!" It was if he'd said he knew one of the Twelve Apostles, and not one of the obscure ones.

"I thought you weren't into computer games," he said.

They settled into the car and she tapped insistently on the clasp of his seat belt the instant she sat down. He put it on.

"Remember one time you told me you'd never read *Gone With the Wind* but you knew what Rhett said to Scarlett because it was in the culture?"

"What a memory. Sure. So Night Dogs is in the culture even if you don't play it."

"It was the biggest thing after the Mario Brothers."

"Who's that?"

"Daddy!"

"Doesn't anybody *go bowling* anymore?"

THE elevator chugged upward. Somebody had hung padded blankets on the elevator walls, which meant movers, and he wondered if the furniture was coming or going. "What do you have against *Gone With the Wind* anyway?" she asked.

"I don't like the values it espouses. To be brutally frank, the Southern gentry can kiss my ass. Pardon my French."

She giggled. "You're being hard on the book."

"If you ever decide to read it, make me a promise. Read a Faulkner afterward. He's hard to read, but he doesn't glorify bunk."

"I better not admit I read *Little Women*."

"No, that's a fine book." He noticed he was getting opinionated again. He'd convinced himself long ago not to carry around all that baggage, and as long as he'd been feeling miserable about things, he'd found the empty shelves a surprising comfort, but now that he had a paying client and was sleeping with Marlena again and things were looking up a bit, he found a sense of zest was inviting opinions willy-nilly back onto their shelf. "Realtors are all right," he said, feeling magnanimous. "They perform a service to humanity."

"Don't *strain* yourself, Daddy."

He laughed as the doors came open on the fifth floor.

Something was subtly changed. Then he noticed the name PropellorHeads was gone from the double doors at the end. The doors came open and two really big guys in company T-shirts that read SIX STARVING GORILLAS carried out a black marble conference table.

"Uh-oh."

He and Maeve stood aside for them.

"PropellorHeads moved?" he asked.

The guy in back jerked his head toward another door. "Reduced circumstances."

The door was unlocked and inside there was a very small secretary's desk with no secretary. PropellorHeads had once had a whole opulent lobby with live video displays of their products. He led Maeve into a hallway where a banner said YOUR FATHER SMELT OF ELDERBER-RIES. The banner had been torn in half and taped back together. A deflated shark hung overhead, like a joke that had gone sour, and extension cords ran along the wall.

"Hello! Anyone here?"

A young woman with acne and lank black hair stuck her head out a door. "Can I help you?"

"I'm looking for Admiral Wicks or Michael Chen."

She popped a finger straight at him, as if he'd just picked the right answer in a TV quiz. "Good choices. They're the only two Joe Codes who survived. Film at eleven." She pointed at another door and pulled back into her office.

A Dilbert cartoon was taped by the open door and the room was obviously only half set up. A skinny young black in a wheelchair was trying to sort out a huge wad of cabling and a young Asian was on his hands and knees under a desk. A homemade parrot cage with a big green parrot hung in a corner.

"Gentlemen."

"Mr. Liffey!" Michael Chen jumped up, banging his head on the desk, and Admiral Wicks whirled around in his wheelchair. He'd worked with them once before, helping them beat off a predatory private eye who'd been working for a predatory Japanese conglomerate. His role in the division of labor had been the private eye and their hacking skills had done serious harm to the home company.

"Mr. Liffey is my dad," he insisted. "Call me Jack. I want you to meet my daughter, Maeve. Michael Chen. Admiral Wicks. Two of the best hackers in L.A."

"In the known universe," Admiral Wicks corrected.

They shook hands gravely. "Hi, there."

"What's happened to PropellorHeads?" Jack Liffey asked.

"We're victims of the big shakeout in CD-ROM. Nobody much is making any money at it," Admiral Wicks said. He was obsessively disentangling one strand of wire from the mass of cabling across his lap.

"I thought you guys were doing okay."

"The boss hit a buzz saw."

"Serve the people," the parrot squawked. It paced gravely inside its chicken-wire enclosure like a short-legged man in a frock coat, but they ignored it.

"Moby layoff," Michael Chen said. He lifted a cardboard carton onto one of the two desks in the room and peered inside. "Bruce's hiding in his office, boozing and trying to forget that his company just had a futurectomy."

"That's really sad," Maeve said. "Did you guys work on Night Dogs?"

Admiral Wicks grinned, and seemed to take her seriously for the first time. "That was elder days. We wrote the first version in *assembly language*." He reached into a pile of trash on the desk. "You know this?"

He held up a cardboard cutout of what looked like a brown bear with a lollipop for a head.

"Huh-uh," Maeve said.

"You never really played Dogs, did you?" He shrugged and set it aside. "Nobody's playing enough of anything these days."

"Correct ideas!" the parrot squawked.

Michael Chen looked over at the bird as if it were something he might soon choose to discard. "This *insect* belonged to Bart Neville, the only Maoist parrot in the United States. It brings to mind a certain Monty Python routine."

" 'The Dead Parrot,' " Admiral Wicks suggested.

"Yawk!" the parrot objected. "Socialism is science!"

Michael Chen frowned and leaned close to the chicken wire. "If it was science," he enunciated clearly, "how come they didn't try it out on *rats* first?"

The bird didn't answer and Michael Chen turned back to Jack Liffey. "What can we do for you?"

"I was hoping to ask a favor but you don't look set up yet."

"Don't worry about all this geeked-out mess. We've got a killer machine up and running next door."

"Remember what you did last time?" They'd hacked into a Tokyo computer room and launched an elegant little vendetta that they insisted would live forever in the annals of computer prankery.

Michael Chen came alive at the memory and did a little dance around the wheelchair as Admiral Wicks put up a hand for a high five. "Do we!"

"Bonk!"

"Oik!"

"Bonk!"

"Oik!"

Maeve watched them celebrate with her jaw dropped an inch. He was used to them and their cyber-rites by now. He thought of them as the children of the New Age, kings of their own universe, and he liked the fact that it made no difference to them whatever whether you approved or understood or not.

"I've got one little favor, and one big favor if you're up to it."

Michael Chen stopped in his tracks. "If we're up to it?"

"It's another telephone job."

"That'd be Michael," Admiral Wicks said. "He's the phone phreak. I'm languages. And soul, of course."

"Come with me," Michael Chen said to Jack Liffey.

"Maeve Liffey," Admiral Wicks summoned.

"Uh-huh?"

"How would you like to be an alpha tester? We have a nice educational game we're debugging. We hope to find a niche in education for our vast talents, and help dehose this poor company."

Jack Liffey left his daughter behind and followed Michael Chen down the hall to a room labeled EAST HYPERSPACE. The room was only relatively tidier, but it had what appeared a working computer with stacks of add-on electronic boxes and two very large monitors. The desk around it was littered with Lego space capsules and an open jar of Jif with a spoon in it.

There was a screech in the hall so shrill it made his hair stand on end, and then a young woman leaped into the open doorway with her arms spread and wailed, "Nobody expects the Spanish Inquisition!" She noticed Jack Liffey and clutched her blouse around her. "*Ooh!* Crash and burn! So sorry!"

Then she was gone, erased out of the air, and Michael Chen shook his head. "That's just Pam."

"Uh-huh."

Jack Liffey shut the door and explained that he wanted Michael Chen to log into the computer that he'd left running in Milo Mardesich's study and nose around to find out what he could. Just as he got that out, the door came open again. "Seen Pam running about? Well, stone the crows, look who's here."

It was Bruce Parfitt, the Australian who ran the company for the absentee Perth beer baron who owned it. He'd cut off his ponytail and put on a business suit since Jack Liffey had last seen him, but at the moment his nose was fluorescing and he was having a bit of trouble standing upright.

"Jack Liffey, as I live and breathe."

"Hello, Bruce, how's tricks?"

"Business is rubbished, to tell the truth, as you can plainly see. A gi-fucking-normous pain in the arse."

His attention was drawn by a wave of giggles down the hall. He raised his eyebrows and pointed in that direction and then pushed off the door frame. "Gotta shoot on through, mate. Come say hello."

When he was gone, Michael Chen got up and closed the door softly. "We were making five CD-ROMs for a big fascist suit-heavy company in Milwaukee, state-of-the-art games with movie tie-ins and lots of expensive graphics and video. They called Bruce back there two weeks ago and he thought he was going to get another big project, and they sat him down and said, 'Sorry, dude, things are bad, no more work. And by the way, we aren't going to pay you for the last three months, either.' One-point-five mill outstanding. Brucie looked like the ghost of Hanukkah past when he got back and he was on the phone to his paymaster for hours. To save what he could of the company, he had to lay off almost everybody. The last group left this morning. We're the skeleton crew, working for half pay. He's a decent guy and he'll make it up to everybody later if he can, but he feels like shit. That's the short version. The long version includes a lot of alcohol and heads banging on walls."

Jack Liffey nodded. "So I noticed."

"Kinda takes the steam out of your enjoyment of life, but you know what computer people say? Ninety percent of *everything* is crap."

The yen to say something smart in reply rose in him and then passed. He felt a kind of easing of all the sour-puss urges inside himself, a harshness passing away. "Sounds a little too high maybe."

"Oh, fnord. Anyway, we're only making games. We're not saving the world." He sat at the keyboard and then seemed to reconsider. "This first hack you want is

Mickey Mouse. Didn't you say something about a tough one?"

"Why don't we complete the first task before you stub your toe on the second one."

Michael Chen's expression grew slowly into a grin. "Real soon now I'm going to be offended."

"I know this guy, thought he was a pretty good hacker, thought he was invulnerable, and they reached back through cyberspace and wrung his neck. Virtually."

They heard a burst of giggling down the hall. It sounded like Maeve.

"Did he take any precautions?"

"He routed his call through the switchboard of a department store and some other stuff he didn't tell me about, and they got back to him and fried his computer. It didn't even look like they'd worked up a sweat."

"Well, let's not underestimate them, then. Let's see if they can find their way back through the CIA and the NSA and the Central Bank of Switzerland. Your friend *thought* he was good. *I'm* good."

Jack Liffey told him about the Theodelphian Elect. All he really wanted now was confirmation that Jimmy Mardesich was with them and where he was.

"I'll have what you want by morning," he promised. "It's when you get impatient that you get burned."

"I am not bloody *Pol Pot*!" echoed along the hallway in a forlorn Australian wail.

"Poor Brucie. He hasn't really got what it takes to be in charge."

"In a world of bad things, it's good to feel a little shame," Jack Liffey said.

As Jack Liffey returned to the first room, the parrot squawked at him. It sounded like, "Oppose the eight-legged essay."

He found Maeve working up a sweat, banging on a little red joystick in front of a busy monitor. She looked like she was having fun, but ten minutes later in the car she denied it.

"Boys!" she exclaimed. "They design a game to teach you grammar, and you know what they do? You know what happens when you put the wrong part of speech in a hole in the sentence? The verb rises up with a machine gun and blows it away! Or the adjective spins around with a sword and cuts it in two. It's called 'Full Combat Grammar.' " She barked a scornful laugh.

"You seemed to be enjoying yourself."

"It's sick, isn't it?"

"Despite what your mom says, not everything that feels good is bad for you."

8

BEHOLD A PALE HORSE

WHAT WOKE HIM WAS THAT OMINOUS DIRECTIONLESS GROWL Loco had, as if a ventriloquist were throwing a dog's voice into the room. The gnarr opened his eyes to shapes and shadows so unfamiliar it took him a moment to remember he'd put Maeve in the bedroom and he was sleeping on the sofa. One of the shadows in particular still seemed wrong.

"Do you own this shithole or are you just renting?"

It was like a bolt of electricity through him and he made a little yelp and sat straight up.

"Neutralize your dog or we'll kill it."

He was wearing pajama bottoms in deference to Maeve and he was glad of that at least. The man was maybe five feet away by the TV. "We," he'd said. Jack Liffey didn't see anything suggesting a second man, but he didn't want to take his eyes off this first one.

"I mean it. Now."

"*Loco.* Sit."

Fat chance he had of getting Loco to do anything by command. He got his hand on the collar and held tight.

"Shhh. Shhh."

He heard the sliding-glass door to the patio come open behind him. There was indeed a second man.

"Put that thing outside."

"C'mon, Loco."

It took only a few seconds to drag the dog out the

door. Loco barked once or twice ineffectually and swiped a paw at the glass. They pulled the curtains. Loco could take care of himself. Jack Liffey was a lot more worried about Maeve, and his eyes kept going to the hallway, but she usually slept the sound sleep of the innocent. The first man snapped on the Lava lamp by the TV that Maeve had given him as a joke birthday gift.

"Fuckin' A, I ain't seen one of these since Ike and Tricky Dick."

It was the redhead all right, a tight brush cut and no facial hair, about six-one. He wore plain gray pants and a gray shirt buttoned to the neck, like a messenger from a far more austere universe, and he carried a 9mm Browning, the pistol all the cops were switching to, except this one had what looked like a soup can stuck on the barrel. It was the first silencer he'd ever seen in person. For some reason, the man just didn't look like someone the Theodelphian Elect would have hired.

"So, you the owner?"

"It's not a shithole."

"It's wall-to-wall nigger out there. *That's* a shithole."

Jack Liffey decided it was not a good time to argue about bigotry.

"God is in the whirlwind," a deeper voice said. The second man came into sight, a stout man with red suspenders and a big revolver stuck in his waistband. He had busy tattoos all down his arms. "The end time is getting real close and the three sixes and all that stuff. You don't wanna get caught up trapped with no mud people now."

"Shut up," the redhead said. "Sit down, Liffey."

He sat on the prickly blanket on the sofa. The light in the room shifted. A big glob of yellow wax had risen to the top of the Lava lamp and sat there refracting its glow out over the three of them. He knew the glob would hang there for half an hour before it melted down and the lamp started cycling. He hoped he'd be around to see it.

"We gotta play a little catch-up here. You called the cops on us out on the street, didn't you?"

"Sure." He spoke as softly as he could without seeming to be suspicious about it. Just the thought of Maeve sticking her head quizzically out the door in the hallway gave him a chill. "You terrorized a friend of mine. You're still way ahead of me."

The redhead gave a broad shrug. "She happened to be here when we came to visit. We thought maybe it would help you get the message. Just in case you're still not getting it, the message is our client doesn't want to see any more trouble from your client."

"Could we be a little more specific?"

The fat one moved into view and picked up one of the cigarettes Jack Liffey left lying around. This was the man who'd burned the hole in his bedroom carpet, Jack Liffey decided. The man studied the cigarette as if it were an omen of mysterious import. "Behold a pale horse: and his name that sat on him was Death, and Hell followed with him."

"Shut the fuck up, Schatzi. We've got plenty of stuff to do before the fuckin' horsemen come riding out of the sky. Does the name Mardesich do it for you?"

"Who's *your* client?"

"Well, if you can't figure that out, my man, just tell *your* client not to give *nobody* no trouble for the next hundred years or so. I can work with that."

The redhead sat on the coffee table only a foot in front of him, considering him like a big cat contemplating something in its food dish.

"Maybe we could talk about this tomorrow at my office," Jack Liffey said.

The redhead snorted once, but instantly there was a faint throbbing sound. The man looked startled and his palm went reflexively to his shirt pocket. He took out a pager and read the number on it.

"Phone?"

"In the kitchen."

"Watch him, Schatzi."

Schatzi nodded and pulled out his revolver, but he only used it to tap his way along the bookcase. He looked at some old English literature texts, a movie guide, some plays, and then he stopped with the barrel resting on three paperbacks that lay on their backs with paper bookmarks hanging out. The phone came noisily off the hook in the kitchen.

"A book sealed with seven seals, that's the only book for you to waste your time." He held the top book up in the underwater light of the Lava lamp as if tilting the cover to a new angle would clarify what it was doing there. In fact Jack Liffey knew exactly what those books had once represented for him—*The Long Goodbye, A Small Town in Germany,* and *Sympathy for the Devil,* books he had read again and again during a troubled time in his life because they validated something deep inside him and did not require new thought. They were books about quiet, self-contained men who were faithfully carrying out what they saw as their duty in worlds that didn't care.

"For indeed the days are coming in which you will say, 'Blessed are the barren, wombs that never bore, and breasts which never nursed.' "

"I don't have a womb," Jack Liffey said.

The stout man looked at him neutrally. "It's a quote from the Bible, *heathen.*"

"That's just a bunch of bedtime stories for children." He hoped to get somewhere by riling the man. "Jesus was a pussy. The devil wins every time."

The man recoiled as if slapped. "Tim," he called weakly. He started breathing heavily.

"The Holy Ghost is a homosexual."

"Stop it."

"God sucks my dog's dick."

The man swallowed heavily and his eyes went wide.

"That's blasphemy!" He was visibly trembling. The one named Tim mumbled away in the kitchen.

"Why would God care about a dumbbell like you? When the trumpet blows and the air catches fire around you, He'll be laughing as hard as He can. *Listen.* I hear wings."

The man's face filled with horror, and he did everything but look around for the angels. Jack Liffey was about to hurl a drinking glass when his hair was yanked from behind back against the sofa.

"Schatzi, calm down." The glass was removed from Jack Liffey's hand. "And you just *shut up.* You two are really terrific. I go out for *one* minute and you can't play like civilized children."

The stout man was still advancing toward the sofa with eyes that seemed to have lost their guiding intelligence, the gun trembling and his free hand clenching and releasing in spasms.

The redhead reached over Jack Liffey's shoulder and slapped his palm against the stout man's chest to stop his forward progress. "Just sit down, *both* of you. Everybody's getting a little too worked up here."

"He said God sucks doggie dicks," the big man bleated, but he backed a pace.

"Now, that's not very nice. Did you do that?"

Jack Liffey could hear the suppressed laughter in his voice.

"I guess that gives us the right to chastise you some. By the way, Liffey, how come you're sleeping out here? Should we have a peek in the bedroom?"

There was no point lying. "My daughter's in there."

"No kidding?"

"Don't even open the door or I'll make it a point of honor to take this somewhere you don't want to go."

"Be cool. Our business don't run in that track. Maybe I'll let the Angel of the Lord here soften you up for the great tribulation. Get you thinking about the Rapture and shit like that. Gimme the tape."

Jack Liffey heard the rip of a short piece of cloth, then the fat man came around and sealed his mouth shut with a strip of duct tape. It panicked him a little until he satisfied himself he could breathe freely through his nose. They dragged him to the dining chair at the head of the table, the only one of the six chairs with arms, and taped his forearms to the wood. He thought of his daughter sleeping peacefully only a few feet away and wondered, irrationally, if his fear would invade her dreams.

The fat man knelt and taped his ankles to the chair legs. A panicky sensation of helplessness rose in him. He faced straight forward at a big blue abstract painting a friend had given him in college for deep-sixing a lot of library fines when he'd worked as a library assistant. The painting hadn't been his purpose for tearing up the fines, just an act of charity, but the kickback was okay with him. Still, the painting was not something he wanted to be looking at just then. He could smell some flowery cologne on the redhead behind him.

"You're maybe not such a bad guy, Liffey, but you got to play by our rules." Something tightened around his neck and held his head back. "We forgive you for all your sins, we wash you clean in the blood of the lamb."

The fat man whooped once, softly. He couldn't tell whether the religious imagery tickled or offended him.

"Go forth and sin no more and tell your client the same. Go take a whiz, Schatzi."

He heard the fat man go into the bathroom and turn the light on. It was becoming obvious that he wasn't quite all there in the head, and he wondered what the relationship between the two of them was. He was a bit dissociated from his own body, with his mind wandering to and fro around the apartment all on its own, investigating points of concern—the bedroom, the patio door. He kept thinking for some reason of Mrs. Gradgrind in

Hard Times saying, "There is a pain somewhere in the room."

"What we're gonna do now won't be so bad, but it'll help you remember us. Sort of a keepsake."

The fat man came back wearing a blue windbreaker zipped up to the neck. He was carrying something that Jack Liffey couldn't see, and when he turned a bit, gold letters on the breast of the jacket spelled out FUGITIVE RECOVERY AGENT. Great, Jack Liffey thought. They were self-styled bounty hunters, skip tracers, the nuttiest of all the varieties of human trash.

The fat man came toward him slowly with a smirk, a can of shaving foam in one hand and a yellow disposable razor in the other. Looking at the man made Jack Liffey sleepy.

"Hold still, pal," the redhead advised. "Remember those doggie dicks, Schatzi."

He saw a switch of mood on the big man's face that frightened him as the razor hadn't. He closed his eyes as they sprayed his forehead and he felt the bite of the razor at the front of his scalp and jumped a little. Even with the foam, the razor clawed and burned.

"You missed that bit."

He flinched now and then when the blade nicked him but he tried not to struggle, figuring it would only make things worse.

"Man, you got a hell of a scar back here. Looks like you went and had a lobe out. What's this?"

He felt a knuckle rap on the back of his head.

"You got you a plate under here. I knew a guy had one. Looks too recent to be from the Big 'Nam. They shoulda put in a trapdoor for a lube and oil change."

Once the hacking at his scalp ended he opened his eyes. They stood in front of him admiring the job.

"Now when you look in a mirror, you just think of us and think of all the worse shit we coulda done. This is no joke, pal. Doggie dicks aren't funny; what's funny is a *six-inch* dick on a three-inch private dick."

The fat man leaned in close to his face. "The Holy Ghost ain't no homo."

Then they were gone and he heard the door close. He heard one brief howl from the patio, where Loco must have detected them leaving, and then he ripped the right arm up off the chair. The furniture set was from his parents' house and he'd disassembled and restored the pieces himself with a glue called Resorcinol that had never really worked. At least he didn't have to sit there until Maeve woke up and found him like a trussed turkey. A *bald* trussed turkey.

He pulled the other arm off and then released the gag, grimacing as it ripped at his skin. He inhaled a big open-mouth breath of warm air. He worked the tape loose on his left arm, and then yelped a little as he yanked off a lot of arm hair. The rest was easy. Foam and hair were scattered all around the chair. He recoiled when the light in the room fluctuated, and then, as the thumping in his chest slowed a bit, he noticed that the Lava lamp had finally started bubbling, big orange globs rising through the blue.

Jack Liffey stared hard at the front door. He wanted to go after them but he thought about Maeve and got a roll of paper towels and cleaned up instead. He wouldn't rest until he evened up the score on them, even if it turned out to be self-destructive, but he wouldn't do it that night. The rule was simple, you had only so much space in the world allotted to you and sometimes people shoved you off it for a while but you had to get it back as soon as you could because you'd never be issued any more.

He went straight to the kitchen and punched redial on the phone. They weren't mental giants, these bounty hunters.

"Yeah?" a man's voice answered.

"This is GTT Night Service. We're having a problem with interference on this line. Have you received any misdirected calls today?"

"No."

"Good. Is this 542-9791?"

"You gotta be fuckin' kiddin'." The man hung up and Jack Liffey figured he would have to get Michael Chen to decipher the beeps and boops and tell him the number, if only he didn't dial anyone else in the meantime.

9

PEOPLE WANT MAGIC

"I'LL RIDE IN BACK, DADDY." MAEVE POPPED OUT THE door, and after he introduced them, she clambered into the backseat in her gangly way and Faye Mardesich settled into the front. Faye stared hard at the navy-blue watch cap he wore. He'd brazened out the haircut with Maeve, saying it was just something he'd tried out but didn't like much, and now he was stuck with that lame explanation.

"It was a bad idea," he said. "I got tired of combing and thought this might simplify my life."

"Did it?"

"Not with all the explanations and sneak peeks." He thought of doffing the cap for a moment to give her a good look, but then he'd have to explain the scar, too.

Maeve rescued him. "Daddy's a bit weird, but you've probably noticed. Buckle up, you two."

Faye laughed softly as she did as commanded. "We're all a bit weird with a sufficiently narrow view of the world."

"How's Milo this morning?" he asked.

"Recovering. They still don't know what it was. They've sent swabs of his mucus to some OSHA lab in Washington."

"Sounds like he was lucky."

"Lucky would be still working at his old job. Lucky would be no gas cloud at all and sitting home playing

on his computer." She turned and looked over the seat
back at Maeve as the car pulled away from her house.
"Maeve, are you weird like your dad?"

"Sure. I like to read books about aeronautical engineering and marine biology. But I don't really like boys
yet." He saw a smirk on her face in the mirror. "That's
what Daddy wants to hear."

"You bet," he said quickly. "Men are complete jerks,
stay away from them."

At the corner a man in a gorilla suit was kneeling to
crack eggs into a cast iron frying pan that rested on the
sidewalk. It was hot out but not that hot. He wanted to
call their attention to it, but the women had tumbled into
an intense communion about dance and music, and he
drove on. Eventually, after exhausting a number of styles
and schools of dance, they noticed him again and Maeve
touched his shoulder and caught his eye in the mirror.

"I'm really not dating yet, Daddy. Honest."

"Good. I have evidence that women should stay separate forever. They're on a higher plane of evolution. I
offer the fact that women do not ever stick up liquor
stores."

Faye smiled.

Maeve seemed to be thinking it over. "I bet that's just
the hunter-gatherer instinct men have. They're going out
to provide for the tribe when there's no other way." Her
voice tailed off quickly and they could all tell she'd realized it was a little too close to home, with a father who
was not doing so well providing for the tribe.

"It's okay, punkin'. I won't rob any 7-Elevens near
where you live."

Faye faced front and squirmed, comfortable. "How
much did you find out about Jimmy?"

"He's at the Theodelphian retreat, all right. My hackers
found that out right away." Jack Liffey had called them in
the morning, and that's what Michael Chen had told him
matter-of-factly. Young Jim Mardesich had reached the
level they called a Summitar in record time, an eighth-

degree Acolyte of the Germinal Idea, and he was at the study center that they had sequestered amidst the protective coloration of all the other quasi-religious retreats and ashrams and wounded spirit zoos out in Ojai. It was Sunday and PropellorHeads was shut down, so Michael Chen hadn't had time to digest the mass of data he'd downloaded from Milo's computer—overnight he'd siphoned off the entire hard disk—but that could wait.

He tried to drive along Van Nuys Boulevard to the freeway but something had it blocked and a cop was turning everybody north or south at Sepulveda.

"What's up?" he asked the cop out the window.

"Keep it moving, sir."

So he pulled to the side to have a peek.

"Sorry, folks. I'm an old fire truck chaser."

He got out and walked to where he could see that a flatbed truck and two VW buses had the road blocked and maybe twenty people were sitting down in the road with picket signs saying STOP THE COVER-UP, and ARREST THE REAL CRIMINAL! On the flatbed there was a big rolling billboard that looked professionally done: COVER-UP! MARK DAVID CHAPMAN DID NOT KILL JOHN LENNON! NEW EVIDENCE SHOWS THE ASSASSIN WAS STEPHEN KING!

There were side-by-side photographs of Chapman and Stephen King, enlarged from newspapers, and the resemblance was startling. THE CIA: FIRST DRUGS AND KENNEDY AND NOW THIS! it said on the side of one of the VW buses. The group sitting down in front of the sign seemed to be chanting something that sounded like "Redrum backward is murder," but he couldn't be sure.

He strolled back to the car, wondering why they didn't realize Stephen King couldn't have done it because he didn't use three names. Maeve and Faye were talking like sisters over the seat and he was happy they'd hit it off. He didn't like bringing Maeve along on a job but there didn't seem any danger in an afternoon jaunt to the squeaky-clean little Conejo Valley where Ojai nestled.

"What was it?"

"Just a normal day in L.A."

The women fell guiltily silent, as if they'd been talking about him. He doffed the watch cap for a moment. "Take a good look." Then he tugged it back down before Faye could get too interested in his scars. "It looks pretty good on black basketball players, but so do chartreuse pants. I learned my lesson."

"It's not as bad as you think," Faye said. "And it makes you look mean enough to eat the bad guys for lunch."

"We're just going out there to reconnoiter," he said pointedly. "We'll look Theodelphia-land over, and maybe we can have a few words with Jimmy if they'll let us." He glanced at Faye.

"I get you," she said. "No kidnapping."

"No kidnapping and no blowing your top."

"How did you know I had a vile temper?"

"I make my living judging character."

She glanced at Maeve once, as if trying to decide whether to share what was on her mind. "That's a chunk of the story I left out when I told you my ballet dreams. I did time in juvie for it. That's what we called it back in the sixties. There's probably some euphemism now, like Troubled Girls' Rancho."

She fell silent and Maeve rocked a bit with interest.

"You can't stop now," Jack Liffey said.

"I know. It all happened after my foot went. I used to be a dancer," she added for Maeve's benefit. "A very good one, but the bone in my foot cracked up."

"That's too bad."

"I was kind of a famous case, actually, for a time there. Good girl gone bad. God had broken His side of the deal, you see—He let my foot go to pieces—and for a while I just decided I had license to break my side, too." She looked at Maeve again, obliquely, as if deciding how graphic to be. "This was a long time ago, so it took a lot less to be shocking." She looked back at him.

"You remember what high school was like back then?"

"When the gout isn't rising," he said.

"Third period, on a Monday, and I'm not feeling much like school. I sneaked out of English to go to the girls' bathroom and smoke. Kools." She shuddered. "God, they were awful."

"It's okay," Maeve said. "I'm not tempted."

"They *were* awful. I avoided one of the teachers on hall duty and got a cigarette and some matches out of my locker and made it to the girls'. I can still see that bilious two-tone green paint with the darker green all round the bottom of the walls as if some kind of vomit flood rose to *there*. I locked myself in a stall and sat on the top of the toilet tank, with my feet on the seat, and lit up.

"I was past even enjoying the sense of rebellion. It was all old hat by then. After a while I heard somebody come in, and with the seat down it was hard to put out the cigarette right away. I crushed it on the porcelain but you could hear it crunching and hissing as it went out and some of the smoke lingered in the air and I figured, *Damn,* I'm discovered.

"And, sure enough, there's this voice: 'Who's *smoking* in here?' and I know her right away, it's bitchy Martina McCarty, who's also a dancer and a real kiss-ass on the school patrol. We never liked each other much. I could see her cordovan Bass Weejuns and white socks under the door, and I can imagine the smug little grin and I was starting to get down into the anger already.

"Martina was a real social climber, sucking up to all the clubbers and going out with the quarterback, and probably doing things with him . . . never mind, and I don't even have any dates yet except this geek who turns out to be Milo's friend.

"So she raps on the cubicle door and says in this I'm-going-to-Stanford voice, 'I know who's in there. Faye Trani's in big trouble, you bet she is.' "

Faye did an imitation of a nasal girl's voice.

"And I say—oh, *why* did I do it?—I say, 'Leave me alone, Martina, I've got to tinkle.'

"So Martina laughs for a while and of course makes a big deal out of the word *tinkle*. And just then one of the teachers comes in, Mrs. Dillard that she's pals with, and Martina explains to her about me *tinkling* and they have a good laugh and finally I flush the remains of the cigarette down and come out and Martina goes in and studies a bit of the ash on the porcelain and says, 'Here's where she crushed the *tinkle,* Mrs. Dillard.'

"And they escort me out of that dreary bathroom just as the bell goes and they walk me past about a dozen girls I know, talking about me getting tinkle on myself and wondering if I inhale when I tinkle and laughing like, What a jerk I am. They take me to the vice-principal, but I don't even care about that, all I can think about is Martina getting together with her boyfriend, the quarterback, that night and telling him about me smoking in the bathroom and talking about tinkling. And they'd have a good laugh about the moron."

There was a small break in the rhythm of her story while Maeve moaned a little in sympathy.

"I sat in the detention office trying to read a *Reader's Digest* article but I couldn't. I know it's out of proportion, but things get that way at that age—sorry, Maeve—and, anyway, my life's ambition had just been dashed by a broken bone and this idiot girl, who was a third-rate dancer, still had two good feet and couldn't even use them right, and she had her hotshot boyfriend and her nasty little off-to-Stanford laugh."

He pulled onto the freeway and headed north right behind a flatbed truck with two huge advertising figures, like something out of a Macy's parade. One was a big top-hatted Fred Astaire in a frozen tap dancer's pose, bent forward and one hand low in front of him and the other crooked behind his head as if introducing a new step. The other figure was a big sheep. The way they were tied to the flatbed, it looked like Fred was goosing the sheep, but he decided not to point it out. Faye's story seemed to be a common enough complaint about high-school humiliations, he thought, but he didn't point that out either.

"I knew Martina was released to dance practice last period, and the Assistance League where she practiced was just down the street from the school. It's where I'd practiced, too. First thing I did, I walked out of detention. Then I took all my schoolbooks and notebooks out of my locker and threw them into the fountain in front of the school. It was just a sort of make-or-break gesture. You know, you can't stop now.

"The one thing I didn't toss out was this twirler's baton with the big rubber bulbs on the end. I was just keeping it for somebody, I wasn't a cheerleader. I went down to the Assistance League and found Martina Mc-Carty in the shower and took a full swing with the baton and caught her a good smack right across her white bottom. For an instant I wanted to kill her, but I wasn't quite that whacked out. It did get her attention, however.

" 'That's a little *tinkle* for catching me smoking!' I shouted at her, and I hauled back and swung again but I missed as she ran out of the shower. 'The next one's for laughing about it!' I chased her buck naked out of the Assistance League building just as half the school was heading home. We ran up the middle of the street and she was dripping wet and had a big splotch on her bottom that was going bright red and then she started screaming for help, just in case there was one person in school who wasn't already looking at us."

Maeve was applauding in the backseat.

"Now, one of Martina's breasts was a lot bigger than the other and she'd always been sensitive about it, she had this special bra that evened them out, and that day the whole school saw the mismatch. I swung a few times as we ran, but the school guard caught me at the fountain and I just gave it up."

"So they sent you to juvie."

"So they sent me to juvie. I finished out my education in a continuation school, and then had a semester at Valley State before I married Milo."

"Are you sorry about beating her up?"

"Not one bit. I hate her just as much today, but I bet she doesn't tell a lot of jokes about the girl she caught tinkling. If I'd walked away, she'd have married her quarterback and had beautiful kids and bought a mansion up in the hills and she'd have been telling her rich friends this joke about me all her life. I'd rather have the year at juvie."

She was trembling a little with emotion, and he remembered how she'd cried after the Theodelphians had interrogated her. She wasn't anywhere near as controlled as she wanted you to think, and he worried a little what might happen if things ever got ragged around her. He didn't like things taking off on their own, not with Maeve around.

As they rose out of the San Fernando Valley into the northern hills, he asked her if Jimmy had inherited any of her temper, and she said no, he was the sweetest boy imaginable, very self-contained, he'd got all that from his dad. He waited for her to say Jimmy wasn't all that bright, either, which she seemed to need to do from time to time, but she didn't do it in front of Maeve.

To their right was the foaming water ladder where Owens Valley water made its way down an artificial waterfall into the basin. They rose along the flank of the transverse range of the San Gabriel Mountains toward the long pass to the north that had once been known as the Ridge Route and then the Grapevine.

He thought of his own temper, which took off now and then on him, too. There had been a theory going around since the sixties that it was a good idea to get the anger out, not let it stew inside, but he found that a little too facile. Why should you have a right to inflict anger on others? Was it any different in kind from say-

ing you had a right to hit people and get out that *need*
to hit? It was just as plausible that letting it out got you
used to it and made it all self-perpetuating.

When the talk wore down, Maeve chirped up and pro-
posed alphabet soup. She had invented the game coming
back from a camping trip, devised it on the spot where
the high desert freeway passed under all the phantom
overpasses that some developer had built north of Lan-
caster for the big intercontinental airport that had never
come. Avenue A, and then a mile later Avenue B, and
so on up to Avenue S, where all that daffy obstinacy
broke down at the San Andreas Fault.

Maeve explained the game pedantically, and Faye
seemed to feel put-upon at first, and then she snapped
herself into another mood, almost like an act of will.

"We don't have alphabet streets," Faye objected sen-
sibly.

"It doesn't matter, just a mile on the speedometer."

"Okay, I want the difficult option, with two different
things. I'll choose trees." She turned to him. "You pick
the other."

"Felonies," he said.

Maeve laughed and applauded. He and Maeve had
pretty well exhausted the obvious categories, the movie
stars, European cities, novels, women of history, and or-
namental flowers. "Go for it," Maeve said.

He glanced at the odometer just as they turned off the
freeway onto the highway west. "*Mark*. We're on A."

Two tank trucks were idling on the narrow shoulder
of the highway, their drivers out on the pavement and
wagging their fingers angrily at one another. He bleated
a short warning to them as he approached. They both
turned to wave, switching abruptly to broad smiles as if
they knew him.

"Time, children."

"Arson," Maeve said quickly, "And ash."

"Assault and alder," Faye said.

"You don't leave me much," he said. "Alienation of affections and acacia."

Maeve giggled. "Dad's a show-off, you gotta know."

"I'm not sure that's a felony," Faye objected.

"No time to argue—on to *B*."

He watched the two of them grow heatedly competitive as they played. By the letter *F* they were struggling to come up with two felonies and two trees each, and he wondered if Maeve had got under Faye's skin in some way or if it was just something in the genes, competing for the favor of the male who was driving. As if to reclaim some advantage, Faye let her hand rest lightly on his thigh, down where Maeve couldn't see it. It made him nervous, but there was nothing he could do about it.

THE car crested the Sulfur Mountains and tipped forward to display the pretty little town of Ojai nestled amidst orange groves and green fields far below. The ashrams and retreats were already accumulating on the hillsides, even the Catholics represented up at the ridge with a gate announcing Thomas Aquinas College somewhere back off the road. It all went downhill from there past the Crystal Vortex Haven and the Sun, Moon, and Stars Blue Algae Farm.

On the lower slopes they passed signs for the Krishnamurti Center, the Ray of Hope Holistic Healing Foundation, the Feldenkrais House, and the Shoong Shai Institute, whatever that was. The buildings were mostly set back from the road, so you couldn't see what lurked there in the trees. Nothing about the Theodelphians. He slowed to read the competing signs on a big professional building at the edge of town that promised acupuncture, shiatsu, aromatherapy, Hellerwork, applied kinesiology, iridology, and noötropic pharmacology.

"I know what acupuncture is," he said.

"Shiatsu is a kind of massage," Faye Mardesich said.

"Maybe Hellerwork is the critical study of *Catch-22*," Maeve suggested.

"I'll make the jokes," Jack Liffey said. The center of town was a long Spanish arcade with upscale dress shops, cappuccino bars, and one Druid art shop. A poster on an arch said MAGNETIZE AND ENERGIZE YOUR WATER. Cursing himself for not getting an address ahead of time, he parked in a diagonal slot and picked up a local paper and read it in a café while Faye sipped a black coffee and Maeve had carrot juice.

The paper was chockablock with ads and vanity articles. He read about goddesshood, the power of coral calcium, how scaler waves and electrical precursors unlock the power of the pyramids, the path to whole brain functioning, spiritual acceleration, flower remedies and spells, rebuilding the immune system through meditation, the Naessons microscope that had revealed the existence of tiny glowing lights inside our cells, Tahitian Noni kelp juice, colloidal silver, Certified Voyager Tarot, and a seminar on new ways to sell a full sense of power and "uplevel" your life.

The lead article was about a pirate school. You signed on for a week and studied classes in fencing, seamanship, and drama, and then you dressed up and actually spent three days at sea playing pirates. It was very expensive, despite an apparent lack of any metaphysical element. Money is far too maldistributed in this world, he thought.

He split the paper in half and handed a part to each of them. "See if you can find anything about the Theodelphians. My tolerance gauge is beeping."

He found a phone booth and was deep in the Yellow Pages when a throaty girl's voice took him by surprise. "Have you accepted Jesus Christ as your personal savior?"

She had long blond hair, a spooky sort of addled smile, and a cotton print dress that covered her neck and her arms down to the wrists and her legs to her ankles.

"You are *just* the person I wanted to see," he said with a grin, and she retreated a few inches in panicky diffidence.

"Do you want to make a personal affirmation?" she asked, but so tentatively that it was if she were soliciting information about some private shame.

"Not precisely." He waited and saw her grow even more uncomfortable. That was one of the main differences between the strong and the weak, he thought with a touch of sadness. The strong could wait and make the weak nervous.

"I need to rescue someone from an un-Christian cult here in town. The Theodelphians."

"Oh, the headers."

"Is that what they're called?"

She hesitated, as if explaining might reveal too much about herself. "Some of them stand on their head to meditate."

He remembered Goodman Hedrick doing his one-hand lever in the pillowed office. Headers. Like the Shakers or Quakers or Holy Rollers or Snake People. There was probably no activity so strange that some religion somewhere didn't espouse it for worship and eventually get named for it. Maybe right here in Ojai. The crotch-grabbers. The water-spitters. The finger-snappers.

"Do you know where their center is?"

She pointed to the east. "Pot John Road, past all the rock walls and the oranges. You'll see the yellow buildings."

"Thanks a lot. Take it easy."

She almost let him go, but her wish to do good in the world got the better of her. "Whoever doesn't acknowledge Jesus shall burn in hellfire."

He stopped. It was remarkable what kindly people could let themselves believe. He watched her for a moment and she flinched as if expecting a blow.

"Do you really think God is more unforgiving than you or me?"

It was actually called Potrero John Road, and it was really remarkable he hadn't noticed their facility from the ridge on the way in. It was an old two-story frame farmhouse and a barn, plus a lower structure built later to join them together, and all of it painted canary yellow just like their center on Melrose. A nice discreet sign at ground level said THE RISING COURSE OF HUMAN EVO-LUTION STUDY CENTER, PRIVATE ROAD. There was a phone number for appointments, but he decided he'd already been down the polite route.

He parked on a gravel drive and had the women wait while he walked up to what had once been the front door of the farmhouse. It let him into a barren reception area with a polished wood floor, a lot of pamphlets and books in racks, and an old desk painted a pristine white. There was no one there, but soon a woman came out of an inner office, walking on eggshells. She had an air of distance and abstraction, as if a lot of her psyche was heavily involved in investigations in some other dimen-sion. Her unlined face could have belonged to someone anywhere from thirty to fifty-five, but long steely gray hair upped the guess.

"Can I help you?" The voice was tender and breathy and came from far away, like Marilyn Monroe on Quaa-ludes.

"Jimmy Mardesich's father is in the hospital. I need to speak to him."

She considered him for a few moments in silence. The watch cap probably wasn't doing him any good with her, but the shaved skull and scar would have been worse. The house creaked and popped in the sun. "We aren't allowed to acknowledge the presence or absence of any of our Summitars in their earthly location."

"Have a heart, ma'am. His father's condition is serious. He may die tonight." It was true, anyone might die tonight.

She looked down and thumbed some papers on the desk, as if a solution to her dilemma could be found there. "Oh, dear. Oh dear. I assume you can marshal certain standards of discretion."

"Oh, sure," he said.

"What did you say your name was?"

"Just tell him it's one of the Dharma Bums."

She slid back through the partially open door as if trying not to touch the wood. He smelled a minty herbal tea from somewhere and someone was strumming a stringed instrument that was not tuned to a Western scale.

After a while the door came open without hurry and a young man stepped into the lobby. He looked like his picture in the high-school annual, though he'd filled out to the muscled build of a wrestler. He folded his arms across a collarless white shirt, but those shirts were becoming popular and it might not have been an affectation.

"I'm Jim Mardesich," he said. "How is my father?"

"He's had an industrial accident. He was caught in a cloud of gas of some kind and they've got him in the hospital."

"What gas was it?"

"They don't know but they had to put him on a respirator."

The boy nodded, as if thinking it over very cautiously. He seemed almost without affect. "How long has he been in the hospital?"

"Three days now."

"Improving steadily?"

"Improving."

"Do you think it would make any difference if I went to see him now?" There was a kind of serenity about the boy that made Jack Liffey want to shout *Boo*.

"Frankly, no. But you might want to do it out of filial duty."

"Thank you for the suggestion." There didn't seem any irony in the reply. "Why did you introduce yourself as one of the Dharma Bums?"

The boy still hadn't stirred a muscle. Jack Liffey didn't really want to admit he'd prowled the boy's room, but it might be worth it to get a rise out of him. "You copied out a long passage of Kerouac, in your own hand."

That brought a tiny smile, but no other response.

"He wasn't a very nice guy, you know," Jack Liffey added.

"He felt America's ache in the fifties," the boy said slowly. "Maybe you didn't have to be a nice guy to do that."

"And you feel it now?"

"Don't you?" His face furrowed in an earnest look that was at least a departure from utter neutrality. "Wisdom may increase with age but I don't think sensibility does. Even Gandhi was young once, and I imagine the young Gandhi had quite a wonderful soul."

Sensibility was a pretty big word for ordinary conversation. Jack Liffey wondered if it was a word they used a lot in the Theodelphian canon. "If you allow that lawyers have a soul. He was a South African lawyer in his youth."

The boy was faintly surprised, but without embarrassment. "I didn't know that. There's still a lot I have to learn. Do you think I would learn more by going back to Van Nuys High School to get my D in remedial math? I never could understand geometry. Or chemistry. I wasn't good for much in school."

He made no excuses and didn't seem chagrined by his failures.

"And magic will make you feel important," Jack Liffey suggested.

The smile again. He turned slowly to see if anyone was eavesdropping through the open door, and then he nodded. "That's their weakness here, most of them.

They want easy enlightenment, from a magic spell, and they want it quick. It's why I've just about exhausted what I can learn here."

It was stunning, the self-composure. The boy had just admitted that major changes were brewing in his belief structure and it hadn't distressed him a bit.

"Your mom is out front. Would you talk to her a little?"

"Not right now. Please come through for a moment. I need a calmer place."

He led Jack Liffey into the inner office, past rows of white filing cabinets, and out French doors into a courtyard dominated by an immense pepper tree. The feathery leaves and little red seeds and the medicinal smell reminded him of his youth in San Pedro, where big pepper trees had lined much of his walk to high school.

"You've been hired to snatch me back and deprogram me, haven't you?" the boy asked.

"Not exactly. I can't compel you to do anything you don't want to do, and I won't try to."

They strolled along a terra-cotta walk lined with tidy vegetables and low-lying flowers like the tranquil courtyard of a Spanish mission.

"We've had science for hundreds of years now, but people still want magic, don't they? They want some pure and meaningful thing to stick up out of all the material fog in their life. Isn't that an urge for the good?"

"It's none of my business what people want as long as nobody's exploiting them."

The boy looked up suddenly, as if he had just had an idea. "You know the sort of world we should be building? One that makes it easy for everybody to be kind. Everybody wants to be kind, but the world makes it hard."

Jack Liffey tried to remember where he had heard something like that. He thought it might have been the Catholic Worker people.

All of a sudden the boy stopped and turned to face

Jack Liffey. He was a good inch taller, and all of his serenity had become focused into a kind of shy intensity. The boy's hands lifted, as if on their own, and reached out to press softly against Jack Liffey's temples. His fingertips pushed under the watch cap and they were smooth and soft, like a baby's bottom.

"I can feel your goodness inside. Bless you with all the force of life, Jack Liffey."

It was the Holy Boy road all right, he thought.

10

THE WARRIOR CLASS

AN OLD MAN STOOD BY THE SIDE OF THE HIGHWAY WITH A cardboard sign. He wore a threadbare dark suit and there were no buildings for miles, no turnoffs and no abandoned vehicles he could have clambered out of, as if he had grown spontaneously on one of the orange trees that lined the road. He aimed the sign hopefully at the car but Jack Liffey was the only one who looked. WILL WORSHIP FOR FOOD, it said. The man had one of those scooped-out Okie-faces from a Dorothea Lange photograph. Sorry, man, Jack Liffey thought as he whizzed past, I'd rather not be worshiped.

Jack Liffey's forehead still burned from where the boy had touched him. It was a pity he wasn't on crutches, he thought, so he could hurl them down and shout his elation. Still, he could joke about it all he wanted, but he figured everybody had a right to a shot at the sacred, as long as he didn't take it out of somebody else's hide.

It was a strange hour of the weekend on that road, with the Sunday drivers finally arrived wherever it was Sunday drivers dawdled off to, and the churchgoers and Sunday brunchers back in their homes, and the high school kids not drunk enough yet to go careening down the farm roads, so the only vehicle traffic as far as the eye could see along the two-lane highway was a single rattletrap stake truck loaded with watermelons.

"This is where they shot the orange-grove footage for

Chinatown," he said. "It pretty well mimics what your neighborhood probably looked like in the 1930s."

Faye Mardesich perked up a little at that and looked around, but in general she was not at all happy about going home empty-handed. He'd convinced her to wait it out by promising he'd stay on top of the boy's whereabouts. He'd already struck a parallel deal with the boy, handing over his business card—a trifle reluctantly because he'd caught sight of the big embarrassing eyeball Marlena had insisted on printing on it—and the boy had agreed to call and let him know where he went when he moved on from the Theodelphians.

"I'll bet retreating to a sanctuary like that can be really satisfying," Maeve offered. She was trying to ease Faye's mind in her own way. "Being a teenager can be such a drag. You know, there's all that ego all the time and all the fuss of worrying about being popular. It must feel good just to bug out and sit down in peace to read the heavy thinkers."

"I'm not sure Goodman Hedrick qualifies as a heavy thinker, but I appreciate what you mean."

"I can't picture Jimmy sitting down with a difficult book of any kind," Faye Mardesich said. "I really can't."

"Maybe it doesn't have anything to do with reading things," Maeve offered generously. "Maybe it's just getting away from other people for a while and thinking."

"And maybe you find out eventually that it's just a grander kind of ego," Jack Liffey said. He'd had an ex-nun as a girlfriend for a while, and she'd still carried a lot of the holy about with her, and one day she'd said to him, "You're really working overtime to be decent today. It's what you've got instead of God, isn't it?"

Maeve was starting to say something earnest and urgent when he felt the steering wheel change. That was the thought that came into his head, but really the word *change* didn't do it justice. Suddenly there was no sensation at all of being able to direct the car. The wheel was flaccid and ineffectual, like something in a dream.

He was off the gas immediately, but they were still doing about fifty on the two-lane road and he could see the old car angling gradually down the crown of the asphalt. There was a gravel shoulder, then a deep dry ditch and the orange grove beyond.

"Brace yourselves," he snapped.

The outside tire was nearing the ragged edge of the pavement. Irrationally, he tried to will the steering to work again and spun it to the left but it did nothing. He put on the brakes lightly and that only speeded the drift to the side, so one wheel crunched off onto gravel.

"Daddy!"

Faye Mardesich put her palms hard on the dashboard. He couldn't remember if the rear seat belt worked but he knew Maeve would be wearing it if it did. A crow fluttered up off the shoulder ahead, squawking mightily, and he thanked his stars the phone poles were on the far side of the road.

He could tell they weren't going to make it. As a last try, he yanked on the hand brake. It only worked the rear wheels and he hoped by some strange vectoring of forces, it might just slew the car back onto the road, but it didn't. Faye shrieked as the first wheel went over the edge of the ditch. He felt the vehicle lean sharply and then bang down as the underside hit, then something bad and loud and disorienting happened all at once as his head snapped forward into the rim of the useless steering wheel.

When things came to rest, he found he was staring at the open glove box and his shoulder was pressed hard against Faye. He could smell her musky perfume. The car seemed to be on its side and he'd fallen half out of his belt against her.

"Maeve, are you okay?"

"I don't feel so hot, but I'm okay."

"What do you *mean*, you don't feel so hot?"

"My stomach is upset. I hate roller coasters."

"Faye?"

"Ooh. I think I've got the window knob under here. There's gonna be a hell of a bruise. What happened?"

He got himself oriented and used the belt to pull himself up and look over the situation. The car lay on its right side in the ditch but was not badly damaged, and Faye seemed to be okay where she lay against the door. There was no blood.

"The steering went out. Just like that."

"I'm glad we weren't in traffic," she said.

"Or coming over the hills."

He used the wheel and the window opening on his side to haul himself up and get his shoulders out of the car. Then his foot found purchase against the side of the passenger seat and he boosted himself straight up until he got his entire torso out the window. He could see that the car stuck up visibly from the ditch. Somebody would be along to notice them. A smell of gasoline prickled in his nose and he decided it would be a good idea to get them all out pretty quick.

He scrambled out and leaned as far back in as he could.

"Give me your hands."

He took Faye's hands and helped her torque herself around. She stood straight up on the passenger door with her head out the driver's window. She smelled it, too, and tucked up a leg to climb the seats and dashboard with some urgency. She was heavy but her dancer's strength helped her wriggle out in one fluid motion. Maeve hadn't moved.

"Punkin, can you get into the front seat?"

"Wooo. I almost threw up there."

"Never mind that now. I want you out here in the fresh air." He hung back inside and nudged her leg where she lay crumpled nearly upside down in the back. "Let's go, soldier."

"Let me just be here a sec."

"Not right now, Maeve Mary. Just swing your legs down and stand up."

"Oooh, two names means you're serious." She stirred finally and started readjusting to the unfamiliar orientation of things.

He got a good look at her face when she wrested herself upright and saw tears streaming down her cheeks.

"You hurting, baby?"

"I don't think so. It's just a funny peculiar kind of crying, like the midnight sillies you get when nothing's really funny."

He helped her into the front seat, and she was so light he lifted her straight up and out and swung her around onto the bank of the ditch. Faye reached down to give him a tug away from the car and the gasoline smell, and they all retreated to the road and then to a culvert where there was curbing to sit on. They felt themselves for bruises and scrapes.

Faye winced at a spot on her side. "That won't be pretty tomorrow. That's my first accident since Jimmy was just learning to drive and wanged into the neighbor's trailer with me in the car."

A small yellow school bus approached and they all stood and waved. It pulled over to the side of the highway and switched on all the red lights as a dozen pairs of eyes gawked out the windows. The door hissed open and a heavyset woman in a leather jacket cranked on the hand brake and came to the door.

"That you folks' car?"

"Yeah, we lost the steering. Have you got a phone?"

She nodded. "You're in luck. I just saw Clyde giving a ticket back there, he's the deputy today. Hope you're good for the Breathalyzer."

He guessed she'd meant it as a good-natured warning. A small boy with leg braces came up behind to peer around her.

"I'm okay. Why don't you call him."

While she was calling, he noticed the name on the bus, MASSIMO'S ORGANIC SCHOOL FOR THE CHALLENGED. He didn't even try to work it out.

• • •

THE name tag said CLYDE D. BOLD and the paunchy middle-aged man wore a sombrero that didn't look much like a regulation part of his khaki uniform, but they were so far out of the Ventura County seat that he could probably get away with any eccentricity he wanted. Jack Liffey passed the routine Breathalyzer and the deputy separated them off in different spots so he could get their stories one by one and make sure they were all on the same page. Then he had a look at the car.

"Hey, pardner, come here."

Jack Liffey joined him in the ditch. Most of the gas smell was gone.

"You got you some enemies?" The deputy pointed to a metal arm that was hanging loose by a front wheel. "Somebody pulled the cotter pin off this here linkage."

"Maybe it wore out. The car's pretty old."

"Trust me, they don't wear out and they don't just fall off. Never seen it. Somebody's gone and bent the ears straight with pliers and pulled it most off and then it was just a matter of time till the link fell off this doohickey."

It was not a good time to explain his occupation, or what they'd been doing in Ojai.

"This car's old enough to vote," Jack Liffey said. "And it's got two hundred and fifty thousand miles on it. I'll settle for wear and tear."

"There's a first time for everything." The deputy squatted down, took a small cloth bag out of his shirt, and started rolling a cigarette. "Since you wasn't so drunk you couldn't hit the ground with your hat, and your passengers' stories all hang together, I guess I'll just write it up as a accident. Unless you got a objection."

"Sounds good to me."

"Keeps the paperwork simple. I'll call you a tow."

Jack Liffey sat beside Faye on the curbing as Maeve followed the deputy to his car to peer over his shoulder at all the electronics and gadgets in the big Crown Victoria.

"The steering was sabotaged," he said softly to Faye. "I think it's another message to me to mind my own business, but I really don't get it. The Theodelphians are famous for getting upset if you pry into their affairs, but I can't believe they did this just because I talked to Jimmy. Did Jimmy ever do drugs?"

"I'd like to say no. I really would."

"Maybe he was caught up with some really bad boys, muling or selling to the high school kids, or maybe turning them in. I can't think of anything else that would merit this." He glanced at her, but she seemed as puzzled as he was.

He waited in a funk, trying to work out the complexities of dealing with the city of L.A. without a car and without money. One thing he had to do soon was get Michael Chen to give him a read on the telephone number stored on his kitchen phone.

THEY left the beat-up Concord outside a repair shop in Fillmore and they all squeezed into the bench seat of the tow truck to ride into a car-rental place in Santa Clarita that was still open. The only vehicle the impatient manager had left was an exorbitant Lincoln Town Car the size of Oregon, and Jack Liffey put it on the credit card he kept for emergencies and took Maeve and Faye home in style.

He was just kneeling down to scratch Loco behind the ears, despite the dog's usual air of barely tolerating affection, when the doorbell rang. Nobody could enter the complex without calling first, so it had to be a neighbor or someone the guard knew. For the first time in years he actually used the peephole and found himself staring straight into the face of a well-groomed man in a stylish beige suit, a man he'd never seen before. He opened up.

"Jack Liffey?"

"Uh-huh."

The man held out a business card that said he was Lieutenant Kevin Anderson of the Special Investigations Unit, Culver City Police Department.

"I think I'd like to see a badge, too."

The man plucked a brown wallet from his coat pocket and flipped it open to show a silver badge and an identity card.

"I'd like to talk to you for a few minutes, sir."

He had the usual trimmed mustache and a handsome chiseled face that made him look remarkably like Kris Kristofferson. Jack Liffey waited a bit before answering.

"Could you tell me what it's about?"

"I'm not a threat to you, Mr. Liffey. I'm here to help you, if anything."

"I'm not sure why I don't believe that. But come in."

The man smiled as he came in, and Jack Liffey shut the door and gestured to the sofa, where the officer sat down decorously. "When you're a police officer you learn a lot about paranoia just by following people around."

"Well, I learn about paranoia when people follow *me* around."

Loco growled softly but the policeman ignored it. He was also ignoring Jack Liffey's bald dome and that was suspicious by itself. "You know, when I go to a party, everybody else is Jimmy or Bob or Douglas, but I'm always introduced like, 'This is Kevin, he's a cop.' "

"Probably so nobody'll offer you dope or underage sex."

"And somebody always throws up his arms and goes, 'I didn't do it!' Could you sit down, too?"

"Sure. What's Special Investigations?"

"A little of everything. Culver City is a small town."

That was certainly edifying, Jack Liffey thought.

"I haven't seen a Lava lamp in years," the policeman said. "I used to have one right under my blacklight poster of Jimi Hendrix."

"I used to keep mine under all the Maoist literature and the bombs."

The policeman laughed warmly. "Okay, okay. I know a bit about you, Mr. Liffey, and I think we could be acquaintances in another world, but, you're right, that's probably another world. The reason I know a bit about you is I had to do some research to find out . . . Well, it's basically a question of your integrity. It's the *sine qua non* of this discussion."

"Better stick with the small words."

"I also know you've got a master's degree. Let's not be disingenuous."

"No, let's all be *forthcoming*."

"I'm getting to the heart of the matter, and I think you'll like it. One of the duties of Special Investigations is what other departments call Internal Affairs."

"So you're the yellow pad in this here town," Jack Liffey said, after a long pause. He knew it was what the police called IA.

The policeman raised his eyebrows. "I'm the yellow pad. I'm it. This town isn't big enough for me and corruption both. I mean that. You've had a run-in with a Culver City officer named Mike Quinn, haven't you?"

"Hasn't everyone?"

"Point well taken. I believe a woman friend of yours was battered by Quinn, but she didn't complain, so there's nothing we can do about that. What's got us worried is the possibility that he's been planting evidence, particularly in dope cases. If even one of them comes out in court, it could compromise years of convictions."

"We've had words a few times, but I've never personally seen Quinn do anything illegal. I hate to disappoint you."

"That's about what I expected. He would remember you, though, wouldn't he?"

"I don't know. I doubt his universe revolves around me. I'm just another civilian who wouldn't drop down and kiss his ass. There must have been others."

"Don't kid yourself. You're a private investigator, which makes you stand out already, and you got in his face at least once in front of witnesses. If that's not enough, we could do other things to make sure he remembers you."

"Oh, great, that's what I want. Let's get him angry and then send him around to roust me."

Kevin Anderson laughed again. "We think you're just the sort of person he'd be tempted to try to plant evidence on. There's nothing to worry about. We'd have you covered and videotaped."

"And after he shoots me, my heirs would get a fortune."

"I promise you'll be safe. And you'd be helping rid this town of a bad cop. I happen to know he's a bully and a bigot. I hate having men like that on the force, they give us all a bad name."

Loco had been standing across the room, looking from one to the other with a little quizzical expression as if trying to decipher the conversation on too little information, which was probably exactly what the dog was doing. Then he made his decision and came across the room diffidently and did something he'd never done before: he pressed his flank against Jack Liffey's leg, almost as if offering his support and affection.

"You know, there's no question I don't like Quinn very much," Jack Liffey said. "If he were out on the ledge of city hall, I wouldn't budge to keep him from falling off. But I don't snitch people out."

"I don't consider it snitching if you're not his colleague."

"I do."

"I don't think I understand your philosophical position. Are you saying it's wrong to track down a rogue cop?"

"It's not my job."

"All I'm asking you to do is offer Quinn the opportunity to plant evidence on you. I'm asking you to be one hundred percent *clean* and let us videotape the encounter and see if he tries to dirty you. Doesn't that give your sense of justice a little thrill?"

"I've got enough thrills, thanks."

The policeman settled back for a moment and looked around him, as if he'd find the answer printed on one of the walls. "You know, Quinn turned your name in to our surveillance unit as a guy to watch. You're lucky his partner at the time scotched it."

He remembered the partner, a black cop who'd seemed a decent guy. "Give him my thanks."

"Somebody told me you had balls. You were the sort of man who stood up for the weak even against people with the power to hurt you."

Jack Liffey smiled. He *had* said something like that once or twice, and it sounded preposterous read back to him, like something an actor in a colored jumpsuit on TV would say. "That was probably just me getting my ego all worked up."

"Maybe, but I believe in what I'm doing. I care about getting bad guys off the street and bad cops out of the squad room. It's a simple philosophy, but it's the best I can do." His eye drifted to the wall of books, and he thought about something for a long time. "You know, American cops are the first warrior class in history provided with weapons but no real belief system."

It was an intriguing thought, but he wasn't about to let himself get hooked by an intriguing thought. "We've all got our problems."

The cop argued for a while longer in a desultory way. Jack Liffey liked the man, his earnestness and the willingness to risk himself, but there was no way in hell he was going to get drawn into cop-verus-cop stuff in his hometown.

"Keep my card and think it over."

When he was gone, Jack Liffey started absentmindedly scratching the dog's haunches, and something strange happened. Loco's ears went back, the neck arched, and the head started swinging very slowly to one side and then back the other way. The eyes seemed glazed over and the rhythmic swing went on and on.

"Should I have done it, pal? What do you think?"

It was easy to imagine that slow sway back and forth was a glacial *no* issuing from the wild coyote unconscious.

11

CHANGING ONE TIRE AT A TIME

"Hey, Mr. Liffey, how can you tell an IBM field
service engineer who's got a flat tire?"

Jack Liffey recognized the bubbly voice on the phone.
It was Michael Chen and he was really pleased with
himself about something.

"I don't know, how can you?"

"He's changing one tire at a time to see which one is
flat."

"I think I get it."

"And how can you tell an IBM field service engineer
who's out of gas?"

"I don't know."

"He's changing one tire at a time to see which one is
flat."

Jack Liffey chuckled dutifully as Michael Chen reduced himself to hysterics at the other end.

"Did you practice your violin today?" Jack Liffey said
in his best nag, and the other end of the line went dead
silent.

"I'm nailed to the wall, dude," he said finally. "How
did you know about my mom?"

"I know everything." Loco was at his feet, looking up
winsomely like a real pet, and Jack Liffey wondered if
the dog was sick. In two years he had never done more
than snarl at him and demand food. Jack Liffey didn't
quite trust this new affection, though, and he looked

around the living room idly for some obvious catch, a gnawed pillow the dog had to suck up for or a big pile of dog shit.

"Every afternoon, the moment I got home from school. All I wanted to do was get back to my computer—I had an Altair back in the elder days that I built from a kit—but Mother wanted me to be the next Yo-Yo Ma."

"That's the cello."

"You know what I mean."

"Uh-huh. I played the trombone, but nobody wanted me to be the next Bix Beiderbecke, least of all me."

"That guy, you know, you wanted me to check out his Internet activity."

"Milo Mardesich."

"Well, I checked him out."

A bit of sun streamed in the top corner of his patio window, throwing one lozenge of brightness on an old pair of boots against the wall like a clue in a bad movie. The architect had cleverly arranged his window in relation to the balcony on the condo upstairs so the sun could only get into his place about four days a year.

"Leaving the computer on didn't help, by the way. His service provider logged him off when it'd been idle awhile, they all do, but I broke his password and took care of that." He paused again, apparently a bid for congratulation.

"You broke his password just like that? Good work."

"It was pretty easy. Amazing how many people use some form of their birth date. Anyway, film at eleven. His bookmarks show he was mostly surfing around in places like Critical Theory and French Philosophy and someplace at Carnegie Mellon with a lot of essays, I've got a list."

"You said *mostly*." Loco lay at his feet and bellied up subserviently for a rub, the first hint ever that the dog might not insist on being the alpha dog. Jack Liffey squatted to rub him lightly, feeling the coarse thick fur.

"Recently he's not into Baudrillard anymore, he's looking up chemistry handbooks and reading syllabi of college courses in organic chemistry. But the really strange part was day before yesterday. I tried to go into his machine for another look. Didn't you say he was in the hospital?"

"Yup."

"Well, about nine I couldn't get into his site because he was logged on."

Jack Liffey stopped petting Loco and stood straight up. "Can you be sure it was him?"

"No, but it was his ID and password. Hold your horses. I tried about ten and he was still on. Then at eleven I got in after he'd quit and I found out what he was after. He was pulling up everything he could find on Bhopal, you know, that place in India where they had the gas leak that killed a whole bunch of people."

"Uh-huh, I have heard of it."

"He was also downloading information on methyl iso-cyanate, and the design and engineering of gas storage tanks, and anything he could get on a chemical called sodium thiosulphate."

A penny was starting to drop. "How long ago did he first start pulling up chemistry files?"

"Just about three weeks."

"And the first Bhopal files?"

"That was all the day before yesterday."

The first time he could have logged on after his accident, assuming he had a way to do it at the hospital. The penny hit and went right on through to the bottom. The bounty hunters weren't worried about anything to do with *Jimmy* Mardesich and the Theodelphian Elect. They were worried about *Milo* Mardesich, the dangerous whistle-blower, and his pal and accomplice Jack Liffey. The dog righted himself all at once and trotted away.

He stared at the disappearing rump of the dog as Loco shouldered his way through the partially open door into the bedroom like a lazy drunk.

"Michael, I've got another favor to ask." He had used a cranky old tape machine to record the beeps and boops off his kitchen redial. "If I play you the sound of my telephone dialing a number, can you find out what the number is and who has it?"

"Ask me something *tough,* dude. Hold on." There was a minute's delay, with a lot of rustling and banging at the other end. "Okay, shoot it over here, big shot."

Jack Liffey played the sound of the number.

"Got it. I can give you the number right now, but if you want the name and address, call me in half an hour."

"Thanks, Michael. I owe you one on this."

"Feetch-feetch."

It was high time he had a talk with Milo Mardesich, just as soon as he returned the big Lincoln and got his car back.

"I kinda figured you wasn't rolling in dough," the owner said. The shop was a big Quonset hut outside Fillmore called Esteban's and this was probably Esteban himself, fortyish and brown and round as a berry, with the sleeves of his greasy shirt rolled right up to his armpits. Ranchera music was beating away from the dim depths of the shop, and Jack Liffey liked the fact that this was one guy who probably wouldn't ask him anything about the weird haircut. "When you said, just get it going, you know, *however.*"

"You figured right."

"The steering was easy to fix, but the rest is pretty . . . *transitorio.*"

"Temporary," Jack Liffey suggested.

He nodded and led him around a huge tangled pile of broken car parts to the wounded Concord in back. On the bad side they'd tied rope around the window pillars to hold the beat-up doors shut and the windows had been sealed over with thick plastic wrap and duct tape.

"I like fixing for cheap."

Jack Liffey couldn't resist patting the roof of the car.

At least the thing got an extended life span with him, and it would fit right in with all the other beaters driven around L.A. by janitors and their families newly arrived from Oaxaca who had hired on somewhere at decent wages only to see their jobs contracted out to some fly-by-night firm that dropped them to minimums. The car of the broken dream. L.A. was full of them.

"What do I owe you?"

He shrugged apologetically. "Can you do twenty bucks?"

Jack Liffey figured a double take wouldn't be a good idea. "I can do twenty bucks. I'll come up here and give you some real work when I can afford it."

"You don't owe me nothing, but I might be able to find you some new doors cheap."

"Give me your card and I'll call you."

"Card?"

"I'll look you up in the book."

"CHEN, Michael, at your service."

He had called from a pay phone in a Mobil station. "This is Jack. What can you tell me about that number?"

"Technically it's unlisted. It's corporate, unassigned. The bill payer is GreenWorld Chemical."

"Bingo. Thanks, wizard. I'll buy you a new floppy disk."

"Twenty-three skidoo. You really *are* out of date."

ON the way back to the Valley, he slowed past the spot of the accident, out of a kind of dark nostalgia. There was a bit of rutting off the shoulder where the tow truck had spun its wheels to drag the car out of the ditch, but nothing else. He wondered how many people would ever see that sign and try to interpret it—acting out a sort of archaeology of bad luck. Farther along he saw other ruts, and scrapes in the guardrail, and black skid marks on the pavement, each a sign of somebody's heartache. The world was funny that way, he thought, chockablock with the scars of events just about everywhere but damned reticent about what they meant.

His new passenger-side windows billowed and flapped whenever he went over forty but they seemed to be holding. Just before the interstate his eye caught on something odd by the side of the road. Somebody had collected a lot of roadkill, dead possums and rabbits and a few cats and a small dog, and arranged them into a regular dot-dash along the shoulder. He wondered if it had been an impulse to order, trying to make the markings fit into a pattern so the world wouldn't seem so haphazard. Like religion.

From the freeway, St. Agnes Hospital looked even more like an office building for accountants. He parked under a sign that reserved a row of parking places for VISTOR'ES and wondered idly how many grammatical errors you could possibly wedge into a single word. He followed a gaggle of nurses in under a long carriage porch that thrust into the parking lot. One of the young nurses wore a beige duster that just whisked the ground, like something from a J. Peterman catalog. He liked the dashing look of it.

A hand-lettered card in a name bracket by the door of the room said *Mardesich* and the second bracket was empty, so he guessed it was temporarily a private room. When he put his eye to the peekaboo window, he was surprised to see Jimmy Mardesich leaning over the bed talking to his father. The boy was wearing a ratty letterman's jacket and he opened and closed his flat palms like a book, as if offering his father something insubstantial but precious. The elder Mardesich was off the respirator but still on an IV drip. One hand clung lightly to the boy's jacket sleeve, as if it was a talisman. Jack Liffey was surprised to see the contact between them and he decided to leave them to it for a while.

Unlike every other hospital corridor on earth, there was actually somewhere to sit, a plastic chair left against the wall, and he sat and folded his hands and went into a kind of suspended animation that let him mull over the events of the last week. He was still working on readjusting his footing to take account of the fact that the Theodelphians were irrelevant, and always had been. If any cruise missiles had his name chalked on the nose cone, they were coming from another place entirely.

A young black man in a filthy white coat came down the hallway, juggling a small beanbag casually off his elbows and forearms and occasionally his forehead.

"Climbers do rope," he said distinctly as he passed Jack Liffey and popped the bag up off the back of his wrist. "Masons do bricks . . . junkies do dope . . . and doctors do dicks . . ."

He wondered if it was a counting game he'd never heard of, something that had been around in the black community for centuries. Down the corridor the man dropped the beanbag and swept it up again nonchalantly. "Damn. Dead twice on dicks."

He decided he'd have to visit Mike Lewis, the only man he knew with a finger firmly on the pulse of the city, and ask the inside dope on dirty chemical companies. But first he had to find out if Milo Mardesich had indeed logged himself on from the hospital and what he'd been up to.

The door to the room swung open and closed heavily with a *wubb-wuff* and the boy stood blinking in the brighter corridor. He looked at Jack Liffey, and recognition slowly filled him like a liquid rising into his eyes, but he didn't betray anything more than the recognition.

"Mr. Liffey. It's good to see you again."

"Have you left the headers?"

The slang name didn't throw him.

"Yes, I have. There wasn't much more for me there. I think I'm on a path in another direction."

"I thought you were going to let me know."

"There's a message on your machine. I needed to tell my father, too." The boy had the same curious atonality to his speech that he'd had in Ojai, as if a drug were taking the edge off everything.

"How did he take it?" The boy was so tall in front of him that he was growing uncomfortable talking up at him from the chair, so he stood up, but the boy was still a couple inches taller.

"He took it all very well. It's the first time in months he actually heard what I said to him. We had a good talk. I told him where I need to go right now."

"Maybe there's a side to his character you never appreciated."

"Maybe. I have a great deal to learn." There wasn't a trace of irony in the boy.

"Where are you going?"

"I think it's important for me to live amongst the poor for a while. I don't think it's possible to appreciate the things they may know about the world if you don't share their life."

"Just how poor are we planning to be?"

"I thought I'd start downtown near the missions."

Jack Liffey raised his eyebrows. "If we're truly planning to share the life on skid row, we're going to have to acquire a couple of blood diseases, some running sores on our legs, a taste for Thunderbird, a gash in the head, and a lot of green phlegm."

Even that didn't get a rise out of the boy. "I hope that's not going to be necessary."

"It's probably going to be unavoidable." He checked his watch. They didn't usually enforce visiting hours, but he had to talk to the elder Mardesich and he couldn't take a chance. "I need to talk to your dad for a few minutes. Will you wait for me?"

"Sure."

"Wait here. Sit *right* there."

"Okay."

"*Will* you wait?"

"Why would I lie?" He seemed nonplussed.

Jack Liffey chuckled. "People have been known to."

The boy smiled, but it was a different and gentler music he smiled to, not cynicism about human nature. He sat like a big automaton winding down and Jack Liffey went into Milo's room.

THE room had that hospital smell of antiseptic and plastic, plus some indefinably human aroma of innocent pain and innocent fear. He noticed that the other bed wasn't vacant after all, but held a wizened figure that lay rigidly in a fetal position with extra pillows propping up his scrawny legs and arms. Milo Mardesich sat up in bed watching a silent TV. He pulled out an earplug when he saw Jack Liffey.

"You may not remember me, Mr. Mardesich. Jack Liffey. Your wife hired me to find your son. I had more hair when you saw me last."

"And you did your job, implacably I bet, like a bloodhound." There was the same mystifying hostility, maybe no more than a reflex against an outside world that disturbed his calm.

"But I'm a postmodern detective, so I probably did it with less authenticity than Philip Marlowe would have."

That got his attention, though he still pretended to be interested in the monitor that sat on a bracket on the wall. Jack Liffey stared at the television, too, where they both watched a man with a television camera stalking into the lobby of a public building.

"I believe," Milo Mardesich said, "that the simple presence of a television camera in a public space creates a high probability of a violent event." He switched off the monitor and turned to look at Jack Liffey.

"Your actions sure increased the probability in *my* life," Jack Liffey said calmly. "Your wife's, too. How did you log on from here?"

"Hospitals are full of computers."

"Somebody was watching your account, and I think they got really upset when you started reading about Bhopal."

His eyes became suspicious.

"Friends of mine were watching, too. Your enemies are now my enemies, so we ought to have a little talk. I think it's probably too late to back down."

"What happened to Faye?"

The man in the other bed gurgled a little, and they both turned to listen for a moment. Something trundled past in the corridor.

"She's fine. We had a little car accident when my steering was sabotaged. There have been other incidents, so I'd like to know what you know or what you've seen or what somebody *thinks* you've seen."

"Maybe somebody's just taking you off."

"Uh-uh. Guys show up and use your name a lot and then they talk like goons in a thirties movie. It's embarrassing."

Mardesich raised his eyebrows. "I don't really know you."

Jack Liffey nodded to the phone on the bedside table. "Call your wife. She knows me. I'll give you some space."

He left the room and the boy stood up, but Jack Liffey motioned him to sit back down. "I'm not through here yet. I'll give you a ride anywhere you want if you agree to stay in touch."

"Sure."

They heard a door open and turned to watch a small group coming out of a room down the hall. A little girl tugged angrily against the arm of a gaunt woman who seemed to have been crying, and a heavy woman walked haughtily behind them both. Her hands were occupied with a black cowboy hat and a toy tomahawk with a feather on the shaft.

"You promised me a pony ride!" the girl complained.

"Shut your bloody cakehole, girl!" the gaunt woman barked.

He saw Jimmy Mardesich recoil slightly from the emotion. The little girl retreated inside herself and let herself be led along, and the boy watched sadly as the grim procession went past them.

"What makes it so hard for a woman like that to be kind?"

"Her own pain?"

"We all have pain."

"I don't think you're going to be able to take it all on yourself," Jack Liffey said.

The boy glanced at him with a worried look. "I just need to understand it. That's why I left the Theodelphians. They couldn't explain things."

"You know . . . I hate to say this, but it's possible the Big Engineer up in the sky never got it right, and things can't be explained. Some people get lollipops and some get shit, and there it is."

The boy took it in, but didn't react. Jack Liffey walked across to glance through the peekaboo window just as Milo Mardesich hung up the phone. "Stick around."

As he entered, he noticed the old man on the other bed was breathing noisily, but it didn't seem to be distress.

"Faye says I can trust you, you're a regular Sam Spade." Milo seemed to have gone a bit dreamy, as if a drug had kicked in.

He'd rather have been Philip Marlowe because Spade had a nasty streak, but he didn't say anything.

"I'm sorry I caused this mess, it's typical of me the last few years. I think I'm the original Hard Luck Kid. Even when I try to do something selfless, it backfires. At some point life just becomes a whole bunch of things you don't want to do but you've got to do."

"Could we explain this in some sort of order?"

He smiled slightly. "Sorry. You know I was working as a night watchman at GreenWorld Chemical. There were always two of us on duty, and every hour one of us would have to do the rounds. You know, you carry that big punch clock on your waist and there's keys on chains in these little boxes all over the grounds. You walk around and insert one key after another in your clock and it records you were there at that hour doing your duty.

"Most of the place . . . Well, I don't know what they do in most of the place, but out in the middle there's an area behind a lot of skull-and-crossbones signs that's got holding tanks for toxic waste, a kind of transshipment yard where I think they collect waste from little manufacturing companies all over and then when the tanks are full, they do whatever they do. Every night I'd see these scabby old tank trucks pulling in and pumping waste into the tanks. Some of them had Mexican plates and some were California and they all said 'Joe's Waste Collection' or 'Ed and Arnie's Refuse' or things like that. Some were GreenWorld trucks and they looked a little better.

"I only had one key station in that area and the smell was pretty bad, like somebody spent about half the day burning cats around there, so I got in and out pretty quick. I noticed, once a week, Thursday about one A.M., a big shiny–stainless steel truck came in and loaded itself up. One Thursday I'm clocking myself into the toxic yard and the driver of the shiny truck tried to bum a cigarette from me. He was a big guy with a kidney belt like a lot of truckers and a strong New York accent and a real fuck-you attitude, even when he was asking a favor. Just to be friendly, I asked him where he takes the stuff he picks up, and right away he turns into George Raft, tells me to mind my own beeswax. That got me to thinking and then it got me to watching for him. And one Thursday I called in sick and I waited outside the gates and I followed him. I must have been flat out of my mind."

The breath rasped across the room and the bed creaked, and slowly Jack Liffey became aware that the old man over there was perfectly conscious and masturbating. The cords in the back of the man's neck tensed, and finally Jack Liffey came around to the chair on the far side of Milo Mardesich's bed and sat so his back was to the busy creak-creaking.

"I followed that truck all the way out to the desert. I figured there was an incinerator or a government dump of some kind out there, but he turned off on a small ramp called Corn Springs Road and then onto an old stretch of Highway 60 that's parallel to I-10. I had to turn out my lights and follow him slowly but he got slow, too. There was nothing on that road but a few abandoned foundations of old gas stations. Then the smell came in my window and I realized what he was doing. He'd opened up the taps and he was dumping his evil concoction on the old road as he drove along."

The air conditioner kicked in and the sound mercifully helped cover the insistent whittling noise from the old man just as it seemed to be coming to a crescendo.

"I stopped when I saw what I was driving on because I didn't want to expose myself to any more of that stuff than I had to, but I'm sure he emptied his whole load on that back road. It's called Chuckawalla Road now, out past Chiriaco Summit, if you want to check it out."

"I'll take your word for it."

"A couple weeks later I followed him again. The same big stainless-steel truck. This time he went up on an old stretch of the Ridge Route that's still there beside I-5 past Castaic. He did the same thing, just motored slowly along with the pipes gushing. I could see the spray in the moonlight. I don't know how long they've been doing this, but I sure wouldn't get out and walk around on any old back roads in Southern California, I'll tell you that."

"Do you remember where you were when you were gassed?"

"Sure. I was walking between A-six and A-seven, they're two low corrugated metal buildings just outside the toxic area. You could stretch out both arms and touch the walls and it was a dead air trap under the eaves, but I don't know any storage tanks there. It was a shortcut I used most nights."

"And when did you get interested in Bhopal?"

"Well, I remember the smell that knocked me on my ass. It was like chili powder thrown in the air and then being walloped with an old gym sock. I've never smelled anything like it. The first day in here, I watched them draw my blood and it was the color of cherry Kool-Aid. It jogged my memory. I remembered descriptions like that from *Time* magazine or somewhere."

"Were you right?"

"I don't know. I'm an engineer, not a chemist. The gas at Bhopal was methyl isocyanate, but they think it reacted with water and gave off lots of products and the real damage to people might have been done by cyanide. What I experienced could have been cyanide. You going to help me find out?"

"Are you planning to go back to *work* there?"

"Next week, if they let me out."

"I think your gassing was deliberate. Somebody probably found out you followed the truck and laid a trap for you."

"The possibility crossed my mind. All the more reason to nail it down. Hey, Mr. Spade, my life hasn't been worth very much up to now. This gives me something to do."

"Woooo." The old man gasped and expelled a long breath as if deflating. Milo Mardesich frowned and turned to look at him and Jack Liffey realized Milo had been aware of the long intimate sonata, too. "What the hell's wrong with this place?"

"It's full of sick people," Jack Liffey said.

12

STAYING ABSOLUTELY EVEN

THIS WASN'T AT ALL WHAT THE BOY HAD EXPECTED. SCORES of unfriendly eyes along the curbs and against the walls followed their progress. Jack Liffey motored slowly down Fifth past Wall Street and then San Pedro Street, well into the heart of the Nickel, L.A.'s Skid Row, and Jimmy Mardesich said nothing. Wind cut around the homeless missions and abandoned warehouses and plucked eddies of paper trash up off the streets into little white whirlwinds. They passed what had come to be called Indian Alley, where homeless Native Americans were encamped in hogans of cardboard and blue plastic tarps, and then they reemerged into the larger tribes of the African-Americans and Latinos. Curiously, the few Anglos they could see were all women. One brown-skinned man with half his face blasted away by some disease reached out ominously for the car.

"Not quite here, I think," Jack Liffey said.

Jimmy Mardesich was too stunned to reply. For some reason even the physical environment was eroded away down here, the fire hydrants losing their last paint and the curbs rounded and chipped away, as if a great burden of something corrosive had hung over the streets and rasped regularly back and forth on tides driven by the last faint currents of the sea breezes that made it fifteen miles inland. The sharp-edged skyscrapers of the bankers' downtown were only six or seven blocks west but they fussed away in their own universe, barricaded into safety by security guards and every wile of street-level grille and blank marble facade the architects could devise. Discreet urban fortressing had become an L.A. specialty, tens of millions of dollars invested in keeping these few thousand lost souls at bay.

The car drifted past a half-dozen black men who sloped along the sidewalk with walkers and wheelchairs like a shoal of the wounded.

"These are real people," Jack Liffey said. "They are not mere circumstances of your spiritual education."

"I understand that. I hope I do."

They passed people squatting to eat beside cardboard encampments, tearing hunks of bread off a hard loaf. A young man hurried along wearing one red tennis shoe and one black loafer, pushing an empty hospital gurney. A dwarf stared back angrily at the car and gave them the finger. A woman clung to a man from behind and reached over his shoulder, shouting and trying to grab something from him, but no one was inclined to come to her aid. He drove on.

"Maybe here," the boy said.

It was the Grace Mission. A sign on the side wall said SLEEPING ZONE and had arrows pointing every which way. The street seemed less chaotic, and a short line of men waited at the door.

"Do you have some money?"

"Enough for a while I think."

"Do you really think this is the way to share their experience? I don't think you're equipped."

The boy seemed to summon his equanimity back from some deep reservoir. "*They* don't have any choice. I have to try."

HE caught up with Mike Lewis at the channel end of Fish Harbor in San Pedro, where he was dangling his short legs over the gunwales of a ratty old shrimper named *The Great Regret* that rode the swells off a con-

tainer ship that was just beating its heavy way out the
channel. Lewis was an L.A. social historian, with a specialty in where the bodies were buried. He'd had a vogue
for a time after a book of his had unburied a few choice
local bodies, but then had fallen out of the public eye
and ended up teaching a few courses here and there at
small art colleges where the deans weren't particularly
sensitive.

"Nice car, Jack," Mike Lewis said.

"I'm running a scientific experiment on the strength
of sheet plastic."

"Nice hair, too."

"That's a longer story."

Mike Lewis did something businesslike with the valve
of his scuba gear and set it aside just as a weathered old
sailor came on deck from below. His skin looked pocked
and unhealthy and he grinned at Mike.

"Jack Liffey. Dusko Marrot."

"Hey."

The container ship hooted as it rounded the end of
Terminal Island, and the old man sat nimbly on a hatch.
He dug out a Popeye corncob pipe and lit it as Jack
Liffey stumbled aboard with his landlubbers' legs.

"How does Mike get you to take him out diving?"

The old man thought about it awhile, scratching his
leathery neck. "He save my boy's bacon," he said finally.

Another Mike Lewis story, Jack Liffey thought. There
were a lot of them, and he didn't really have room for
any more. The last time around someone had told him
how Mike had been desperate to find out which bureau-
crat the L.A. School Board was grilling in closed session
over a leak about one of the many district breakup
schemes that percolated up out of the whiter reaches of
the Valley. So Mike had phoned in a bomb threat and
then videotaped everyone scurrying out of the big gray
building above Grand Street.

"So I will do the world for him." The old sailor subsided, and they all seemed to endorse his reticence, though probably for different reasons. Mike Lewis never talked about what it was he expected to find down in the channel bed between Catalina and the shore, but whatever it was, it was probably there.

A sudden breeze swept across the boat and caught his car where he'd parked behind a mountain of seine netting, and they watched the plastic on his windows flash and ripple in the sun.

"Dusko used to be a Yugoslav," Mike Lewis said. "Then he was a Serb for a while, until he got fed up with what they were doing."

The old man puffed a bit, a kind of European huff of contempt, like steam leaking from a pot. "Not just in Bosnia neither," he said. "Right here in town, too. Throwing pipe bombs and calling names, 'You fascist Eustache Croat bastard.' 'You commie Serb baby-killer bastard.' Guys been friends for forty years, they eat at Ante's every Tuesday, their kids play football at San Pedro High together, it's all so moron. It makes you want to bring Tito back. For a little peace, I would even drive a Yugo."

"Don't go overboard."

Jack Liffey wondered how Milo Mardesich fit into the Balkan feuds. It was a Yugoslav name of some variety, but he seemed so far removed from it all, with his engineering degree and his home up in the mongrel suburban vastness of the Valley. He tried to imagine his own Irish heritage catching him up in the same way, reduced to feuding with some Scots-Irish Presbyterian in his condo complex over what was going on in Northern Ireland, but it was too ridiculous. It would be like fighting over TV shows or the size of the cuffs on your pants.

"I sponsor a petition. We got the Jugoslavian Club in town, you know, with the *J*, and I know we can't use that name no more and I say, 'Let's make it the Dalmatian Club, we all from the Dalmatian Peninsula,' but then Disney make the damn movie and we all suddenly damn spotted dogs."

Mike Lewis laughed. "What are you now? Adriatics?"

"I'm a southern Slav, but I don't know. It's all too moron."

"This guy might not be all that magnanimous," Mike Lewis explained. "Most of the other 'southern Slavs' in town here are Croats, from the fishing coast around Zadar and Pag, and he's an inland Serb and distinctly in the minority."

Dusko Marrot waved the pipe and hissed contemptuously. "This hatred goes across the ocean by magic waves. It's in the air. It sneaks into brains like virus and these little bitty brains swell up like a blister. Somebody say one word, 'blubba-blubba,' and the blister burst open, and the virus fly out and look for enemies."

"That's two words, blubba-blubba," Mike Lewis corrected.

The man shrugged. He seemed to have talked himself out on the disturbing topic for the moment.

"Corruption's two words, too," Jack Liffey said. "Cor. Ruption."

Mike Lewis frowned and turned toward him, and Jack Liffey could see him coming into focus. It was the kind of word that did that to him. Mike Lewis smiled a kind of feral smile. "You look like a man with a question."

"That's me," Jack Liffey said. "Men with questions form a distinct fraternity in this town."

"And all the others are heavy drinkers." He knew Jack Liffey was on the wagon. He produced a bottle of single-malt scotch and shared it with the boatman. "I won't offer."

"It doesn't burden me. I need to know about the toxic-waste business, or about GreenWorld Chemical out in Burbank."

The boatman put down his pipe and took a packet of Twinkies out of his canvas jacket. He stripped off the cellophane and poured scotch fussily onto one of the

Twinkies, dribbling it slowly from end to end so the spongy cake had soaked up as much as it could hold. Then he began to eat the Twinkie with satisfaction.

"GreenWorld. Formerly a subsidiary of ACI, the third largest chemical corporation in the world, part owner of the state of New Jersey. But I think I know what you're really after. Remember when napalm became unpopular, and Dow spun off their subsidiary that made it? When DDT became illegal, Du Pont shipped the production facility to a maquilladora just south of the Mexican border and then cut it loose. Manville waited too long to get out of asbestos and they damn near went under with the lawsuits. Spin off the bad stuff, send it to the third world, let the Thais eat rat poison—it was the corporate game of the eighties."

"What was GreenWorld's poison?"

Mike Lewis laughed and took a big swig off the bottle. "Their poison was poison. They began with reclaimed motor oil and picking up old photographic chemicals to dredge out the precious metals and they got into storing really bad industrial waste, taking it off the hands of other corporations. Then ACI pioneered ways to neutralize PCBs and dioxins and nerve gases by burning them at very high temperatures, preferably in big incinerators in the working-class end of your city. With all the Superfund money around, it was a growth industry for a while."

"I thought they stopped those incinerators."

"Most places did. I worked on the campaign to stop Lancer in Watts. This is a mighty litigious country, and when the poison game started getting more risky than profitable, ACI cut their industrial waste group loose with a pat on the back. Actually they spun it off to a group of VPs and some venture capitalists who liked the gamble. They had the common touch, some of these new owners. There was a lot of corporate bonding with some shady types, I hear."

The old sailor started flavoring his second Twinkie.

When he had it well soaked, he offered Mike Lewis a bite, but Mike shook his head and took his straight out of the bottle instead.

"Sicilians used to be big in reclaimed motor oil," Jack Liffey said.

"Or what passed for Sicilians out here in the west. Guys like Mickey Cohen. These guys like any kind of gig where you can cut corners and muscle a lot of little guys."

"How's this for cutting corners? Somebody pays you a pretty penny to haul off their toxic waste and neutralize it and you just dump it down the drain."

Mike Lewis shook his head. "They monitor the drains. EPA, city agencies, the state."

"It's a metaphor, Mike. You put it in a truck and dump it at night on a desert road where nobody much ever goes." That got his attention all right.

"That's not a metaphor. That's a felony."

Inexplicably the old sailor had started to cry. He stared at half a Twinkie in his hand and wept silently, tears rolling down his cheeks.

"Oh, Holy Moses," Mike Lewis said.

At first Jack Liffey thought he was reacting to the old sailor's tears and then he noticed Mike was looking down at the water, bending forward, his eyes open wide.

"I thought it was just a tire."

The other two joined him at the gunwale and they all stared overboard at an oil sheen ruffled by the wind, and then faintly, beneath the surface, a darker shape turning slowly in the current that tugged past the mouth of Fish Harbor.

"Waterlogged," the old sailor said.

When the shape of the long neck became unmistakable, they could see that it was a Thoroughbred horse, drifting just beneath the surface, though all the legs had been chopped off at the knee. Or eaten off, Jack Liffey thought.

"Not good," the old sailor decided, and wept some more.

AT the end of the dock there were three pay telephones in their little phone-company plastic bubbles. One phone was missing its handset, the second took only credit cards, and the third had its coin slot jammed with bubble gum that had hardened to concrete. He trudged back to the boat.

"Mike, let me borrow your cellular."

"What makes you think I've got a cellular?"

"Same thing makes me think you don't take ginseng supplements."

"Okay." He dug in his gym bag and something clumsy in the motion made him look younger, more vulnerable, but it might just have been the sickly sea light on his pale skin.

On an intuition, Jack Liffey asked, "How's Siobhan?"

Mike Lewis gave a little shrug as he tossed the phone casually over to him. "She went back to Ireland."

"See her family?"

"For good."

"Oh, shit, I'm sorry, Mike." Siobhan and his own wife had been best friends. Mike Lewis didn't look very happy about it.

"I hope it works out for you."

"I'm learning to like losing. It has fewer responsibilities." He saluted with a hoist of the scotch bottle. "A dark disenchantment prevails for now."

Jack Liffey wanted to step back aboard and give his shoulder a squeeze or punch him lightly, but it would have been too awkward. "I hate it," Jack Liffey said. "Life won't leave you alone."

"Nothing scares me anymore," Mike Lewis said. "I've got that."

Jack Liffey walked a ways up the dock before calling Art Castro's office. He recognized the secretary's voice. She was the one with the big eyebrows who was always eyeing your shoes and wristwatch, something they taught in receptionist school to sort out the losers and make them wait. Art Castro worked for a high-class detective agency and they didn't do a lot of work for losers.

"This is his old buddy Jack Liffey, so you can tell me where he is."

He heard a dull electric hiss for a bit.

"You remember me, Timex and Sears loafers."

"Oh, I remember you." Still more phone hiss.

"Art told me if I ever really needed to get through to him to tell you, '*Murieron tres toreros el año pasado.*' "

She corrected his pronunciation fussily but he could almost hear the disappointment in her voice. "I bet you don't know what it means."

"Three bullfighters turned in their lunch bucket last year." They'd set up the password because Art was holding something important for him, some evidence he would probably never need, but if he did, he'd need it in a hurry.

"He's up in Hanson Dam on a stakeout. He'll be in the wild land up in the far north. That's all I can tell you."

"If I don't make it out in a week, send the sled dogs."

HE thought a moment and then dialed a second number. He asked at the switchboard and finally got through.

"Quinn."

"You don't know me, but I have some information for you."

"The hell I *don't* know you. You're that fuckhead Liffey."

Jack Liffey waited a moment, but it didn't change anything. "I'm that fuckhead Liffey who's warning you that IA is after your ass. Don't do anything I wouldn't do."

He hung up. He'd thought long and hard about this call and he could not quite come to grips with why he felt compelled to make it when he disliked Quinn so and would be perfectly happy to see someone pull him down. Bending over backward to give a hand to your worst enemy was a moral imperative of some sort—in his finicky conscience it seemed to have something to do with staying absolutely even in an ambiguous world.

13

BLOOD WILL TELL

SOUTHERN CALIFORNIA MANAGED TO NORMALIZE ITS DIS-
asters by making up scientific scales for them. The
equivalent of the Richter scale for wet-season floods was
based on anticipated frequency, and in the world of rush-
ing water the Big One was a hundred-year flood. The
massive earthen Hanson Dam was almost two miles
long, meant to keep a hundred-year flood sweeping
down out of the Tujunga Canyons from obliterating the
whole northeast Valley. On the safe side of the dam
there was a manicured golf course for the rich, but on
the inner, danger side they'd left a couple thousand acres
of wild chaparral, boulders, dirt parking lot, and the kind
of rough parkland that the city offers up to its working
poor.

He cruised slowly down the winding access roads.
Here and there dusty pads off to the side held a handful
of cars and Latino families cooking at portable barbe-
cues or playing soccer. Art Castro drove a big silver
Lexus but Jack Liffey guessed he'd have some sort of
beat-up agency panel van for surveillances like this. The
Lexus would stand out here like a gorilla in church. He
smiled, thinking of his woeful Concord with its flapping
plastic, which would fit right in.

On one of the parking pads about fifty Asians of all
ages were standing under a banner with a big cross and
a lot of Korean script as they belted out Christian hymns.

He wondered who on earth Art Castro was spying on out here.

And there there it was, a gray Ford Econoline so old the driver's seat was forward of the front axle, the only American van ever made that was as dangerous to drive as a Volkswagen. MANNY'S SEWER-ROOTER, it said on the side and it even had a pipe clamp on the hindquarter as window dressing, but it was backed up to the edge of the parking pad so the rear windows would look out over the chaparral to the west and Jack Liffey couldn't think of a single rational reason to go to the trouble of backing that van into the parking slot except for the view.

He parked in front of the van and got out to rap on the side door. "Liffey Pizza," he called. "Anchovies 'R' Us." There was a scurrying sound, like unleashing a big animal, and then the door came open.

"Fucking-A, Jack, step inside quick."

Art Castro helped boost him up and then shut them in, and it was a remarkable shift, like falling through into another dimension. There was a rudimentary bar, a lot of radio gear, and two easy chairs facing back. The light coming in the back windows was so subdued he guessed they were one-way glass.

"So this is the sort of fancy toy you get when you work for the big boys."

"You should see the private jet. What are you doing out here?" There was a crazy glisten in his eyes, and Jack Liffey guessed he'd taken something to stay alert.

"I used the magic word on your secretary."

Art Castro groaned and motioned him to sit. "Dr Peppers in that little icebox. Try to keep your voice to a gentle roar." He picked up a pair of binoculars with the biggest lenses Jack Liffey had ever seen and gave the area to the west a once-over.

" 'Course, I could ask what you're doing out here, too," Jack Liffey said.

"That's kind of on a need-to-know basis, Jack."

"Couple jackrabbits cheating on their disability?"

"Something like that."

Jack Liffey borrowed the glasses and peered out the back window. Surprisingly, the binoculars weren't as powerful as he'd expected, but all that optical glass made the scene brighter than day. They had a weird resistance to being moved and he felt the faint tremble of spinning gyros in the image stabilization mechanism that was making the picture rock-solid.

In the distance a strange game was going on in silence, and it was like peering through a thick glass window into another world. Thirty or forty small brown men drifted in shoals behind a ball the size of a cantaloupe that was punched back and forth by men who seemed to have bricks strapped to the punching surface of their fists. One man with a tall pole marked out a position in their midst, and he drifted back and forth regularly to replant his marker without apparent reason. It was like an ancient ghost of some Aztec contest reasserting itself on the face of the land.

"What the hell is that?"

"I don't know much more than you. It's called *ball,* and it comes from the far south."

"Way past Mason and Dixon."

"Oh, *way. My* south, Chiapas or Campeche. I don't think you tracked me down to ask me anthropological questions about Mayan ball games."

Jack Liffey described his bounty hunters and asked if he knew who they were. Art Castro went uncharacteristically quiet, then he hummed a little bit, like a machine resonating.

"What are you taking, man? I thought you were clean."

"Just a little crystal to stay on top."

"Special Forces popcorn."

"Nah, those were those green-and-white amphetamines, but there it is."

"You going to tell me about the redhead and his pal,

or you going to go on humming some more?"

"So they fancy themselves bounty hunters now. They're the kind of guys who start out reading *Soldier of Fortune* in high school and recruit themselves into private armies. They leaked down here about a year ago from some militia in Idaho or South Dakota and showed up at the office one day, because we're the best known name, and they wanted a job with us. Rosewood himself threw them out, and when they threatened to blow up his mother and all her friends with C-4 he had them checked out for good measure. Remember BWT?"

"Bacon with tomato?"

He smiled a thin smile and swept the west with his binoculars again. "Blood Will Tell, I think it stood for. Christian Identity guys, whatever the hell that is. I'm Catholic and I *know* who I am. These guys declared the Deadwood Republic up in redneck land and slapped liens on everybody's property who didn't swear allegiance along with them. The liens are bogus but it can cost you a fortune in lawyers to get them vacated.

"These two you're talking about weren't smart enough to run the scheme, but their commandante came up with a nasty twist on this scam. He'd file all these liens and then at Christmas he'd send his enemies a forgiveness notice that he was giving them back a portion of their debt. Then he'd send a 1099 to the IRS announcing the amount of the forgiveness as *income*. The poor schmucks. Some of them are still trying to straighten it out with Uncle Sam."

Jack Liffey laughed. "Man, I wish they'd put a lien on my condo. It's worth half what I owe. I'll FedEx them the paper tomorrow."

"Don't fuck with these two guys. They're stupid *and* clumsy. It's a bad combination, Jacko, guys who never know when to back off. If they think their macho is in question, they'll shoot their own foot off." He rooted in a small Styrofoam lunch bucket and came out with a sandwich in a plastic bag, which he investigated with a dubious look. "Want some?"

"What is it?"

"Velveeta on white bread. My old lady's grand plan to make me more American." He started tearing the sandwich into pieces, crushing them down to small white marbles and dropping them back into the Styrofoam.

He liked Art Castro but he didn't much like being with anyone on speed. It was like being left out of the joke. "Do you think these guys registered a home address when they applied for work?"

Art Castro stared hard at him. "Don't do it, man."

"They tried to kill me, Art. They messed up Marlena." He took off his watch cap. "They even shaved my head."

"I wondered what that was about."

"There's a code about letting guys do that to you."

"I used to subscribe to that, too, but now I just kick back and say *nam myoho renge kyo* about ten times. It does wonders for your longevity. These guys are just pond scum, man."

For just an instant he experienced a terrible sensation of futility. Maybe Art Castro was right. What was the point of spending so much energy to even things up with a couple of miscreants who subscribed to *Soldier of Fortune*? And for that matter, what was the point of tracking down missing children at all, most of whom would just go missing again first chance? Then the feeling passed, just vanished into the ether. A Dark Thirty Seconds of the Soul, he thought. Everything was devalued these days. He wondered if there was a random electron that fired from time to time in the brain, making you feel there was no Real Meaning in things.

"A man's got to do what a man's got to do," Jack Liffey said.

"Do-be-do-be-do," Art Castro said. "You got to mellow on down."

"Thanks for the advice." He could see he wouldn't

get any more help, even if Art Castro knew their where-abouts. He got up to go.

Art Castro smiled without much humor and spread his palms wide in a gesture of cosmic acceptance. "Just be yourself, man."

"And if you can't, at least try to be someone rich with a Maserati."

It wasn't all that far south to the industrial area at the back end of Burbank Airport. Milo Mardesich had told him the address and there it was, a couple square blocks of low buildings and giant Tinkertoys behind chain link. A tall louvered structure boiled off clean-looking steam and a number of rusting chemical tanks looked like they would start leaking if you glared hard at them. He couldn't see a nameplate anywhere.

He parked and strolled around the perimeter, up an alley that took him close to a thrumming corrugated metal building. He stood on a Dumpster to see a com-pound containing hundreds of rusting fifty-five-gallon drums, some of which seemed to be toppled and leaking. Finally he saw a pair of low buildings close together that might have been the place where they'd caught Milo with the gas. There was no sign of life anywhere inside the wire.

Out in front a black guard sat in a glassed-in guard shack at the service entrance. He seemed to be playing solitaire on a surface that was out of sight. A half-dozen cars were parked in a little lot that was across a few feet of grass from what must have been the office. The stucco over the office door was a brighter yellow where a name had been painted out, and one big glass window showed an empty lobby and a counter where no one stood, like a set for an end-of-the-world movie. There was no pickup truck, but he noted the license number of the big black BMW 750 parked nearest the door—RECLAIM.

Just as he got back to his car, he saw a little blur coming toward him down the middle of a dreary industrial street. The figure gathered reality, framed by a broken sidewalk along one side of the street and weeds on the other, until Jack Liffey made out a slim, almost weightless athlete, tumbling hands to feet to hands, then cartwheeling and twisting and tossing in a back flip now and then. He wore shorts and a tank top and had a big green number on his back and he came to a stop with a last twisting flip facing Jack Liffey's car window.

"Geroot-patoot," he said, or something like that, his arms flung up in Nixon's victory V.

"Nine-point-seven," Jack Liffey said.

The athlete laughed and did a standing back flip before cranking up his strange progress again.

SULTANATE Street was eerily quiet, but somewhere inside the house behind all the screwy gingerbread eaves something was pounding the floor over and over. The sound was odd, mostly vibration coming up through the porch, and he couldn't quite put an image to it. A tabby cat was on the porch and it was confused by the sound, too, its head cocked to one side.

The cat fled when he rang and the pounding stopped abruptly. Faye Mardesich opened up, something a little off in her eyes. He wondered if she'd been sharing drugs with Art Castro.

"Eeep." She gave a little sound in her throat and then cleared it and a real presence seemed to gather substance and come forward to peer out her eyes. "Jack, am I glad to see you. Come on."

She backed away and he saw she was wearing leotards and some kind of stretchy top that was made of big bands of elastic that crisscrossed. He'd always liked those tops because you could imagine slipping a hand in easily, but he wasn't thinking along those lines at the moment. Her feet clopped on the plank floor and he saw that she was wearing her husband's big cordovan wing tips. They were laced tightly but her feet still slipped about in them a bit.

"You had to ask," she said, but he hadn't asked anything.

The kitchen floor was littered with shattered bright-colored crockery and she crunched across it with a mischievous extra little pump of energy from the wing tips to pound the jumble down some more. She retrieved a generous drink she had going. "I dropped the first plate. I mean, it was an accident, the first one. I mean, it slipped. I'm not clumsy. I'm *not*. It made me so mad, I threw the next one, and the next."

Suddenly he felt trapped and nervous. Something was going wrong in this house. She sipped and glanced up at the ceiling. "Aren't we dysfunctional, one and all. Let me count the ways."

Thankfully, she didn't. He was not going to tell her about Jimmy now, even though that was why he had come. She was in no condition to absorb it without looping off in some unpredictable direction.

"Maybe you ought to lay off the sauce for a bit," he said.

"I never liked Fiesta Ware anyway." She set the glass down with exaggerated care and took up a dance pose that didn't quite work with the brogans. "And one, and two . . . *plié*. The black keys are called the chromatics, the sharps and flats. You'd think they were superfluous, but they're the true secret of Western music, the sharps and flats." Tears were rolling down her cheeks, but she didn't seem to be crying. She offered the empty doorway a ludicrous grin.

He hated scenes like this, absolutely hated emotion gone sloppy and melodramatic, but he would stay and deal with it. If he'd learned one thing over the years from all the nasty little lessons life forked up for you, he'd learned that whatever you'd managed to absorb of the honorable, you we're never given the opportunity to deploy it in grand ways, with cheering crowds and a sense of satisfaction, but only in small, messy, and unwitnessed rags of duty like this.

"Let's sit down for a while," he said.

"I don't even know what to cry about," she said. "It's like I'm trying to write my own back story. I'm crying, so I have to find something hideously sad to cry about."

She clomped past him dance-wise, then crossed her arms to grasp the shoulder bits of her stretchy costume and wrench them apart and down so her breasts spilled out. She turned to show extremely large brown nipples and white stretch marks where the breasts plunged. "You could have me, Jack. Milo doesn't come home until to-morrow."

He held her the way a priest would have, enclosing and comforting and immobilizing. "Let's talk about things."

She tilted her neck up and tried to squirm around to get him to kiss her, and he pressed the back of her neck to push her face against his chest.

"I'm sorry," she said finally, going slack. "I need something so much that I get angry and the anger makes me crazy."

He walked her to the messy sofa and brushed aside a number of magazines. He sat her down and she pulled her stretchy top back up and crushed her arms to her chest in an exaggerated pose of modesty. "Oh dear, oh dear, oh dear."

"Try to tell me what you were thinking the moment things snapped."

She barked a single laugh, like a cough. "I was think-ing it was *unfair* that only four months have thirty days, and seven have thirty-one. I know that doesn't make any sense. Maybe there's just a sense of injustice that blows in with the Santa Ana winds. 'All the rest have thirty-one, except February which . . . doesn't.' It doesn't even *rhyme*."

There was a loud bang in the kitchen and he waited for another, but nothing came and he decided it was just one of those noises that a house made. Something smelled a little strange, but he let that go, too.

"Long ago I met a guy in Laos," he said. "He was British and he showed me the way they count off the months in England. Watch." He made a fist and counted along the knuckles and valleys as he named off the months. "January, February, March, April, May, June, July-August . . . You've got to count two months on the last knuckle before you start back. All the up knuckles are long months, and the valleys in between are short months. September, October, November, December."

Her eyes focused on the demonstration as if he'd just disemboweled a house pet, and then on him. "Jesus, Jack, I'm not some bar pickup that you have to charm with tricks."

He dropped his hands. "You *are* angry."

She seemed to soften. "And I have enthusiasms and I weary of them. I go through things too fast. You know, I can't even believe in our crusade to save Jimmy anymore. He's a big boy and he can take care of himself. It's Milo I worry about. It's *me*. I've got to have something that doesn't wear out right away."

She picked up his arm and brought it up to her face and bit his wrist softly. "We are such failures in this family. World-historical failures."

"That's hopeless talk."

"It's a place to start. It's not self-deception."

"You can say that again," but she didn't. She only shook her head.

A screech filled the house suddenly and they both bolted upright. He noticed the smoke rolling out of the kitchen doorway up at the ceiling, and he was on his feet in an instant. He got to the stove before her and cranked off the knob. Then he picked up the aluminum pot with a towel and got it under the faucet, where the blackening mass sizzled for a while, sending up another surge of smoke that kept the smoke detector going until he reached up with a magazine and fanned the smoke away from it.

"Chicken noodle soup," she said as she stared mournfully into the pan. "Once. Failures. In my family, we can't even boil *soup*."

The exaggerated remorse struck him as funny, and his laugh started her laughing, too.

"I'm sorry I embarrassed you," she said. "I would have been good to you but I know it was the wrong thing."

They opened all the windows and the back door off the kitchen. The cat stared quizzically in at them. They sat down on the small back porch and talked for a while of neutral subjects—pets, grease fires, childhood. She kept medicating herself with booze and it was getting her sleepy.

"Oh, wow, I'm so ashamed. You can go now, Jack. Don't worry. I'm okay."

"You look better. I want you to know I'm off the clock. I know where Jimmy is and I'll look in on him and make sure he's okay but there's no charge for the service."

Her eyes were closing of their own will. "I have to nap. I'm sorry about all this." She went in and crunched away across the crockery and disappeared into the back of the house. He let himself out. He stood in front for a while, wishing he still smoked. It was one of those moments of relief that a cigarette would have completed.

HE left Sultanate in a different direction than he usually took, and in a block he braked to a stop in the middle of the road. It was the camouflage netting covering the entire backyard that had caught his eye, all the little peanut-shaped figures worked into the net that probably did make it look like foliage from way up in the air. A black POW-MIA flag flew over the netting, and a concertina of razor wire that ran along the top of a tall chain-link fence marked the entire perimeter of the lot. The front yard was a flat expanse of pea gravel, and poking up through the gravel there were a couple of Claymore mines realistic enough to give him a chill. A wooden gate into an interior motor pool stood open, and when he let the car drift forward he could see a couple of mannikins with M-16s crouched beside an armored personnel carrier. An olive four-by was parked in a gated driveway. It was either a perverse art project of some kind or a guy who'd never really made it home. He wouldn't want to try delivering the mail there.

THEY were lining up along the outer wall for the bubble and treat, the five o'clock sermon and free dinner, but if you were paid up for the room you didn't have to get in line. He found Jimmy Mardesich in a utility room down the corridor from the cafeteria sitting on the edge of a beat-up table like a college professor facing a half-dozen men in folding chairs. A huge Latino sitting beside Jimmy like his keeper had his T-shirt sleeves rolled up high to show off jailhouse muscles and blurry jailhouse tattoos, one of which said FUCK PEACE. Something about Jimmy appeared different.

Everybody was listening intently to a skinny kid with a Mohawk and a mannered haughtiness. "So he goes, 'When I find her and tell her what you did, you little fuck, she's gonna kick your ass back on the streets.' And I go, 'Look, *whoa* man, I know I been a screwup a lot but I didn't *do* this one, I swear,' and he pulls off this big fat leather belt and says he's going to teach me not to lie all the time, and I must've been on something because I say, 'And I didn't ask my mom to go remarry no imbecile biker dude who can't find his ass with the toilet paper neither,' and I get this."

He torqued his torso around and pulled up a frayed shirt to show fresh welts along his back. His pants hung low to reveal a lot of his blue-striped boxers. Then for a moment or two he made guttural sounds that were not even distant relatives of words. His head jerked around in a petulant little rage, or a fit of some kind, and then he seemed to readjust himself to reality.

"Okay, wheet, I used to be a happy kid and Mom and

me'd spend hours listening to the Grateful Dead and she'd talk about all the years she been a Deadhead and gone from place to place to follow them and selling hash and hubba, and we used to snuggle up and she'd close her eyes and let me play with her tits a little, and we'd eat Cheez Whiz out of the jar and we were both happy as Larry until Godzilla comes along and takes over her mind like the fucking Body Snatchers. I swear, he musta put a big pod in the basement. Now he goes, Marcella, you go stand on one leg and sing 'Dixie' and she goes and stands and sings fucking 'Dixie.' Anything he says. He gets her fucked up on speed and turns her out to his friends—" The boy's head jerked around again, as if a giant were shaking him.

"Hold on, Low Pockets," Jimmy Mardesich said.

Low Pockets, Jack Liffey thought, was probably two or three years older than Jimmy, but he was a good eight inches shorter and gaunt as a Depression photograph. When he stopped twitching, Jimmy locked eyes with him for a full minute, and Jack Liffey couldn't tell what was passing between them. "We need to focus on what's true, what you know is true," Jimmy said very softly.

Low Pockets rose up in a threatening way, and so did the big Latino.

"Don't fuck with the man," the Latino warned ominously.

Jimmy calmed the bodyguard, and Jack Liffey noticed a smell of vomit wafting down the corridor, warring with cleaning fluid. Somewhere down the hall live music started up behind a closed door, bad Christian rock on an organ.

Low Pockets let his stiff neck fall forward and he gobbled like a turkey once. "Sure, okay, the last stuff's BS. He never turned her out, and he never hurt her. This Clarence probably even likes her some, but he sure hates my ass." His voice was starting to break. "He took away my mom. Abba-dabba." The boy choked back a sob.

"Come here," Jimmy said.

The boy stumbled across the intervening space, Jimmy's Latino guardian alert to pounce at any sign of trouble. Low Pockets started to weep and hugged Jimmy, and Jimmy placed his hands on the sides of the boy's head. "Let it hurt. This is the man who stole your mom from you." The sobbing redoubled and the boy trembled and had another little fit.

After a while, much softer, Jimmy said, "Don't worry so much about what your mother said in the church. If there's divinity at work in the world, it's not located in some building, it's inside you and me and her."

Jimmy let the boy cry for a while as everyone sat and watched, one or two fidgeting, and then he took his hands off the boy's head and reached for about half of an uncut loaf of bread that Jack Liffey hadn't noticed sitting on the table. He ripped off a piece and pressed it into the boy's hand. "Eat this bread and remember its taste, it'll be the taste of your letting go, your beginning to heal."

Tentatively the boy took the morsel of bread and chewed.

"I think they want us for dinner," the bodyguard announced. Only then, with the men rising and mumbling to one another, did Jimmy Mardesich acknowledge Jack Liffey's presence. He glanced up and nodded a greeting as the bodyguard looked the newcomer over.

Two men brushed past him at the door, one saying over and over, "I'm indicated, I tell you, I'm really indicated. I saw the papers."

Jack Liffey nodded back to Jimmy. *I told your mom I'd check up on you* didn't quite seem appropriate after the messiah performance. He knew what was different about the boy now. He'd always seemed calm and distant, but now he was well beyond that, as if he'd withdrawn some part of himself into a world where it couldn't be touched at all.

"How are you?" the boy asked, as if Jack Liffey were the one in jeopardy.

He laughed softly. "Fine, thank you."

The boy didn't see the humor, but it didn't seem to worry him any more than anything else did.

"I'll check in tomorrow," Jack Liffey said. "See if you've risen yet."

As he left the shelter, he struggled with the pesky feeling that there was an ambience of fraud in what he'd just seen. He wondered how he would respond if there really were holy men and some latter-day Moses appeared before him. Perhaps it was just that so much bogus religiosity condensed out of the smog in L.A. that it tainted the real thing when it arrived. *Real thing*—he smiled at himself. As if there were such a thing as a *real thing* in the holy-man business—short of megalomania.

BANDS of fire and purple struggled in the western sky as he walked to his car, silhouetting the fancy skyscrapers downtown. It was a gaudy stage set for an end-of-the-world movie, and with a sudden whirring, a big man with an even bigger motion-picture camera passed overhead walking on air just above the roof. The line of men and women waiting for supper gawked upward as an amplified voice bellowed and crackled, "Don't look up, don't look up!" to no avail.

Jack Liffey made out the cable and then the arm of a crane from which the man dangled. For some reason, two white seagulls, turning rosy pink in the dusk, wheeled around the cameraman like performers who'd wandered in from a different dream.

"I don't think the kid needs your help," Jack Liffey said to whatever god was orchestrating all the symbols.

THE noises behind his front door made him hesitate, but he didn't really think the bad guys had come back, and they hadn't. Marlena was cooking something in his big iron frying pan as Loco watched with interest.

She'd been a little anxious, too, peeking out the blinds at the sound of his key.

"Hi, Mar. Brave of you coming back here," he said.

She waited for it, so he kissed her and she kissed back but didn't push it.

"I got this now." She took a tiny purse automatic out of the pocket of her apron. Something was odd about the way she was dressed, but he was distracted by the pistol. He took it gently from her.

"Let me hang on to it for now. You're scaring Loco." The dog had stirred, but now it relaxed and sauntered away.

"I'm making you fajitas, *querido*."

He peered into the pan, but that was refried beans. The sliced steak and vegetables were laid out on a cutting board on the counter.

"I love fajitas. Where did they come from, anyway? Ten years ago they didn't exist, and then like some bush telegraph, every Mexican restaurant in the U.S. put them on the menu in the same week."

"I think it was invented at some resort, maybe Cancún." She switched the fire off and turned to him, and before she had the housedress half off he realized what had been odd about it. Only one or two buttons had been fastened and under it she wore the black merry widow she'd bought from Victoria's Secret plus the garter belt and black nylons. He found it all a bit silly, but knew better than to say it.

She looked down demurely and then up at him and then down again, and he liked the way her face changed from a bit plain to beautiful each time, and he liked the comforting sense he had coming home to her, and he figured he ought to just marry her and get really used to it.

She let the housecoat fall around her feet. "I want you to take all this off with your teeth," she said huskily.

14

IF A FLAME DOUBTED, IT WOULD GO OUT

"**YOU THINK I'M SMART ENOUGH TO DO THIS?**" ROGELIO asked him. He handed Jack Liffey a matchbook that promised a rewarding and fulfilling life after fourteen weeks of General Computer Repair School. To prove it, there was a picture of a grinning youth soldering something together on his kitchen table while a young woman looked on proudly cradling a baby. The scene had everything except a beaming Ike giving his blessing.

"I think you can learn the same stuff for free at JC."

"Not in fourteen weeks."

"What especially makes you trust an ad on a matchbook? If you look close, that's not even a computer he's working on."

Rogelio ducked under the table and fed the cables from the Mac around behind the rear panel. "I dunno. I seen it on TV, too."

Jack Liffey took the ends of the cables where Rogelio passed them up and bundled them with the PC cables. Marlena was trying to expand her Mailboxes-R-Us into a small service bureau, and she'd bought a secondhand Mac and PC and an old laser printer, and he and Rogelio were setting them up at the back of the shop where she used to keep the mailing envelopes, notepads, and cheap pens. It was good to be able to do a favor for her for once, but he didn't know half as much about computers as she thought he did.

"Where did you learn electronics?" Rogelio asked.

"The army taught me everything I know." Jack Liffey stretched a thick black power cord in two clenched fists. "*Men,* this is a power cord. Think of it as a pipe. Think of the electrons as little PFCs like yourselves running along the pipe. Voltage is how hard the men are running. Amperage is the number of men in the pipe. Resistance is how narrow the pipe is, which forces the little men to bend over and rub their shoulders along the walls as they run." He couldn't quite keep up the drill-sergeant voice, and he chuckled once. "A short circuit is when the little enlisted men turn and frag their officers."

Rogelio had picked up a gray cord and was sitting in a lotus beside the table, staring at it, as if he might actually see the little men. "Cool. What's inductance?"

Marlena bustled in with a white tub of the day's mail. She was wearing a tight low-cut sweater and you didn't have to know her all that well to see she was really glowing.

"The U.S. Army does not recognize inductance. It's not a muscular concept."

Marlena was showing quite a bit of chest muscle. She bent a little more than she had to to set the tub down by the letter boxes, and a bright red bra under the black sweater flashed at him like a traffic light. "Rogelio, you can go on to your game now," she said huskily.

"Thanks."

"Jackie can finish the computers."

He figured people for miles around could hear the endearment she varnished over his name, but if Rogelio noticed, he was keeping it to himself as he grabbed his baseball windbreaker and saluted himself out the door.

He booted up, but as usual couldn't get the computer to find the printer. "It's right *there,* dammit. *I* can find it. Computer, meet the printer."

He felt her hand hot on his neck and something large and soft pressed his ear, and he had to close his eyes and swallow.

"I forget how good you are for me," she whispered.

She went into the storeroom off to the side and left the door open. No one in the shop could see her, but she was only a few feet away from him when she pulled the neck of her sweater to the side and showed him one cup of the lacy red bra. It was semitransparent, another purchase from Victoria's Secret, and he could make out her dusky nipple clearly. She really had her pilot light going and it was having an effect on him, too.

"*Querido . . . querido . . .* " she mouthed softly.

She ran one finger softly around the shape of her breast, watching him. He smiled as she mouthed more words at him. He couldn't make out the words but it hardly mattered. She kept her eyes on him with a kind of fixed ferocity and let her hand drift south. He was beginning to wonder if he ought to reciprocate in some way when the deep male voice boomed over his shoulder.

"Do not be affrighted, my child. The cleansing that is coming soon will be great, but all who have stayed in the light and gathered up their grace shall be saved. We have not shared Communion with you recently at the barn door."

Marlena had stiffened like a deer hit by one clean shot, then turned away as if looking for a particular box of red pens on the shelf. Jack Liffey turned to see a gaunt man in a black robe and dog collar. He had one of those Swedish beards that ran in a thin line along the rim of the jaw, framing skin so white and pasty that blue veins showed in his cheeks. It looked like the wrong face had been poked into one of those photo props you saw in carnivals, with the bodies of princesses and cowboys.

"Our Redeemer's tears are falling upon nations as the end days draw nearer and the world will be cleansed in a baptism of fire. My child, we miss your bright face in our congregation, among the righteous." The preacher glanced down at Jack Liffey with an unyielding dark gaze.

"Nice to meet you, too," Jack Liffey said.

"Have you accepted that Jesus Christ is filled with love for you?" he asked. "We approach the millennium," he added darkly.

"You know, the zero point was pretty arbitrary. They usually reckon Jesus was born somewhere between four and six B.C., so I figure we've already survived the millennium."

"The Bible does not make *mistakes*."

"I didn't realize the Gregorian calendar was referenced in the Bible."

A tiny breeze of puzzlement wafted over the man and then vanished as a door slammed shut to return his mind to its accustomed stasis. The heathen sitting on the floor winked out of existence for him, and he lugged his ponderous attention back to Marlena, who was slipping guiltily out of the storage closet, carrying a ream of paper.

"Hello, Father Paul."

Jack Liffey remembered her telling him that she had been raised in some fundamentalist sect, and she had toyed recently with another one. It was a mistake to think all Latinos were Catholics, particularly since Protestants had made such inroads in Central America. L.A. was full of Templos de Nazarenos Evangelicos de Ultimas Dias and the like.

"The smoke from the bottomless pit that blots out the sun in Revelations eight is every false doctrine that obscures the light of the Gospel. The barn door is still standing open."

Jack Liffey wondered if that was the one they would lock after the horse escaped, but he decided not to ask. "I'll see you later, Mar."

Her eyes looked a little desperate. "Call me, Jack."

He nodded and went out into ovenlike stifling heat and then upstairs to his office. Somebody had shoved a flyer under the door for a local Festival of Recycling Household Waste. It seemed an unlikely subject for a festival. The faltering answering machine winked at him and then played back so slowly he couldn't recognize her voice at first.

"Jack, pleeeease give me a caaaall when you get in. I neeeed to apologize and I neeeeed to tell you sommmmmething Milo said to me. Heeee's back at work nowwww. They put him onnnnnn swing, from threeee to midnight. I'll try your hoooome, too."

It was Faye, her voice so distorted that he couldn't make out the emotional undertow, but he got her machine when he called right back. He guessed she had just stepped out for a bit and he decided on a whim to drive up there. He still needed to tell her about Jimmy anyway, and he hated doing things like that over the telephone. In fact, he hated doing any business over the telephone since you couldn't gauge the feelings of the person you were talking to. He needed that edge.

COPS were stopping traffic along Venice for a parade of gaudy gold-and-red wagons drawn by horses. Banners and flags hung over the wagons like the trappings of a gypsy army. Crowds of young people with tambourines and orange robes danced on some of the wagons and with a twinge of irritation Jack Liffey realized he was being held up by the Hare Krishnas on one of their pilgrimages from their Culver City parking lot to Venice Beach to feed the homeless.

All at once a group of dancers ducked as one, and a girl pointed excitedly up into the air. He squinted and looked where they were all looking, and at last he made out a model airplane and then, not far from his car, he noticed the grinning twelve-year-olds with the radio control unit. The plane banked over his car with a ratchety fizz and then dived to buzz the dancers again. As it rose for another pass, a cop spotted the boys and started in their direction. They laughed wickedly and took off.

Jack Liffey gave them a V with his fingers out the window, but he doubted whether they saw it. It was nice to know he wasn't the only person in L.A. who wasn't on some sort of holy road.

SHE was out on her patio staring mournfully at a wilted red impatiens in a clay pot. "They're so sensitive," she said. "Hi, Jack. Unlike me, I mean. I never wilt, I just get angry. I've done that all my life and it's always cost me."

For a moment he wondered if she was going to smash the plant down on the brick patio for thwarting her wish that it be healthy, but then she blew softly on the leaves and set it back on the little iron tea trolley with the other plants. She was wearing jeans and a work shirt, which made her look like someone who'd found a bit of comfort in herself.

"Sometimes it costs more when you don't get mad," he said. "It's probably just a question of deciding which time is which."

She stared out at the ivy-covered embankment at the back of her yard. "It's hard to believe the universe is expanding, isn't it?"

He laughed and she smiled finally, but there was no humor in her, only tension. "I'm glad you came. I'm sorry I was such an embarrassment the last time. I'll be good, I promise. I'm all under control. Can I get you some lemonade?"

"I don't think so."

There was a rustle in the ivy and an opossum waddled out onto the grass, looked them over carefully, and then waddled away as if deciding they didn't measure up. It was like a dismissal by some alternate reality. The animal lumbered back into the ivy and crackled there for a while and a couple of neighboring dogs started up. She winced when a leaf blower came on like a chain saw next door.

She turned and met his eyes but he had no idea what

her look meant. "Milo is back on the job, believe it or not, straight from his hospital bed. He called and said the tank truck is coming this evening at seven. He wants us to follow it so we can back up his story about the dumping."

"Actually, I was hired to find your son and I did. I'm off the clock now."

"I don't think this was ever just about finding Jimmy. I need to put my family back together." She thought for a moment. "You know, Milo actually asked for my help."

"These guys aren't juvenile delinquents, Faye. I think they're the guys who sabotaged my steering. They're the kind of guys who see a big federal building and right away think of dynamite."

The way her hands were fidgeting against one another, it didn't look like he was going to be able to tell her about Jimmy's slumming this trip either. A cat yowled once and came over the fence and then hightailed across the yard. The cat stopped suddenly near a stunted cherry tree and snarled at it, and Faye scowled after the animal. "I don't really care what I'm facing, Jack. Something tells me this is just about my last chance to do my duty for my family and I'm going to do it, with you or without you."

A mockingbird fluttered up out of the tree, squawked horribly, and then did a dive-bomb run that sent the cat over on its back in self-defense. Faye Mardesich made a little run after the bird and cat and stamped her feet until they both fled. When her voice came, it was shrill and tense, ready to break through a crust into another register altogether. "One more distraction and I'm going to kill something! I swear it!"

It was good she had her anger under control, he thought.

She put her hands on her hips and looked up at the heavens for a moment. Then she slogged back to the patio, and he saw that he would either have to go with her on her crusade or tie her down to prevent her. He felt trapped. There was this limitless obligation to a code that was always there, like a relentless fate, and he could see it would carry him across a lot of life's boundaries whether he acknowledged it or not. His life was a story that was only allowed to unfold along a single path. What if he cut the thread? he thought. What if he veered off in some arc he had never taken before? Walk away from this and let her drive into danger alone.

"Let's do it," he said.

There were two hours until the appointed arrival of the waste truck at GreenWorld, but neither of them wanted to hang around her house. Out front she came to a halt when she saw his car, the sheet plastic rippling lightly in the hot wind. "I'm not riding in that. I'll drive." She led him to a good square Volvo station wagon and then drove to a coffee shop called Deep Shaft Miners. Every coffee shop in L.A. had to have a theme, and he was worried a bit about double entendres with this one until it turned out to be literal. They went in through a mine adit, complete with timber shoring, and sat in a brown plastic booth under crossed pickaxes and headlamp helmets as the place filled up for early supper and he ordered apple pie and coffee. She stared for a long time at the menu and then ordered fried zucchini strips and fried shoestring onions. "I feel like picking at things," she explained.

Across the aisle, a teenage boy had his hand discreetly under the skirt of a girl with an old-fashioned pageboy haircut and a dreamy look. They thought they couldn't be seen.

A sad-looking woman came up and left Jack Liffey a little card explaining the American Sign Language alphabet and then moved silently on. He put a dollar bill in its place and wondered if the manager would catch her before she got back for it. He noticed that *K* would make a pretty serviceable fuck-you in England and *T* would do fine everywhere else in Europe.

"Did you ever have a clue how your life would turn out?" she said, and the burden of dejection was still there.

He was beginning to work himself down into the attitude where you just longed to get the next few hours over with. He liked Faye Mardesich well enough, when she was under control, but he didn't want to deal with the bounty hunters and a nervous breakdown at the same time. The girl with the hand up her skirt gasped once faintly.

"I don't think it's turned out yet," he said. But it hadn't really been a question.

"I'll tell you, I never thought I'd be a grumpy frumpy housewife, and if I ever did entertain even the vague suspicion that was what lay in store for me around the big corner, I certainly wouldn't have imagined such a hideously dysfunctional family. It's like being caught up in a soap opera that's so bad you know it'll be canceled in midseason."

She clacked her teeth once, like a dog snapping at flies.

"There was always something a bit dangerous waiting outside my window, something that offered a whole lot more, and I never seized it. I wanted to conquer worlds and I moved to Van Nuys. I wanted to do something that mattered, I wanted to be excited and challenged. I heard the call and I didn't go. You can't blame anyone but yourself for that."

Now and again he was hearing a little sound that he couldn't identify, a pop, like a cork coming out of a tiny bottle. He looked casually around but all he saw was a dozen busy families and the young couple across the aisle who were pretending they were there to eat hamburgers.

The food came and he didn't have to look very close at the limp battered zucchini to decline her offer.

"I dreamed last night I was trying to write a letter and every time I tipped the paper up the words would come loose and slide off the page. My car was lost in a huge parking lot. Milo didn't know who I was. Some other boyfriend was laughing at me. And every time I tried to dance, I slipped on a wet spot."

He heard the little pop again. This time he waited a half minute and then dropped his napkin. In turning to pick it up, Jack Liffey caught the eye of a ten-year-old boy two booths away who was shielding a soda straw in the crook of his arm, aiming it at the teenage couple. Jack Liffey wasn't the only one in the room who'd noticed what was going on. The boy stuck his tongue out at him, then put his mouth to the straw and fired a spit wad into the wall just over the heads of the couple. They were oblivious.

"Life is so *gruesome*. It's full of ridiculous people doing awful things to other ridiculous people."

"You could say that," he agreed. "But with the right perspective, it can all be pretty funny."

But she had an unstoppable urge toward misfortune. "You know, it's not so crazy I feel this way right now, now that Milo's back and Jimmy's been found. I've noticed that when you've been sick a long time and the fever finally breaks—it's right then that things start looking grim. You've been looking forward to feeling good for so long and you think it'll be the answer to everything, and then the fever does lift, and you're face-to-face with the fact that the *real* problem is you're unhappy . . ."

A spitball hit the side of the booth and ricocheted across the floor. The girl in the pageboy was sucking in little breaths, and he resisted the temptation to tell Faye that what she needed was a little of what the girl was having. In fact, what she needed was to learn how to cut her losses, but he'd noticed long ago that women had a hard time doing that. It was probably a good thing for the race but it was hard on the individual case.

Faye dabbed at her eye where a tear had formed. "I'm

sorry. I know I'm doing this to myself. My hour is up, doc."

"I'm sorry I'm not more help," he said. "You need to talk to somebody who knows how to deal with unhappiness."

"A therapist?"

"Why not?"

"It's so humiliating."

"Oww!"

The girl with the pageboy wrenched around in the booth, rubbing the back of her neck, but she was too late to catch the boy. She readjusted her skirt and she and her boyfriend both got up and left their untouched cheeseburgers. He tried to imagine being that age again and unable to wait even a few minutes for a little grope and tickle.

What he remembered instead were those first years with Kathy, when he was desperate to give her a life so rapturous and satisfying that everything in it would remind her of him. He knew now that a feeling like that could only be a sign that something underneath was wrong, that his own insecurities were seeding trouble left and right, slow-acting poisons, but everything had seemed to be scudding along so happily that he hadn't noticed.

He watched Faye take a pill and he hoped it was a tranq but he didn't ask.

"At least I can domesticate the pain," she said to no one.

THEY were parked in front of a big offset printing factory that was still operating. The printing plant took up both sides of the street, and now and then forklifts trundled across the road in front of them loaded with big rolls of paper or pallets of cardboard cartons that glowed in a peculiar orange light from the sun that was going down behind the car. They had a perfect view of the front of GreenWorld Chemical two blocks away. She said it was

Milo in the guard shack, though you couldn't have proved it by him. The BMW 750 was still there by the door. Faye had calmed down and seemed to be on task. Better living through chemistry, he thought.

Inside GreenWorld's fenced complex, the big rusting tanks were partially obscured by a plume of steam that drifted off the louvered tower and billowed east on what little of the evening onshore wind leaked over the mountains into the Valley. A red warning light on a tangle of pipes that stuck up four stories began to flash ominously, and then up at the top of a tall thin chimney there was a flare of burning gas so bright it hurt his eyes. The flame sputtered a bit and then flared brightly again and wavered upward in a picturesque pennant like Liberty's torch. They could hear a faint rumble on the air. Then the flashing light went out and so did the flame and, a moment later, the sound. It was as if somebody had given up on a recalcitrant cigarette lighter.

"I read somewhere that belief is very delicate," she said. She smiled. "If a flame doubted physics for just an instant, it would go out."

He watched as the warning light came on once more and the flame tried and failed. "I'm rooting for physics."

A young worker in a ponytail came out of the printing plant and sat on the trunk of a Thunderbird to smoke. He rapped the cigarette on his thumbnail a few times and then fiddled with it long enough to make it clear he was adding something to the tobacco.

"Thanks for not being sanctimonious with me, Jack." She sighed once as if gathering some kind of newfound energy. "It feels like people have been doing things for me for years and years, and I guess I'll be all right if I just give something back."

"It's a plan," he said.

A battered black tank truck came around the corner, made a wide turn as it clashed gears, and rumbled right past them. There was no name on the door and it looked like generations of chemical spills had collected on the tank itself and crusted on the piping along its flanks. It wasn't the shiny stainless-steel truck that Milo had described, but behind the wheel he'd seen the stout bounty hunter named Schatzi. Jack Liffey's scalp crawled and he actually ran his hand over the fuzz that had grown back. The redhead wasn't in evidence.

He thought back to that evening in his apartment and how Schatzi had talked so much about the Four Horsemen of the Apocalypse. He wondered if Schatzi had anything to do with Marlena's goofy millenarian priest, but L.A. was full of people who talked apocalyptic stuff like that. Every few years some group or other gave away their possessions, put on white robes, and clambered up onto the roof to wait for Jesus, or the bolt of Holy Lightning, or the Martian spacecraft, or the Black Helicopters of the Next Life. They always assumed the next deal would come out much better for them, but he figured things could always get a lot worse and it was best to play the hand you had.

"Is it . . . ?"

"Oh yes."

The black truck idled at the gate a moment and Milo came out to look over a sheaf of papers Schatzi dangled out the window and then he unlatched the long gate and rolled it aside. The truck stalled once and then pulled inside. Evidently, he wasn't much of a driver. Milo stared after the truck for a while and then closed up the gate and went back into his guard shack. Nothing further happened until seven-thirty, when one of the lights went off in the long window in the office block and a small balding man in a business suit came out and got into the BMW. It was RECLAIM, he thought. He needed to have a talk with RECLAIM soon.

The last of the daylight was fading away and they took turns doing the *L.A. Times* crossword in the faint light from a street lamp down the road. "Three letters for salt?" she asked.

"Tar," he said.

"Tar?"

"They're both nicknames for sailors."

"Oh, crud." She threw the paper down. "That's ghastly. It's too dark, anyway."

Just after eight, a stake truck full of fifty-five-gallon oil drums arrived. As the stake truck pulled inside, the black tanker reappeared around the office building. He nudged her alert behind the wheel.

"Time to rock-and-roll."

You could tell by the way the truck rode low on its springs, and by a heavy inertia that it suggested in its starts and stops, that it was loaded to the gills now.

"Don't start up until he's past. He's not going to lose us in a forty-ton tank truck."

When the dark truck rumbled past, they could feel its weight in the ground. It was still Schatzi sitting up stiffly in the high old-fashioned cab. She gave it a long count and then did a U-turn to follow him slowly to San Fernando Boulevard, where he turned north to parallel the freeway. She missed the light and then had to wait nervously as a flagman got in front of her while half of a big church approached up a side street. Jack Liffey couldn't believe his eyes. A nave drifted slowly across their bow, towed by a big house mover bedecked with red flags. They stared straight into the right half of an American Gothic church that seemed to have been cut down the middle, complete with stained-glass windows and blond wood pews, all lit up by their headlights. A big sheet of plastic was nailed across like the plastic that sealed his missing windows. Running behind was a truck that said WIDE LOAD.

"Let's not wait for the other half," he suggested.

She maneuvered her way past the church despite an angry wave out of the wide-load chase truck and caught up. The tank truck was in no hurry and Jack Liffey had already noticed that it had four distinctive red taillights, round and bolted on the bumper like something from

Pep Boys, so it was easy to follow on the wide city boulevard.

The truck stayed off the I-5 all the way to the pass, trundling slowly up what was now called the Old Road. At Newhall, Schatzi had no choice and he ground onto the freeway at about forty. They stayed well back.

"Where do you think he's going?" she asked.

"Somewhere where we're going to be damned conspicuous, I'll bet. When he pulls off, I want to take over."

She nodded grimly and he could see her knuckles white on the wheel. She was as tense as he'd ever seen her.

But in the event, the truck carried on all the way to a busy truck stop at the top of the Grapevine, where it pulled behind the gas pumps and parked between a Shell tanker and a long refrigerator truck. A sign at the edge of the lot said mysteriously DO NOT SWAT. Schatzi got out and went into the restaurant. They parked two roads away in front of a closed motorcycle repair shop, where they had a good view of the truck stop.

"How long do you think he'll be?"

"If he's not out in half an hour, he could be a good long time. He may be waiting for the wee hours."

He took the driver's seat, and Faye walked to a 7-Eleven up the road. He left the car door open and wedged his foot against the trip button to keep the dome light off. Far away he heard the distinctive slap of a screen door closing. It was the kind of taut heat on the air that carried sound a long way, and a cicada was sawing away somewhere. She came back with sandwiches in plastic tubs and coffee in Styrofoam and tore into her food hungrily.

"Do you know why Milo launched this crusade of his?" he asked.

She shook her head. "I don't know why I'm such an emotional wreck, either, or why Jimmy's playing Jesus. I thought we were a normal family, dealing with everything the way normal people are supposed to, and then Milo got laid off and it was like a virus falling from outer space on all of us, like a time bomb going off in our DNA. Maybe we weren't as normal as I thought we were. Or maybe there's a lot of families so near the edge that all it takes is a little push to send them running for cliffs like lemmings, I don't know." She looked away and shrugged. "You can't really talk seriously sitting in a car."

So he let it go.

IT was a long wait. They took turns napping and he was nearly dozing on his watch when a little jolt of guilty electricity went through him as the dark truck's headlights came on. It was three A.M.

"Here we go, Faye."

He followed as the truck ground onto the freeway, surprisingly turning back south toward L.A. Traffic was light, running in dots and dashes in the darkness. Trucks with onions and tomatoes bound for the big produce market, a few beat-up commute cars heading into L.A. from beyond the farthest reaches of the sprawl, loners on the last legs of their thirty-seven-hour drive from somewhere. It was a time he'd always loved to drive, private and peaceful, the hour of the super-dependable, the outcast, or the fanatic.

There was a good thirty miles of high mountain pass between the Grapevine on the north end that led steeply up from the central valley and the more gradual descent into L.A.'s San Fernando Valley on the south, and it seemed Schatzi was going to take I-5 all the way back to L.A., but at almost the last moment he pulled slowly down a ramp and turned west. At the bottom of the ramp, Jack Liffey turned out his headlights and waited. A two-lane road led off into a desolate canyon in the foothills. There were no shops or houses, only rolling hillsides that would be yellow and dry in the day, dotted with sumac and stunted live oaks. There was just enough moonlight to make out the silvery road leading off toward the taillights of the truck that dwindled ahead.

He started up the road slowly without lights.

"Whoa." She clung to the dashboard.

"I can see well enough."

He followed the road very slowly as it curved gently away from the freeway. On the left was a bland hillside that rose maybe a hundred feet above the road, and on the right there was a ditch of indeterminate depth that was to be avoided at all costs. At one point the truck seemed to stop for a while and he hung back until the lights started to dwindle again.

They smelled it before there was any other clue, a rich tarry odor on the air that prickled the nose with little hints of ammonia, old photographs, and rotting citrus. When the taillights disappeared around a bend, he stopped and opened the car door. The interior light showed a damp sheen that seemed to spread out from the middle of the road. He used his ballpoint pen to poke at a tiny gob of damp tar. The pen tip came up blackened and he sniffed it and tossed the pen away.

"I don't want to drive on this much more."

A dirt track rose shallowly up the slope to the left and he used parking lights to take the track very slowly up to a flattened dirt pad maybe fifty feet above the road, where he parked and shut the car off. They stepped out into the bloodheat air, and from the edge of the pad he could see the truck's taillights winding up the canyon. There were no other lights. Even far above the road his eyes smarted from the chemicals.

"I know where we are," he said softly. "Just over this hill is Val Verde."

"What's that?"

"Long ago it was the only rural black community in California. They came first to work in the oil fields around here. Then, back when all the big resort towns were still segregated, they put in little cabins and it became known as the Colored Palm Springs. The only whites who even knew of it were the Communists who used to come through to leaflet."

"I've never heard of it," she admitted.

"Once they broke the color bar at Vegas and Palm Springs at the end of the 1950s, Val Verde died a pretty quick death as a resort, but there's still a lot of poor black and brown folks amongst the yuppies looking for cheap land."

"And that truck is poisoning their environment," she said indignantly. "Why are they *doing* it?"

"Money, of course. Disposing of toxic waste the right way is expensive. I'm sure GreenWorld is making a pretty penny taking the stuff off the hands of other chemical companies."

"Bastards."

After a while they saw the headlights of the truck coming back down the road. "I'm surprised he's willing to drive over his own dump site," Jack Liffey said. "Maybe he hit a dead end he didn't anticipate."

"Maybe he's just too stupid to know the danger."

The truck ground slowly past and stopped on a wide bit of road just fifty yards away. The big man got out and smoked for a few minutes. It was Schatzi all right, still wearing his suspenders. His cough echoed clearly off the hills. Then he fiddled with some controls on the piping on the flanks of his truck and drove away.

Jack Liffey drove down to where the truck had stopped. A puddle had formed, deeper than the chemical slick that had sprayed the rest of the road, and it was slowly spreading. "Have you got anything like a container in the car?"

"There's a quart of oil in the trunk."

"That's it."

He retrieved the yellow plastic bottle from a plastic bag and let it glug itself empty into the ditch. "Of course, this is toxic waste, too."

Holding the bottle gingerly, he scraped it across the puddle again and again to scoop up what he could, then he capped it and wrapped it carefully in the cello bag that the oil bottle had come in.

The sky in the east was just beginning to lighten as they drove down out of the San Gabriel Mountains. When he got off the freeway at Victory, the early commuters waiting at the metered entrance looked just as bleary as he felt. The first sun was just peeking out between low office buildings. She let her hand rest on his for a moment.

"Jack, we've just spent the night together."

He smiled. "I hope Milo doesn't misinterpret."

"I'm not sure he cares enough to care."

"I'm going to put your family back together," he heard himself promise. It startled him and he turned to look at her and he could see she was confounded, too. It had just tumbled out of him, like a sneeze or a long-forgotten name, but it seemed like the right thing to do.

15

SEND THE GUNSELS PACKING

IT WAS ALMOST EIGHT BY THE TIME HE'D RETRIEVED HIS own car and fought his way south with the commute traffic to Culver City, and he could barely keep his eyes open. For a while he had worried at it, wondering what he'd been thinking about when he promised to put the Mardesiches back together, but now there was only a heavy stillness inside him. Weariness was in charge, and trying to get his mind to budge in any direction was like trying to shift a huge soft mass that flopped back over your wrists wherever you pushed. He was too old to go all night without sleep.

Both Loco and Marlena were in the kitchen and they looked up with identical scowls.

"Morning," he said.

Loco gnarred softly in the back of his throat, and Marlena probably would have done the same if she'd known how. "Good morning," she said with a frosty tension in her voice.

He sensed something was wrong but he had no energy for it. He set the plastic bag containing his loot of toxic waste on the table. "Don't anybody touch that," he said with his last flicker of energy. "It's dangerous."

"Do you want some coffee?"

"I have to sleep. Sorry. Talk later." He staggered down the hallway to the bedroom, where the bed had been made tidily for the first time in weeks. He kicked off his shoes, and was astonished when he didn't drop off the instant he hit the bed surface. He was still wired, and some strange brain chemical was fizzing away, keeping him going on nervous energy.

"Jackie." He sensed her in the doorway. "Were you with her?"

Her?

"Staking out . . . toxic dump," he managed to say.

He felt the bed give as she sat, and his hand was plucked up into the air. He opened one eye to witness her smelling his hand carefully, thrusting her nose along the fingertips.

"Don't do this," he said.

"I can't help it." She seemed about to weep, but mercifully he fell sound asleep.

HE awoke in a sweat with a hot light pouring in the bedroom window. Loco was beside him, half asleep but still watching with a slitted eye to ward off any retribution for partaking of the forbidden bed. It was just past noon.

"Partner, you take chances."

Marlena had left a small plate of flan on the night table for him. She knew he loved it, but it was subsiding to a puddle in the heat. He passed the yellow mess across to Loco, who roused and sniffed it suspiciously, then licked once and made a face, if a dog could be described as making a face.

"Hey, that's good stuff. But I suppose I wouldn't like your kibbled kidneys either."

He showered and made coffee, changing his mind about four times along the way on how to deal with Marlena's jealous snit, and finally decided just to leave it alone. She had a forgiving nature, even if there was nothing to forgive. He dug through his medicine cabinet and came up with a little yellow plastic tube that had two Tylenols rattling inside. He dumped the pills and then downloaded an ounce of toxic sludge into the container. In another mood, the irony would have entertained him: whoever tested the sample might report that someone had adulterated the poisons with a little Tylenol.

A crossing guard flagged his car down at Overland with an octagon-shaped stop sign as a gaggle of little kids crossed to the boop-boop of the east-west light. The north-south signal went *bleep-chirp*. Something at the edge of his consciousness seemed wrong and then he noticed that the crossing guard had a guide dog and he held his gaze off in no particular direction, the way blind people often did. At the far curb the last of the little kids announced loudly that they were all across. They trooped up Overland toward the rec center as the crossing guard's dog came about on the sidewalk like a tug with the *Queen Mary* in tow and waited diligently for the next green. Jack Liffey believed wholeheartedly in affirmative action, but this seemed a particularly dubious application.

As he left Culver and passed into L.A., he had that strange steely taste he got in his mouth whenever a police car was pacing him, but he watched carefully in the mirror and there were no police cars, not even a plainwrap, unless the cops had started using cement trucks. He decided it was just a taste after all and he needed to clean out his coffeepot. He couldn't think of the last time he'd done more than rinse it under the tap.

He found he was squinting as he drove, his eyes burning, and then he realized that only a few blocks away buildings were fading out into the ocher air. It was one of those days where the parking-lot exits of all the big aerospace companies would be posting a first-stage smog alert for the next day, but what could you do, bicycle thirty miles to work? On a day like this, the city lost its ring of mountains completely and seemed to have been whisked up out of its basin and dropped back into the flattest reaches of the Mojave, where it belonged.

Downtown didn't even show up until he turned off

the Santa Monica Freeway and headed up the harbor into
the small nest of skyscrapers that L.A. had thrown together in the 1980s out of insane jealousy of New York.
He looped around the downtown and came down the
east side into the Nickel. An old guy with one tennis
shoe and one bare foot was banging on the wall of the
Grace Mission with a coffee can, but no one paid any
attention.

A bored-looking woman with a pencil in her hair sat
behind the chicken-wire hatch, and she told him Jimmy
was out.

"Ya think he stays in here hanging around the Polo
Lounge?"

He asked a number of people on the surrounding
streets, showing them Jimmy's photo, and finally a
midget waved his arms in an animated way and said he
knew "Cousin Jimmy," and he thought he was preaching
over in Indian Alley.

Cousin Jimmy. Already he was preparing the ground
for his TV ministry.

The alley ran uphill shallowly off Fifth, just enough
of a slope for an overpowering reek of urine to flow
downhill around him off the blue plastic hogans and
lean-tos. One forlorn seagull came streaking out of the
alley as if chased. At the entrance, an old man sat against
the brick of an abandoned building with his head
slumped forward, rocking lightly, showing the back of
a neck that was fantastically crosshatched by cracks and
wrinkles. A woman sat dully beside him, her hand
wrapped with bloody gauze. About fifty yards up the
alley, he saw a half-dozen middle-aged Indian women
sitting in a semicircle of boxes and pails and battered
folding chairs. Jimmy Mardesich faced them, half sitting
on the detached fender of an old car that was propped
against the wall. He wore a Hawaiian shirt with yellow
pineapples against red, and his Latino bodyguard hovered nearby.

"I can't offer you a thing." Jimmy's reedy voice

drifted down on the heady air with its usual serene tone, like a heavy dose of Quaaludes. "Everything you need you have within yourselves already. It's all there in your heart or your soul or your mind—whatever you choose to call it. All you need to do is detach yourself from the baggage that's dragging you back toward doubt and let out your ability to love yourself. You've already learned the lessons you need from all the things you've experienced and you only need to tap into that wisdom and appreciate who you are. It's not always easy, I know that. For many of us, it's only when we've come to the end of the path of self-destruction that we're caught on, that we're ready to turn and move in a new direction. I realize that, and I make no effort to force-feed anyone beliefs that don't make sense. What you hear has to set up rhythms in your own heart before you hear it properly and use it. But some of you may be ready right now, and if you are, I'm here to try and help you find your way back to God, or back to that sense of comfort and safety you felt in your first home, or to that warmth you feel when you genuinely help your fellowman."

He went on and on like that, and Jack Liffey was torn between the desire to go bang the boy's head a few times to wake him up and send him back to high school and a kind of reluctant forbearance because of the obvious urge to something generous and virtuous that was welling up in the kid. He wondered if he really was witnessing the first ministrations of somebody who would found a new religion, an Aimee Semple McPherson or a Joseph Smith launching the New Thing right before his eyes, and he could tell his grandchildren, *Honest, I was standing right there in the alley that day . . .*

The boy had definitely found a Sinai to test himself on. An old woman with a reddened leathery face watched him with curiosity but the rest seemed more taken by the things they saw in the distance or on the ground at their feet. It was not even clear if any of them understood the words he was using. One old man sat cross-legged on the ground, almost within reach of Jimmy Mardesich, arranging and rearranging small bright objects on the pavement in front of him.

"And what if there is no big floaty place above the clouds filled with saints and angels with white wings and harps, what if this life is all there is and we all reap what we sow right here and now? If that's true, if the here and now is all we're going to get, is it any reason to make ourselves even unhappier than we are in the here-and-now? Joy is a state of mind, it's unique to each of us, and all you need to do to help find your own joy again is to remember one splinter of happiness from your past, one little ray of sunshine, and build it up again. Think back, get in touch with it, and detach yourself from everything that's denying you that feeling now."

A man with long shiny hair in braids came out of a plastic lean-to and glowered at the boy, the Latino body-guard watching him like a hawk. He said something too soft to hear and strutted away down the alley. As he passed Jack Liffey, the man with the braids muttered, "Pecker Christer greaseball." Jimmy hadn't even noticed and the mild, imperturbable voice droned on and on.

The old man sitting on the ground finally seemed to decide he had achieved the perfect arrangement of bottle caps and stones and cigarette wrappers, and he looked up hopefully like a bower bird expecting a mate. The piss smell was getting to Jack Liffey and he pulled out. He'd look in tomorrow, and when he did, he'd probably find the boy troweling in the cornerstone of a shrine to himself—the Church of the Big Floaty Place—or pounding on foreheads to hurl out devils, or patiently explaining to the homeless how to levitate. There were some processes that you had to let work themselves out on their own. He just hoped the boy didn't stumble into something he couldn't handle.

● ● ●

OUTSIDE the Nickel he started trying pay phones until he finally found one that still had its phone book inside the dangling fiberboard clamshell. There was no listing under the federal government for a local office of the Environmental Protection Agency and he had to settle for the city Environmental Affairs Department, which he knew had moved into the old city hall into offices the mayor's staff had fled during the big earthquake retrofit.

He realized he'd never actually been inside it—that wonderful L.A. version of the Mausoleum of Halicarnassus that he'd probably seen several thousand times embossed on police badge 714 opening *Dragnet* and he'd seen destroyed almost as many times by Martians and giant lizards. Some of his image of city hall still had to come from his imagination that day because the top half of the tower disappeared up into the smog. Inside there was a four-story Byzantine rotunda full of colored tiles and mottoes on the walls and then the elevator took him up to an ordinary hallway in two shades of institutional beige.

A bit of cardboard taped by a door said *Environmental Affairs,* and he had a momentary image of a man and woman coupling in the woods but he guessed the people inside had already heard that joke a few times too many. A low wooden fence penned him in a reception area, and mostly empty desks filled the rest of the open space. A young woman with a crooked nose had her feet on an open lower drawer as she read a tabloid paper that seemed to be called *Moxie.* He saw a big headline saying:

EXTREME SKY SURFER
PECKED TO DEATH
BY STARVING CROWS

It seemed to be illustrated but he couldn't make out the picture. He tried the clearing-the-throat trick and when that didn't work, he announced himself, "Hello there."

As she looked up, he saw a second headline:

NAKED MAN
THROWS LARD
ON INTERSTATE

She offered him a pleasant enough smile and he decided he liked the crooked nose. It made her look congenial, the way imperfection always did.

"They're all at a conference. I'm just holding down the desk."

"You like that paper?"

She glanced at *Moxie* and seemed to look at it in a new light, as if seeing it for the first time. "I dunno. It's not highfalutin, like some of them."

She brought her feet to the floor and tugged demurely at an extremely short red skirt. "Where else would I learn that Japanese people got yellow skin because they eat so much fish? I always wondered."

"Actually, I don't think that's true," he said. "Many scientists feel that it's because they're genetically descended from bananas."

"Wow, cool."

"I like your nose," he said.

For just a moment there was a reflex to cover it. "Really?"

"Really. It makes you look friendly."

She smiled warmly. "My little brother hit me with a cast-iron skillet, rigged it up on a rope to fall when I opened the door, the jerk. What can I do for you?"

He set the Tylenol tube on the wooden rail, on one of his business cards.

"I believe this is toxic waste that a company is dumping illegally. You might want to have it tested, and then I'll tell you who's doing it."

She eyed it suspiciously. "I dunno."

"It won't bite. Just pass it on to somebody when they get out of their conference, okay?"

"How do they reach you?"

He showed the card. "They can call the number here or they can fax me." It was Marlena's fax number. "I'm not highfalutin either."

OUTSIDE city hall there was a small commotion. Somebody had left a large dead thule elk on the grassy knoll that led up to the building. A half-dozen rubbernecks and two puzzled cops stood around it. One of them was laboriously copying down the message that was hand-lettered on a placard attached to the beast's antlers.

NATURE WILL BE BACK, AND SHE'LL BE PISSED

A boy poked at the animal with a stick and one of the cops waved him back. As Jack Liffey walked past, he heard the boy ask the cop, "Is there anything on Mars to kill?"

He drove up the 5 to Burbank, attending to his finely tuned sense of dread, which seemed to be firing again. This time he didn't suspect a cop following him, but something spookier and more malignant that waited out there in the smog. The last time he'd had this feeling, L.A. had been hit by a seven-plus earthquake and someone he loved had died. He didn't believe in the supernatural, but he did believe there was a faint possibility that his unconscious could tune in to signs the rest of him ignored. Dogs that whined a little too often, people on edge from too many positive ions in the air, a sky just the wrong shade of orange, the birth of just one more religion than some cosmic register could tolerate. He looked around cautiously for signs, but nothing suggested itself. Maybe it was just the dead elk. Somebody had gone to a lot of trouble to move it two hundred miles from the nearest elk reserve in the Owens Valley.

The big black BMW was outside the GreenWorld of-

fice when he parked just where he'd waited with Faye
the night before. If the car hadn't been jet-black it would
have disappeared completely into the smog. He had an
hour or so to kill before quitting time, but he didn't want
to take any chances on Mr. Reclaim taking off early.
The plastic over the right side of his car was beginning
to get smoky and translucent for some reason, but the
smog was so bad that the view wasn't that much better
out the windshield. Someone was in the guard shack,
just a shape moving in a window, but there was no way
to tell who it was. He could barely make out the louvered condensing tower in the center of the compound,
the steam boiling off it seeming to bleach out the smog
in the vicinity. Once in a while a glow up in the orange
air gave away the location of the flare stack.

Moods swam at him out of the smog. At dead times
like this he couldn't help drifting into thoughts about his
life, the failed marriage, joblessness, missed chances, a
daughter he could never do enough for, places he'd
never been, and books he'd never read. Sometimes it
seemed that everything he had done since leaving high
school had just happened to him; he'd fallen into things
without willing any of them. They had nothing to do
with who he was at root, with the person he had been
at eighteen.

Stay long enough in this mood and you'd look at the
trash collector, or the security guard, or the guy in the
pickup who fills the newspaper vending machines and
say to yourself, *I* could do that, why not? I could be
happy in that life. He knew he'd reached the age where
the way you'd always looked at yourself and justified
things didn't work any longer, and you had to step back
and find a new place to look from.

To fight off the funk, he tried to bring to mind a situation in which he had been an utterly absurd butt of
the fates. The day he'd reached out to secure Maeve onto
the Redondo Pier and tumbled off himself, thirty feet
into the Pacific below, with Maeve's scream following

him all the way down, or the belt sander that had ripped out of his hands and taken off across Kathy's dresser to wreck ten feet of hardwood floor before ripping its own plug out of the wall. He chuckled for a long time. The absurdity of the picture was important, he thought, not just the defeat. It was as if he had to make himself small and comic to sneak up on the gods, and then one day he might be able to look over their shoulder and see what they saw. It was the only way he knew that he might find out what it was all about.

He shrugged off his rumination and worked at an old crossword puzzle until he got hung up and angry about a compound derived from ammonia that could have been *amine* or *imine* or *imane* or even *emine*. Just after five P.M., the main body of paper-pushers left the Green-World office all at once. Clock-watchers, he thought, and he didn't blame them one bit. By half-past, the ass-kissers and supervisors started coming out, too, and then, after the BMW had sat there all by itself for about fifteen minutes, the boss himself made his appearance. Mr. *Reclaim.* He wore a dark suit and even a fedora, like someone who'd wandered out of a film noir.

Jack Liffey followed him easily to Studio City and then up into the hills above the Valley. Near the crest the Beemer slowed and then pulled off abruptly and disappeared down a steep drive that seemed to pass under a roadside parking pad. He caught a glimpse of the swing door coming down and saw that the pad was the roof of a garage. It was also an entry walk that led alongside a row of potted foliage to the windowless cedar wall of a hillside stilt house that probably had a hell of a view out the other side. Jack Liffey went on another quarter mile before he found a spot where he could park on the narrow road.

He strolled back, with glimpses here and there out over the Valley through the allotted spacing between the blank street sides of the houses. The road had risen only a few hundred feet, but he was above the smog, and there it was like a thick brown fur covering the land below, hiding all the features and ribs and scars except where a few tall buildings poked up through it. The sunset off in the west was going to be spectacular, banded in a dozen hot colors. There were no people anywhere in this hillside world, and here and there a dog barked as he walked past, but he didn't see any of the dogs either. Finally he saw a man straining upward with a fat brush to paint a high concrete wall, but as he approached and the man didn't move, he realized it was only a *trompe l'oeil,* a statue someone had stuck in his front yard as a joke.

"Missed a spot," Jack Liffey said softly as he passed.

He approached Mr. Reclaim's house cautiously. There was a pretty good gap to the next one and enough foliage on the hill to let him scramble down the slope a ways unseen. Then, if he went over a low fence into a neighbor's flower garden, he saw he'd have a bit of a view of the front of Mr. Reclaim's house. He climbed down the slope and then over the fence, but what he hadn't noticed was that the neighbors were out on their patio drinking martinis and enjoying the view of the smog, so he settled quietly onto the dirt between rows of dahlias and waited.

"You can take the race baiting?" The woman's voice was dry and raspy in her throat and she seemed annoyed, as if she wanted to be somewhere else.

"It's of its era. And there's not that much of it. Even Graham Greene had a bit of it, too, back then. Hell, are you going to throw out *Huck Finn* because of the N-word?"

"You can't say it, can you? If I were just a little lighter-skinned, could you say it?"

"That's not fair to me, Marjorie."

"Poor misunderstood man."

Jack Liffey found a comfortable spot to rest his weight on his hand and settled in for a bit of a wait. He could see some of Mr. Reclaim's narrow deck, and the light spilling out over the deck shifted and pulsed from time to time to indicate something was going on within.

"I was going to tell you about the little game Chandler had with his editor. That was over a forbidden word, too."

"Oh, go ahead. I'm all right about it, really, I'm just tired."

"In those stories that he wrote for the pulps, he was always trying to slip in a little something about pederasts, but every time he did, the editor would yank it out."

Jack Liffey could hear the clink of ice and liquid pouring in the gathering gloom.

"It was a pretty Puritan time, after all. He'd sneak in a child molester as a minor character and *out* it would come. Just one reference to a perky little bottom in passing, zip, eagle eye would spot it and blue-pencil it. He'd write about a character who liked to watch young boys playing football, and yank, out he would come. Finally he had an inspiration and he made Marlowe call one of the hoodlums a 'gunsel' and the editor let it pass. Chandler and his pals had a real yuk about it in private but they never gloated publicly."

An odd whoop-whoop siren complained far below and they fell silent for a moment as they listened.

"So?" the woman's voice asked finally.

"If you look in the dictionary, you'll see that the dictionary folks define 'gunsel,' in their piquant way, as a boy who's kept for immoral purposes. Ironically, of course, Chandler was so popular that his little joke ended up making gunsel into a synonym for gunman."

The woman laughed for a moment, a laugh with a nasty cold edge. Jack Liffey listened to them for a while longer, wondering idly about their relationship, homeowner and date? Houseguest and wife? As the sky darkened up, a man's voice hailed them from the house and they went inside. He sat quietly for a while longer, smelling the flowers and earth, plus a hint of mildew and wild sage.

A little spur of hillside stuck out in a crumbly cliff and when he felt it was safe he risked edging out there, clinging to a tall sumac bush, until he had a view into a slice of Mr. Reclaim's living room. Something flashed by the window, as if thrown, but it happened too fast for him to make it out, perhaps a small pillow or a book. Then a lithe blonde in a black bra and panties ran past and bent to pick the object up. It startled him and then made him uneasy, and he looked around to see if somebody might catch him peeping. By the time he glanced back, the blonde was gone.

The lights inside were full on, and moving shadows continued to spill out onto the deck. Then Mr. Reclaim marched into view, whirled around to point back at someone and shout angrily, his face red as a fire engine, before trotting back the way he came. That wasn't the odd part. The odd part was that though he was still wearing the fedora, he wore nothing else but boxer shorts with big hearts on them and black knee-high socks with black oxfords. Just before he disappeared from view he did a little high-knee running in place, like an Olympic long jumper limbering up.

Jack Liffey was tempted to edge out another few feet, but one glance at the tile roofs far below dissuaded him. Movement caught the corner of his eye and brought his attention back to the house. This time a dark-haired woman in a short blue-black slip strutted haughtily into view and whirled to bend forward until she touched the floor with both hands. Her buttocks waggled once, thrust up into the air provocatively, and Mr. Reclaim sauntered up behind her and pushed his hips against her for a moment. Then he bent forward, too, bobbed his head a couple of times, and she hiked a football to him. Mr. Reclaim backed two steps and passed the football out of sight in a perfect spiral. They both took off after the ball and Jack Liffey worked his way back through the garden with a big grin on his face. He imagined himself at the front door: *Hi, I'm a pollster doing research on assholes.*

He rang and rang and heard the two-note chime somewhere in the house. Finally a porch light came on and the door opened on a heavy-duty chain. The fedora was off and a lime-green smoking jacket was on.

"I think you know me," Jack Liffey said. "I'm the guy your two gorillas have been beating up. We need to talk."

It shouldn't have worked but it did. The man stared impassively for a long time and then turned and barked into the room, "Go bake some cookies, girls."

"Aw, Nick."

"Now."

He slipped the chain and ushered Jack Liffey in with a dismissive flourish of one hand. This level of the house was one big room with a silvery-blue wall-to-wall carpet, and it was furnished with the most garish rococo gold-on-white furniture he had ever seen, though at the moment the furniture was mostly pushed to the side walls. The football was not in evidence, nor any spare articles of clothing.

He spoke again, and his voice was so soft and so out of key with what he said that Jack Liffey wasn't quite sure he heard it right. "You got to be the dumbest fucking shit the face of the earth," Mr. Reclaim said. "Coming here."

"Nick!" a wail skirled up from an open stairwell that led down to the lower level. "There's nothing but lousy beer in your icebox."

"Shut the fuck up!"

"Interesting word, 'icebox,' " Jack Liffey said.

Mr. Reclaim kneaded the back of his neck with one hand, just a fidget. His round face was red and he still seemed a bit winded.

"I'm a small businessman," he said. "Not a big-businessman. Do you know the difference?"

He seemed almost reflective, but then his black eyes

found Jack Liffey with a flat cold gaze, like a hunter trying to select the very best weapon for the kill.

"It means you pay for everything, guy. Every mother's son's got a hand out. It means the big-business guys go to the bank in a fuckin' road train of limos, get waved up to the first-class dock, and borrow big money, and they got a partner for the duration. I go to the bank in my little car, sneak in the back door to get some chump change, and I got a shylock ready to fuck me over for the vig."

Little car? Jack Liffey thought. What was big in his world, a battleship?

Mr. Reclaim kicked a straight chair away from the wall, but the gesture was spoiled when it fell over and he had to stoop to pick it up. The chair had a satin patterned seat and the frame was carved and curlicued white wood with gold leaf worked into the recesses. He sat and pointed to an identical chair. "Help yourself. I got to fucking sit down here, I been moving furniture."

Jack Liffey moved a second chair away from the wall and sat facing the man across an expanse of carpet. He felt like an emissary from one clan of the Borgias to another.

"Nick, you ought to hear what Ginny just said about you!" The voice from down below choked off as if someone had clapped a hand over a mouth. The man glared in the general direction for a moment. "Kids. They all just go hairy ass apeshit these days."

"Nick what?" Jack Liffey asked.

He wasn't even hesitant. "Giarre. G-I-A-R-R-E. That's JAR-ay, okay, not fuckin' GEE-arr-ay. Get it right. Half the fuckin' wops in this country don't even know to pronounce their own names. So, what are you gonna hold me up for? Get to the point."

"My name is Jack Liffey. Pronounced Liffey. In my experience, the Irish know how to pronounce their own names, usually. I'm the guy who followed your tank truck up into a Santa Clarita canyon last night and scraped up some of the toxics it dumped there. The driver was a guy who broke into my house last week . . . but you know all that. Two guys actually. I imagine these gunsels report in from time to time and tell you what they do. That's a lot of felonies on the table, but I still think we can make a deal."

"That's what you think. I don't."

He heard someone slam the fridge down below and the women's voices whickered back and forth, arguing over something. Nick Giarre didn't even look toward the stairwell.

"I gave the EPA people a sample of the toxics, but they don't know where it comes from yet."

"So you thought you'd come jerk my fuckin' chain? Are you absolutely fuckin' nuts, tryina hold me up in my own house?"

"I don't want money. I don't want any kind of trouble at all. I just want you to send the gunsels packing. And I want you to start disposing of waste the way you ought to. That's not much to ask."

"Listen up, Jack Liffey. Your first mistake is thinking those two cunt-hairs, do stuff for me now and then, mean shit to me. So they don't follow the rules on what they do with some of the stuff, I don't know a damn thing about it, and by the time the government agencies get around to getting up off their thumbs that are stuck up their asses, we'll both be rolling up our pants in a Florida nursing home and these two Huey and Dewey guys will be back in Nazi-land, Idaho, wearing bib overalls. Your second mistake is coming to my house, getting in my face. Your third mistake is making the first two mistakes. I want you should get the fuck out right now."

"Is that your final word?"

He looked off into the middle distance like a cat seeing things nobody else could see. "This guy—this *dumbshit* wants me to be an albatross around his fucking neck the whole rest of his life." He cocked his head and looked curious for just an instant. "I used that thing all my life and I don't even know what an albatross is."

"It's a guy who keeps little boys for immoral purposes," Jack Liffey said as he stood up. Just before he
left he said, "You've got a hell of an Alley Oop pass."

16

DEEP INSIDE HIS PROMISE

HE WASN'T SURE WHY HE'D FIGURED THAT GETTING IN NICK
Giarre's face would work, but he *had* expected it to
work and now that his visit hadn't panned out very well,
he was feeling a bit clueless. He felt like one of those
TV detectives who started every show by threatening the
bad guy at the top of his lungs, on behalf of the client,
so the bad guy would spend the next forty-five minutes
beating up the client.

Giarre was probably right, the environmental agencies
would take forever to act and they wouldn't threaten
GreenWorld with anything more than a wrist slap. Jack
Liffey worried it all the way home without coming up
with an answer, and when he got back into his complex
it was almost ten at night and there was a sack of potatoes on his doorstep, but he'd seen this particular sack
of potatoes there before. It was Maeve curled up asleep
on the rope welcome mat with a can of Pringles in one
hand.

He picked her up, surprised how light she still was,
and felt a little pang deep inside at the vulnerability that
suggested. She came blearily awake.

"What's up, punkin'? Lost your key?"

"Mom took it away." She hugged him. "Oh, Daddy,
it's awful!"

Uh-oh, he thought. "What is it, sweetie?"

It was so terrible she couldn't get it out right then.

Loco was happy to see her, first sniffing someone different on the air and then looking up as Jack Liffey
carried her inside, and then actually wagging his tail,
like a real dog. He deposited Maeve on the threadbare
couch and gently removed the can of Pringles.

"I hope this wasn't dinner."

Loco got up on the sofa, another no-no, rolled his eyes
quickly to Jack Liffey to make sure he was getting away
with it, and then snuggled up to Maeve to commiserate
with whatever it was the dog sensed was bothering her.
She balled up her fists and rubbed them against one another, then caught herself at it and clutched her knees.

"Mom's getting married. To her new man." She shuddered, as if the new man were Robert Mitchum with
LOVE and HATE tattooed on his knuckles.

"Whoa," he said, almost involuntarily. He got out two
diet Cokes, mostly as a delaying tactic as he thought
about it, and sat on the orange canvas captain's chair
that was the only side furniture he could afford. He ex-
amined what he was feeling and found he wasn't so
much bothered by the thought of some new man sharing
Kathy's bed, or her mealtimes, or her closet space, but
of someone else playing father to Maeve.

"It had to happen sooner or later," he said evenly.
"The divorce has been final for two years. You knew
we weren't going to get back together."

"But, *Daddy,* he treats me like a little girl, and he
watches stupid TV shows." She thought a moment and
then decided she had to reveal the worst. "And he picks
his nose in the car."

Jack Liffey laughed. "It's amazing how many people
think a car's a private space for things like that. If that's
his worst trait, you'll be okay."

She didn't want to be consoled. "Daddy, he teaches
social studies. Only *dorks* like social studies. And he
believes it all."

"Somebody's got to believe it. If everybody was cyn-
ical like us, who would we have to rebel against?"

She huffed a moment. "You're just being contrary."

"Actually, I think I believe it. I grew up with Ozzie and Harriet and the Beaver, and it gave me some reference for normality. It's a kind of pastoral vision, that world. What's going to happen to kids who only see the Power Rangers and Beavis and Butt-head?"

"I don't want to talk about philosophy."

"I'm sorry, punkin. Let's talk about Butt-head while I make you some dinner."

She giggled.

"What happened to the last guy, the real-estate salesman? And, by the way, how come I've never heard about this guy and already she's marrying him?"

"I didn't think it was serious, so I didn't talk about him. You know, they just teach in the same school. I thought he was her friend."

He knew there wouldn't be much in the tiny pantry off the kitchen, or in the shelves over the sink, but maybe the freezer. He came to a full stop when he opened the freezer door. Here was a little reference for normality all right, he thought. Marlena's .25-caliber purse pistol was sitting on the frozen peas right where he'd left it. He put it in his pocket and pried a couple of frozen chicken breasts out of the frost and put them in the microwave, packaging and all.

"You feel like Parmesan chicken?" As a rule he'd pound out a couple of breasts and sauté them with some Kraft cardboard Parmesan and spices, and they usually turned out all right. And Kathy wouldn't complain too much that he was wrecking Maeve's health because it wasn't red meat.

"Sure. I'm famished, I guess."

Speaking of Kathy, he thought. He checked the answering machine and there was the message, blinking up at him over and over as if it was trying to scratch an itch. She was undoubtedly worried about Maeve and he'd have to get back to it, but he'd let it go on itching for a while yet. He hunted up the spices and a little butter. "You're going to have to find some way to make your peace with this guy," he said. "Your mom likes him enough to marry him and she's not an idiot."

"She probably just likes the sex with Butt-head."

His eyes went wide staring down at a pat of butter on a saucer, but he didn't say anything right away. This was going to be an issue with Maeve sooner or later, he thought, and he shuddered to himself theatrically because he knew she couldn't see him. A part of him made a stab at imagining Maeve asking to borrow a condom while a zitty teenage boy waited at the door, then it went worse on its own and he saw a big pink vibrator tumble out of her purse. He cringed and made a face, and the rest of him chased the images away.

"I'm sure she likes sex well enough."

The doorbell rang and mercifully cut off that particular line of discussion, and he wondered if he'd see a zitty teenage boy through the peephole.

"Want me to get it?" Maeve asked.

It was probably Kathy, he thought, frantically waving an arrest warrant for kidnapping. "I'll get it."

He didn't use the peephole first and it wasn't a gawky boy, nor was it Kathy, it was Quinn, in his full spit-polished Culver City police uniform and a grim look on his face. He wondered if he was about to be arrested for whatever they called it short of kidnapping—violation of custodial agreements, or custodial interference, something like that.

"Liffey," Quinn said, about the way he'd probably name a dead possum in the driveway.

"Still here."

Quinn seemed to be thinking something over.

Just so the policeman wouldn't embarrass himself with some obscene outburst, Jack Liffey said, "My daughter's here for a little while, too, then I'm taking her home to her mother."

The cop's eyes picked out Maeve, then dismissed her presence. So it wasn't about that, he thought with relief.

Quinn gestured Jack Liffey outside, but rather politely for him. "I got something to show you."

It was Jack Liffey's turn to think things over. "Uh-huh. You're not gonna sandbag me down the trail a piece, are you? You've actually got something for me to *see*?"

Quinn almost smiled. "Don't be a guy with a problem." He gestured again and Jack Liffey shrugged agreement. The microwave was still burring away.

"Punkin, check the thawing chicken, okay?"

"I'll take charge."

He followed the policeman out of the entrance bay that his apartment shared with three others, and suddenly his neck iced up as he thought of the illegal purse pistol thawing in his pocket. Wouldn't Quinn love to catch him with that, he thought. Of course, he could always shoot Quinn four or five times and head for Mexico.

The young guys who hung out on the retaining walls bouncing basketballs were a bit more subdued than normal as the man in uniform strode past. A big jet that was still on its power climb passed overhead. Some nights they took off from LAX out to sea and then U-turned east to pass right over his condo and some nights they seemed to be making their big turn somewhere else and he could never figure out what the difference was.

"It's in my car," Quinn said. The big black-and-white Caprice was parked in one of the emergency slots near the entrance. "Do you believe everything we do comes back to haunt us?"

"No, not really. Things don't have purposes."

"Well, I reckon they do." He swung open the rear door of the squad car and there was the redhead with the buzz cut glaring at him. Tim something-or-other was the name, if he remembered right, the brighter of the two bounty hunters, but right now his hands were handcuffed behind his back and he just looked angry.

"Marlena complained to me about a guy fitting this description who pushed her around."

A guy fitting *your* description did the same thing, Jack Liffey thought, but he decided not to pick a fight until he found out what was going on here.

"I caught him skulking around her place."

"Skulking," Jack Liffey mused. "That got an official number, like a four-twenty-two or something?"

"So what do you think? Ever seen the guy?"

"What was it about this guy put you in mind of events coming back to haunt us?" Jack Liffey asked.

"I rousted him a couple weeks ago and he said he was after a bail skip. Never mind about that. Marlena said you had some trouble, too."

"I always have trouble of some kind."

Quinn was getting impatient. "Let's just don't do that now. Here, you're a sensitive kind of guy. Check this out." He wrenched up the redhead's sleeve.

There on his arm were the usual SS lightning flashes, a swastika, the letters BWT, and a death's-head. It was all professionally done, not the blurry blue jailhouse tattoos you saw on a lot of jailbirds.

"That's not all," Quinn said, and he pulled open the man's shirt. Across the top of his chest it said in Gothic letters:

> I WANT SOME PLACE I CAN SETTLE,
> ALL I NEED IS HEAVY METAL.

Under that it said SKINS FOREVER and then, beside a big dagger with a snake around it, KILL KIKES, NIGGERS, AND LIBERALS.

"It's all spelled right," Jack Liffey said, with incredulity.

"You ought to like this, you're a liberal, right?"

"Sometimes I'm angry about the way things are, it's not quite the same thing."

"Fuck both you guys with a square fence post," the redhead muttered.

"Another country heard from," Jack Liffey said.

"What country would that be?" Quinn asked, taking him literally.

"The country of the assholes. I don't know this guy and I don't want to know this guy." He could see a glimmer of surprise in the redhead's eyes, which clouded over quickly. Sooner or later the muscles in his jaw were going to get tired from all the teeth-clenching he was doing.

"Have it your way." Quinn opened the front door and took out a book-sized parcel wrapped in Saran and duct tape. "This is sell-weight of the big H. It's worth a mandatory fifteen years sleeping with a lot of convicts."

He tossed it on the redhead's lap and the man wriggled away as if it were burning hot. The package slid down his thigh and rested there on the worn and stained upholstery. The man's eyes went from the package to Quinn and back to the package, but he'd apparently decided there wasn't much percentage in protesting.

"All you got to do is say you saw him with it. You just did."

"I've got food thawing," Jack Liffey said, and he started walking away.

Quinn followed as far as the steps that led out of the parking area.

"What's your problem here, Liffey? I know this guy played bold with you."

"My ideas don't go in that direction," Jack Liffey said. "And you've got enough trouble as it is with Internal Affairs."

"Mrs. Quinn didn't raise a boy stupid enough to let IA get him. Keep that in mind if you ever decide to snitch me out."

"I already told you my ideas don't go in that direction. I don't snitch."

"Maybe I'll just turn sunshine loose around your pad."

"Do what you've got to do."

He wondered if he'd ever get Quinn out of his hair. Even when the man was trying to be helpful, he was a pain in the ass. When he got back, Maeve had the chicken breasts thawed and pounded and ready to go, but she was sound asleep in a gangly tangle of limbs on the sofa. He carried her into his bed and called Kathy and swore on several stacks of Bibles that he'd bring her back first thing in the morning, very very early, for sure before Kathy went off to work.

"LISTEN, it's not a good idea. We won't ever call your future stepdad names again," were Jack Liffey's last words to his daughter when he dropped her off at 5:45 A.M.

"Who? Oh, you mean *Butt-head*," were her last words to him, then she giggled and ran off into the house. It was already warm out, the sun barely up and the air at blood heat.

It was so early he got a cup of coffee and toast with the early birds at a dingy coffee shop, where a boom box set to the news station was up on the counter beside the iced-tea machine, rattling away with some commotion that was going on, but he didn't pay any attention. He decided he'd do his daily look-in on the boy downtown after a while and then figure out what to do about GreenWorld. He wondered if Chris Johnson or one of the guys at PropellorHeads could help him somehow, but GreenWorld didn't seem the kind of business that relied heavily on computers.

Two stools away there was a bleary-eyed man staring into his coffee cup as if even this wouldn't be enough to wake him up. That was ordinary enough, particularly for the hour, except this guy had a big bloused white suit with large yellow polka dots and full clown makeup with a round red nose. Maybe they really were all crying inside.

"Refill?" the waitress asked.

"Hit me hard."

The bounty hunters were a separate problem for him. He probably should have let Quinn set them up with the dope, but if you started doing stuff like that your whole world might just corkscrew down out of the sky in some haywire death spiral. The world would always encourage things toward the in-betweens and grays and ambiguous zones, but you had to resist it. He figured it was better you either stuck with the truth or you went all the way the other way. He didn't want to be part of the modern predicament, but there it was.

MEANWHILE, Faye Mardesich was just then experiencing a flood of relief at the firm knock on her front door.

She'd just hung up from talking to her son for the first time in weeks. It had been a disturbing phone call. The boy hadn't called to talk about coming home, he'd simply identified himself and asked abruptly where his father was. When she told him Milo'd taken a second shift at GreenWorld that night and wasn't back yet, Jimmy had sounded funny. He said he thought there was some sort of trouble at GreenWorld, it was on the news, but he'd go listen and get right back to her, honestly he would. She'd felt a chill go all the way up her backbone and she started worrying seriously about Milo, imagining a dozen terrible fates, but then the knock, Milo's knock, she'd always know it.

He'd forgotten his key, that was it.

She hurried across the room and opened with a smile. It hadn't been Milo's knock after all, and her smile collapsed all at once like one of those big buildings on the eleven o'clock news, brought down surgically by dynamite. It took a moment to recognize him, heavyset and grim, wearing red suspenders. She'd only seen him that once, and it had been at night as he smoked his cigarette beside the tank truck.

"Hallelujah," Schatzi said as he showed her a pistol in his waistband. "Step back inside, woman at risk."

IF Jack Liffey had turned on the radio on the way, he might have found out sooner. As it was, all the geezers standing around the lobby of the mission watching an old TV alerted him. Even then it took him a moment to focus, as he was distracted by the sight of an old man with a deep scar on his cheek who was wearing a pair of women's glasses with rhinestones in the winged corners.

". . . There seems to be no letup, Dave. The plume is still boiling up to about a thousand feet and then spreading out and sinking under the inversion as it cools. There's almost no wind and it's still spreading in all directions from the epicenter. Maybe there's a little preference for being blown west . . ."

He pushed his way as gently as possible into the midst of the old men, the aromas of piss and vomit and stale bad whiskey almost overpowering him. It was hard to tell what was being shown on the screen, except for a logo in one corner that said 5 NEWS LIVE and an inset of a pretty-boy news anchor in an untidy polo shirt. It seemed to be a helicopter shot of an unnaturally yellow cloud, lumpy on top like cumulus stained the color of fresh marigolds. It didn't look much different from any angle as the camera chopper circled, though there was a fat pillar rising higher and brighter at the center. The camera zoomed back and tilted toward the horizon and you could see that the cloud started thinning and paling some way in the distance.

The little talking head touched its ear and stirred. "Walter, we have no word on the chemical composition of the cloud yet, except the initial report from the fire-department spokesperson who said he'd been told it contained 'several reaction products from a runaway chemical process' and some of the products are presumed to be toxic. The highway patrol is increasing the evacuation zone to include all of Burbank north of Olive. Burbank Airport was shut down fifteen minutes ago and inbound flights will be diverted to LAX, Long Beach, or Ontario . . ."

The word *Burbank* had gone through him like an electric shock. Jack Liffey glanced around and there was Jimmy Mardesich, on a window ledge by the wall, staring off into the middle distance with a dependent, hangdog look as if he'd lost all his willpower. He also had a bad black eye, a real mouse, and a scabbed-up abrasion across his forehead. Jack Liffey made his away across and knelt in front of the boy.

"What happened?"

The boy shrugged dully.

"It all got a bit real," Jack Liffey suggested. The boy focused long enough to send him a single flash of fury. It was so uncharacteristic he hardly recognized it. Then the boy settled back into his grave inertia, and Jack Liffey realized something was wrong beyond a bit of random violence he'd suffered.

"What is it?"

"I talked to Mom. Dad called her about midnight and volunteered for another shift. He never came home."

"Is that GreenWorld?" Jack Liffey gestured to the TV.

"Yeah. Yep, it is."

Jack Liffey put both his hands on the boy's shoulders. He could feel himself going onto autopilot. "Van Nuys isn't far from there, either."

"I tried to call Mom again a couple minutes later but there's no answer. She probably saw it on TV and got out."

"You may not realize it yet, but you are just about to enter the critical part of your life's story." Jack Liffey knew the boy had a hunger for the dramatic and that got his attention, all right. "Let's go get your dad."

Was it just vanity, he thought, that made him assume he and the boy could do something? He'd promised to rescue the Mardesiches, that was all he knew for sure, and he was deep inside his promise and couldn't find another way to go.

17

ALL DEATH IS LOCAL

HE SHOWED THE BOY HOW TO POUND ON THE DASHBOARD every minute or so to cuff the radio's one functioning speaker back to life. Luckily when the old slide-rule tuner had jammed, it had chosen L.A.'s all-news station.

". . . Speaking with Dr. Marvin Symons, professor of industrial chemistry at Caltech."

"Actually, that's *organic* chemistry. With what little I've been told, it's difficult to say exactly what the Burbank chemical cloud might contain. MIC has been suggested. That's methyl isocyanate, the notorious compound that escaped from the Union Carbide plant in Bhopal, India, and killed over six thousand people. Rumors have also mentioned cyanide, and phosgene. Everyone knows what cyanide is, it's the gas used in San Quentin's gas chamber, and it smells a little like almonds. Phosgene is a serious lung irritant that was used in gas warfare for a time in World War One. It smells like new-mown hay or fresh young corn. All three can be deadly in sufficient concentration. If the initial reports of a reaction running out of control in a large toxic-chemical storage tank are true, it's probable that the cloud contains many different reaction products including all the gases we've mentioned plus many others that we know even less about."

"Oh, great," Jack Liffey said.

"But what's your best guess, Professor?" As usual,

trained up on lying politicians, the radio reporter treated scientific reticence as a form of cover-up.

There was a silence and then a prissy little sigh. "I'm afraid it would be worse than idle for me to speculate right now without more information."

"That's the best we can do from here, Curtis, talking to Marvin Symons, professor of industrial chemistry at Caltech."

Jack Liffey glanced at the plastic sheeting over the right side of his car. It was not the ideal window to seal out a toxic cloud.

"Just when you begin to think your world is getting on track, oh man," the boy said. He shrugged with resignation and Jack Liffey noticed the black eye again. It was mottled dark and almost swollen shut but probably wouldn't get much worse. "I feel like such a child."

"Don't let melancholy start doing your thinking for you. I'm going to need you."

Rap-rap. "The northbound I-5 is shut down completely at the Ventura, and a massive traffic jam is building back past the four-level downtown. In the north, the 5 is blocked at the Sunland off-ramp and all southbound traffic is being taken off there, but we're told the highway patrol is in the process of moving the roadblock even farther north to the Hollywood Freeway split. The evacuation order has been extended to the city of Sunland to the north of Burbank, and to parts of North Hollywood as far west as Lankersheim Boulevard, and the toxic cloud continues to spread through the San Fernando Valley with no end in sight."

The boy slowly became aware of his surroundings and glanced around critically at the world outside, as if he might be asked to rent one of the buildings they were passing. "This is an odd route to the Valley."

"We've got to make a pit stop."

He drove into the northern foothills of Glendale, where Mike Lewis and Siobhan had moved only six months earlier, apparently just before she had fled back to Ireland. He could see helicopters and small planes circling and circling far away to the west like buzzards waiting for something to die. It was still early enough that he had to pound on the door for a while to wake him up. Finally a bleary-eyed Mike Lewis in a bright red nightshirt opened the door a crack.

"I need your scuba gear. I haven't got time to explain."

"Jayzus, Jack." He pulled the door open and rubbed his eyes hard. He was as wan as an earthworm, and he'd started looking old all of a sudden.

"Do you have two kits? Are they full of air?"

Mike Lewis nodded and then banged his head with his fist, as if clearing it. He yawned and pointed to a door. There was a blast of warmth and dust as Jack Liffey threw open the door that led into the attached garage and went in, and Jimmy Mardesich followed a few steps behind. Mike Lewis stared after the boy with a bemused look. "Good day to you, too."

"Hello," the boy said belatedly over his shoulder.

Mike Lewis caught them up and pointed to a rickety loft hung from the rafters just overhead. "There are two of them up there. Siobhan used to go out with me. Do you know how to use them?"

"Long ago. It's like riding a bike, you never forget how to fall off."

Mike Lewis checked the gauges on one of the consoles. "It looks like most of a charge."

Jack Liffey pulled the second one down and shoved it into Jimmy Mardesich's arms. "Masks?"

"Right here." He grabbed them off a nail.

"Let's go," Jack Liffey said, and then they were outside hurling the tanks into his backseat.

"Might I know what's going down?" Mike Lewis called from the door.

"Turn on the news."

"Uh-oh. Keep your powder dry."

•   •   •

SCHATZI was farting loudly, and it wasn't doing anybody any good. Every time he'd fart, he'd look straight up at the ceiling and shout, "Onions!" and then tilt his head back down with his rambling anger stepped up another notch.

Faye was eyeing the roll of silver tape he'd set on her table, and beside it a bottle of spray shaving cream and two yellow disposable razors. She didn't like what was going on one bit, especially since she was worried about Milo and wanted to try to find out what was happening to him, but this crazy fat man kept cursing and pointing his pistol at things near her.

"It is only through much tribulation that we will enter the Kingdom of Heaven."

"This is starting to get pretty dopey," she said.

"Shut your mouth," he said. He was trying to sound resolute but his voice betrayed the petulance of someone who had a certain familiarity with being ignored. "There will be much weeping and gnashing of teeth!"

The phone rang and he went rigid. Two rings, three.

"Do I get it?"

"No! Don't you budge!"

The machine wasn't on, so she wasn't even going to be able to monitor the caller. It was probably Jimmy calling back.

He farted. "Goddamn onions!" He pointed his pistol at the phone and said, "Bang! Bang!"

The phone stopped. Now Schatzi pointed his pistol at her grandmother's oak rocker, but this time he seemed to be doing it just as a pointer. "Take that roll of tape there and sit your bottom down in that rocker chair and tape your lower arms to the wooden arms of the chair."

"You've got to be kidding." Your *lower* arms, she thought. The *rocker* chair. It was as if he were reading his orders off a printed sheet of instructions translated from the Japanese, and having a little trouble with it. She tried to remember what you were supposed to do with an assailant, something about establishing a sense of rapport and acknowledging them in some way. She'd had a class in women's self-defense at the Y but it was a long time ago.

"We're going to discuss this like two adults," she said. "Are you upset at Milo? At Jack Liffey? Is that it? It can't be me."

"He is a lamb and a lion!" he bellowed, "And He brings us a sword, riding on a powerful red steed!"

"Don't take things too literally," she said calmly. "A lamb couldn't possibly ride a horse and a lion would scare the horse to death. Those are just symbols."

His eyes went blurry for a moment. He had to put down his pistol to pick up the tape and run off a foot of it and then tear it with a sizzling sound. Perhaps it was her self-defense class, or perhaps the dance training, or, too, there was her anxiety at not knowing what was happening to Milo—and maybe it was just her own monumental temper snapping once again—but the instant he advanced on her with the tape, she blew a fuse. She wound up and kicked upward into his crotch with a full extension swing of her right leg. Her foot connected perfectly, driven by what felt like a whole lifetime's frustration, and the blow brought back a very satisfying sense memory of the cheerleader's baton in her hands and that little shiver when it had walloped Martina McCarty's bottom in the shower room. It probably helped, too, that just that morning, on a whim, she had forced her feet into the last pair of dance slippers she'd ever bought and the packed toes were hard as concrete.

His mouth opened as he fell, clutching himself, but no sound would come out of his wide-open mouth. Handcuffs clattered across the floor, and since he didn't seem to be getting up anytime soon, she grabbed up the cuffs and manacled one of his ankles to the steel bed frame in the sleeper sofa right next to where he lay. Then she used his pistol to demand and get his keys, which she threw up on the roof as she ran to her car. She could use the car radio to find out what it was that had so worried Jimmy about Milo.

JACK Liffey kept the old Concord on streets that skirted the hills as he headed westward, and before long they could see the bright yellow cloud ahead, like a furry curtain hung from the summer inversion. They started to see cars coming away from the cloud, very fast, drivers and passengers holding rags and bits of cloth to their faces.

"Radio," Jack Liffey said.

The boy came out of his reverie and hammered on the dash again. ". . . Believes something called the relief-valve vent header has sheared away and there is no possibility of ending the leak until all the reacting gases have boiled off into the atmosphere. The assistant plant supervisor said the tank in question was known to the employees as Big Bertha and has a capacity of nearly two thousand tons of liquid wastes. By comparison, the Bhopal spill released only forty-one tons of toxic gas. A chemical-warfare team with gas-proof armored personnel carriers has been dispatched from the marine-corps depot near Barstow but it will take them an hour and a half to arrive. The L.A. County Fire Department has lost contact with their lead hazmat unit which was sent out forty minutes ago. They don't know what has happened to it. Another unit from the city fire department seems to be caught in the gridlock of the huge tie-up on the Hollywood Freeway. Two other teams with breather equipment have been dispatched from Ventura and Orange counties, and the national guard is reported to be assembling a chemical-warfare team at the West L.A. Armory. Cleve, I think this is a remarkable response in— what?—only one hour and twenty minutes since the spill was first reported . . ."

There were more cars now, speeding away from the yellow fog with occupants hunched forward into wet rags, and there was something else coming at him, shielded by an RV so he couldn't quite see it, and then he pulled to one side as he cleared the RV, making way for a lone riderless white horse galloping down the exact center of the street and then a moving remuda of a dozen more horses in a hurry. A shiny black Arab passed only a foot from the car, with a panicked glaze on its eyes and nostrils flaring. He guessed someone had opened a stable to give them a fighting chance. After the horses there was a steadier flow of cars, and soon little knots of people on foot, hurrying eastward with birdcages, suitcases, and cardboard boxes. A big white goat trotted along with determination, past an old woman in what looked like a Shaker dress who sat on the curb, vomiting, while her family hovered around her.

There was a yellow glow on the air now. It didn't suggest smog, for some reason, more a color photograph that had been processed a bit wrong. There seemed to be an aura around objects, or a gold radiance from within, and he hoped the boy wouldn't mold it into some religious parable. He hammered all the vent latches on the dashboard as closed as they would go.

"My eyes are smarting," the boy said.

"Get the masks."

A big pack of dogs ran steadily along the curb, avoiding the flow of refugees on the sidewalks. A man tugged an exhausted woman along, arguing as they went, and a policeman stepped out into the Concord's path for a moment to try to warn him back, but Jack Liffey honked him out of the way.

The boy hung over the seat to retrieve the scuba masks and they strapped them on. The straps were set for a smaller head and the rubbery edges felt sharp and uncomfortable. Under the rubbery smell, faintly, he thought he detected one of Siobhan's musky perfumes. The burning in his eyes gradually eased.

The boy was watching him. "You're a brave man," he finally said, his voice distorted by the mask covering his nose. Something had finally torn him out of his self-absorption.

"I can mimic it. I'm not brave in my bones."

Refugees were jamming both sidewalks now, carrying bundles and supporting one another. People dragged wagons, walked bicycles, and carted incapacitated loved ones on wheelbarrows. It was like one of those wartime photographs of whole European nations retreating ahead of their defeated army. Before long his was the only car, and the crowd spilled out into the street. He had to slow to give the refugees time to part for him, and now and again someone tried to wave him back or shout something at him. A boy slapped the side of the car.

At a big intersection a long block ahead, he saw tanks and armored personnel carriers. A soldier with an old-fashioned canister gas mask was doubled over at a barricade coughing, his rifle lying in the pavement at his feet. Other soldiers were double-timing away. They all wore gas masks, but the masks didn't seem to be working and a few soldiers were tearing them off. Troops at the side of the intersection were abandoning their rifles and tumbling back into the personnel carriers in a panic. No discipline but plenty of firepower, he thought: the American condition.

The yellow glow had become a palpable haze in the air and he could taste it now, like rotting tropical fruit somewhere in the car. He saw that Jimmy Mardesich was dripping with sweat, and his eyes looked frightened inside the mask. It was stiflingly hot but that couldn't be helped. The gas burned in his throat and he hammered at the vent latches once again. He had to slow the car another notch because people had begun staggering blindly into their path.

They were truly inside the toxic cloud now and there was a chilling sense that everything had changed, they had entered another moral universe. There was no longer any question whether the world around you was hostile, no question of fate giving you an inch of grace, no relaxation, and no exemptions; everything you did mattered. The yellow cloud had erased the existential lie: the future of every person in this new world was distinctly provisional and you might just not make it.

". . . If you're still in the exclusion area, stay in your homes and close all the windows. Roll up wet towels and place them along the bottoms of your doors. If you're in a car, close the windows and set your air conditioner to recycle and leave the area immediately. There is a slight wind from the north, and the cloud is spreading most rapidly south and west. Drive directly out of the exclusion area, north or east if you can. But do not drive *toward* the Burbank industrial park. If you are near the hills, climb as high as you can. The gas cloud appears to be slightly heavier than air. Cover your face. A wet cloth may be of some use. It appears that the standard-issue police gas mask, intended for CS or CN tear gas, is ineffective. Do not attempt to use a gas mask unless it is a positive-pressure self-contained respirator with its own air supply . . ."

The refugee crowds were thinning and more of the people were old and infirm, as if the young had hit the lifeboats first. By the time they wound their way through the fleeing knots of people to the guarded intersection, the military personnel carriers were driving away. One soldier lay in the street unconscious, and two others had been abandoned beside a bus bench. The gas masks were definitely making it worse. A man had torn off all his clothes and ran through the yellow fog cursing and screaming. They could see people who had given up now, sitting on the curbs holding their heads or lying full length on patches of lawn.

A woman lay in front of the broken window of a jewelry shop vomiting on the sidewalk while an infant stood beside her wailing at the top of its lungs. Small knots of drugged-looking people hurried past them, intent on their own escape. Jimmy Mardesich dragged a scuba tank into the front seat, but Jack Liffey shook his head. "Not till we can't stand it."

It felt cold-blooded to be driving past all these people he could have saved, in order to rescue Milo Mardesich, but he couldn't help very many people and one of them might as well be the boy's father.

"Man, this is frightening. It's the sense of being helpless—you don't really have an inkling from a disaster movie."

"No, because you're sitting in a comfortable movie house."

"When you grew up," the boy started, then faltered. "When did you start to know for sure what you were doing?"

"Very soon now, I think," Jack Liffey said.

The fog grew so dense he could barely see the surrounding buildings. Then, all of a sudden, he noticed there were only a few people left, as if the flood of humanity had passed or just ebbed away. The few who remained seemed deranged, no longer human—a man standing at a vegetable stall mashing tomatoes into his face, one after another, like some kind of windup toy. A very tall boy loped blindly along the parkway until he ran full tilt into a ficus tree and knocked himself out. Then Jack Liffey saw through the golden mists to where the ebb of humanity had washed ashore. Bodies lay every which way on the sidewalks, many still crawling or groping along. A few tried to help one another. Here and there a figure was trying to struggle to its feet.

"This is *awful*," the boy protested. He made a contorted face, and Jack Liffey wasn't sure if it was a reaction of empathy or a reflex against the gas. "How could God allow this?"

"How could God allow cancer?" Jack Liffey said irritably. "How bad does pain have to be before you notice it?"

"What do you mean?"

"I mean my perfectly innocent eleven-year old cousin

was killed by a drunk driver. Ask your God why He allowed *that*."

"But look out there—this is terrible!" the boy insisted plaintively. "There must be thousands of people dying. There's too much death, it's everywhere."

"All death is local," Jack Liffey said angrily, and then he shut up. His lungs were on fire and he could feel a kind of panic rising as his body told him the air he was inhaling was no good and he was soon going to be gasping and bug-eyed like those he saw outside the car. The yellow fog around them was like layer after layer of hot suffocating blankets piled over the earth.

His fears took form: a man's face materialized out of the yellow air, pure terror in the eyes, then fell away as if the man had gone down a hole. Jack Liffey could barely see the buildings to his right and he had to drive more and more slowly. His wheels passed over something unseen and he winced.

By the curb, a man with dreadlocks shuddered and spasmed uncontrollably, as if all his muscles were firing at once. A small boy went by fast on a bicycle too big for him, rocking from side to side as he pedaled hard.

"My throat's on fire."

"It's time."

The boy jammed the mouthpiece into his mouth and cranked the knob on his air tank. Jack Liffey could hear a hiss and the boy settled back and closed his eyes like an alcoholic offered one more drink.

"Hey. Me, too."

Jimmy Mardesich nodded and retrieved the second tank for him. The rubber tasted salty in his mouth. He settled it against his gums and then turned the knob and felt a startling rush of air when he inhaled, like a lover suddenly breathing into his mouth. It had been a long time since he had used scuba gear and it took a moment to get used to the way the second-stage regulator responded to his intake of breath.

He knew he was close to GreenWorld. He recognized

the big offset printing plant where he and Faye had waited to follow the chemical truck. A small ambulance had rammed the chain-link fence in front of the printing plant and the driver sat slumped over the wheel. Two people who had apparently tried to reach the ambulance lay in the street.

Jack Liffey drove carefully around the bodies in the long block until he came to the parking lot in front of GreenWorld. It was eerie—a scene that was familiar but utterly transformed by the threat that was everywhere. The big black BMW was in the lot. Good, he thought. At least Nick Giarre was hoist by his own petard, and he hoped the bounty hunters were there, too. He parked beside the guard shack. No one was visible inside, and the gate to the plant stood open.

The boy took out his mouthpiece for a moment. "Mr. Liffey, I'm scared to death," he said.

He nodded in reply and shut off the car to create a profound silence, broken only by a faint hiss from the boy's air tank. I'm always scared, he thought, but I'm trying to lose the knack.

18

PROUD OF HIMSELF

NOT FAR AWAY A SIREN WAS HOOTING ON AND OFF, ON and off. It was like a finger pressing again and again on a sore spot.

A black man in a security-guard uniform lay on the floor of the kiosk with a telephone handset clutched to his breast like a prized possession. He looked quite dead, with his mouth wide open and his chest arched up impossibly as if trying to break his own back. A row of clipboards hung from nails on the back wall of the guard shack, and there was one empty nail under a piece of adhesive tape with *Milo* scribbled on it, so Jack Liffey surmised he had taken his clipboard and gone out on his rounds. Over the clipboards there was a foot-square slab of Masonite printed with a dashed red line that traced a looping route through a series of rectangles and circles that seemed to represent what he knew of the geography of the tanks and buildings of the compound. Spaced out evenly along the route there were little red stars. Jack Liffey ripped the square of Masonite off the wall.

The siren was still hooting, but he noticed another sound on the air, a powerful vibration, like some piece of heavy machinery turning over deep in the earth. He wriggled the air tank comfortable on his shoulders as he stepped out of the guardhouse into the fouled air. From the moment he had clambered out of the car, the air had

prickled his cheeks and neck and forearms like fine needles tormenting a sunburn.

He looked around to orient himself to the map and
then gestured so the boy would follow. The yellow fog
swirled around them in slow filmy eddies, but for some
reason he found that he could actually see a little better
here than on the streets outside the compound, like being
in the eye of a great storm.

The first building along the route was a low corrugated iron structure with wired glass windows. The corner of the building corresponded with the first red star
on the map and he found a little cast-iron shelf with a
lid on it that was screwed waist-high on the wall. He
flicked idly at the lid and a big black key on a chain
tumbled out and dangled, the first check-in point for the
security guards.

Jimmy Mardesich gripped his shoulder and pointed at
a wooden cabinet fixed to the side of the building a few
feet away. It said EMERGENCY RESPIRATOR on a metal
plaque, and showed a line drawing of a man wearing
some kind of breathing mask. He tore a breakaway plastic tab off the latch and wrenched the cabinet door open
to reveal an empty Pepsi bottle and a yellowing tabloid
newspaper. It might as well have had a big note saying
Ha-Ha.

As they skirted the side of the building, the throbbing
became much louder, an ominous roaring of some kind.
The map led them to a flat bundle of pipes of many
colors that ran overhead like some modernist interpre-
tation of a rose bower. They followed along under the
pipe arbor that led deeper into the compound. Here and
there a single pipe, silver or red or yellow, made an
abrupt loop upward and then back down, or several of
them would drop down into panels of pressure gauges
and valves. He was tempted to start turning off everything in sight, but he had no idea what that would do.
The noise grew louder and louder as they advanced until
he could no longer hear the hooting siren, only a furious

roar like standing behind an old prop airliner cranking up for takeoff.

A steel ladder tracked up to a high node in the progress of several of the pipes, and thirty feet overhead a man in overalls hung upside down from a safety belt attached to a small platform at the top of the ladder. His mouth was wide open as he swung lightly and a tool kit lay spilled on the ground at the foot of the ladder.

The red line on the map led them to another key station on a big panel of gauges and then out into the plant's central driveway. Parked along the roadway he saw a black tank truck just like the one he had followed up into Santa Clarita, maybe the very one. A driver in a red flannel shirt was slumped forward with his arm out the window. In front of it was another tank truck, and then another. One of the drivers had got out and now lay in a heap beside the road. He followed the roadway past two more trucks that stood with their cab doors open and the cabs empty, then a much longer truck in stainless steel. All the while the eerie roaring grew louder until it was a steady explosion going off in his ears, just passing into the pain register.

Ahead of him the curving shape of a large chemical tank took on substance out of the yellow fog. It had the number "104" on the side, and he wondered if this was Big Bertha. The roar was so loud now it had no direction at all but seemed to emanate from the center of his head. Beside the tank there was a vertical cauldron, like an upended Winnebago, with a tall chimney rising out of it that was guyed in place by heavy cables. When he looked up he found himself awestruck. Far overhead, a bright yellow column of gas shot straight up out of the chimney like a rocket exhaust. The plume went up another fifty feet before billowing out into the cloud and rolling outward. He had never seen any massive physical process so urgent and angry, and so obviously out of control. Now and again, there was a flash of light inside the relentless exhaust, just above the chimney. It was the flare tower, he guessed, desperately trying to burn off a hundred or a thousand times more gas it was built to control.

The boy prodded his shoulder and tugged him out into the roadway, pointing upward. Following the finger, he could see a second jet of the yellow gas that was venting directly from a crack in the big tank itself. The metal had torn open near the top and a plume of enraged gas shot sideways into the air. As the furious jet slowed, it billowed into a fatter column that swelled and then crested, rolled back on itself, mutated into animal shapes, and finally disappeared horizontally into the fog. Where the gas was escaping the tank, a fold of metal had been torn back like aluminum foil and a thick brown liquid dripped down the side of the tank, like wax down a candle. He could see that nothing was going to turn off this disaster until every ounce of the toxics stored in Big Bertha had boiled off into the air of the Valley.

At the foot of the flare tower, a red tank truck was hooked up to a hose that came off the cauldron. He wondered if some act involved in plugging in this truck had touched off the disaster, and then all of a sudden, with a chill that shot up to his shoulders, he knew why all the tank trucks were waiting up the lane. His late-night visit to Nick Giarre had spooked the man after all, and he had set to work to dump the evidence. And that meant there was a good chance that he, Jack Liffey, had unknowingly set the catastrophe in motion. The disorienting roar and the terrible realization left him dazed and inert, staring vacuously off into the burning fog.

The boy jostled him to life again and pointed to the far side of the road, then hurried across to retrieve a clipboard that lay there. Jack Liffey finally came alive and trotted after him. Under the spring clip was a pad with a preprinted grid that said *Traffic Log* and the boy pointed to *M. Mardesich* typed onto the form at the top right. He saw that the boy's hand looked badly burned against the paper and he noticed that his face, too, was cherry red where it was unprotected. Jack Liffey checked his map, trying hard not to look at his own hands, and saw that if they carried on in that direction, past the discarded clipboard, it led to the office building.

He gestured and they took off in that direction. One of the truck drivers had made it this far, and he was stretched out now along a dashed chartreuse line on the pavement like an additional indicator pointing the way.

As they trotted away from the thundering flare tower, he started to hear the siren again, over and over, like a submarine forever announcing its dive, and he wasn't sure which sound was more deeply terrifying. Then he noticed that on each inhale he was getting a little less of a forced breath and he caught up to the boy to check the gauge on his tank. There wasn't much air left, probably even less than his own. Their fear and exertion was drawing down the supply too fast.

They shortcut through a farm of smaller chemical tanks and around a fenced-off equipment yard full of hoists and rusting pipe. He saw the small stucco office block ahead and figured if they could get inside, they might be able to seal themselves into an interior room and wait for the fire department. Which might be exactly what Milo had done, after all his research on Bhopal.

Jimmy went straight for a steel door at the corner of the office building that had a push-button digital lock. He tugged and yanked and stabbed random buttons with an angry desperation, but it wouldn't budge. To the left a four-foot-high concrete-block wall defined a little private patio enclosing green awnings off the back of the building. When Jack Liffey boosted himself up the wall, he saw a sight so strange he couldn't take it in for a moment. In the middle of the patio, Nick Giarre sat calmly in his dark pin-striped suit in a high-back leather office chair with a grim look on his bright red face as his chin jutted forward. An inch-wide row had been shaved in his hair from front to back, and his forearms were duct-taped to the arms of the chair.

All the other chairs on the patio were the usual molded resin buckets from the Home Depot. Nick Giarre wasn't moving, and he stayed just as still when Jack Liffey leaped off the wall and winced at the smack he got in his back from the air tank. The high chair had casters and he guessed Giarre had been dealt with indoors and then pushed out there by someone with a macabre sense of justice—so his own chemical spill would deliver the *coup de grâce*. No, not *someone,* he thought. The shaved track in his hair and the duct tape meant that Quinn hadn't hauled the redhead off to jail, after all. He wondered if the man was still hanging around, or if he'd found some way to escape.

While Jack Liffey was busy studying Giarre, Jimmy came over the wall. He wrenched open the sliding-glass door and tugged Jack Liffey quickly into a small lunchroom, lined with sandwich and Coke machines. They were hit by a blast of immensely hot stale air. When Jimmy slid the door shut, the glass mercifully muted the siren and the roar of the gas flares. The boy yanked out his mouthpiece and went down on his knees, gasping in a breath. His tank had apparently drained to zero, and he breathed deeply several times, rocking on his knees.

"Oh, thank God, thank God," he sputtered after a moment. "The air stinks in here but you can still breathe it."

Jack Liffey shut his valve off to save the last few minutes of precious air. He kept the gear on his back, though, if only for a sense of security.

"That was scary," the boy said. "The thing's been fighting me for a minute or two. Toward the end, it was like trying to suck a Ping-Pong ball up a garden hose." He took off the mask, too, and took in a large breath through his nose.

Sweat was already prickling on Jack Liffey's burned skin. "Somebody had the sense to turn off the air-conditioning," he said softly.

He opened the lunchroom door quietly and saw a drab

corridor with several other doors, mostly open, and a lot of yellow light from the far end, which was probably the reception area that you could see from out front. The hair on his neck went stiff when he heard a rattle and scrape along the hall—like a sound that shouldn't have been there except in a nightmare. He looked back and saw that the boy had heard it, too. They tiptoed slowly down the bare hallway. The first door opened into a tiny Xerox room, with a rack of paper, a fax machine, and a big calendar with information scribbled all over it in grease pencil. No one was there.

The next was a double office with desks on opposite walls and a library of black ledgers haphazardly racked in head-high industrial shelving, and no one was there, either. There was another scraping sound ahead and his hackles rose and stayed up. He heard a file cabinet come open and someone going through folders hastily, then a muffled wail, like an angry complaint from a deaf-mute. He thought he smelled marijuana but it must have been some trick of the gas spill.

"Look, asshole, if you don't shut the fuck up, I'll push you outside right now."

It was the redhead's voice, and Jack Liffey's eyes went to an ashtray stand along the hall that would make a passable weapon. He might have had a chance with it, but the redhead barreled straight out of the room into them and startled all three of them so much that Jack Liffey yelped, the boy gave a squeak, and the redhead dropped the burning joint out of his mouth.

"Kee-rist, you guys gave me the jim-jams!"

Unfortunately the redhead had a Browning automatic pistol in his hand, and he showed it off with an eyebrows-raised look to back them up while he retrieved his joint. He brushed the little cigarette off on his sleeve before popping it back into the corner of his mouth. "That's more like it. Mmmm. I don't know what the hell you two are doing here." His eye caught on Jack Liffey's air tank. "What have we got *here*? An *air* supply. Right,

right, right. Just what the doc ordered. *Breathing* is still in fashion, and another few years of living for the Idaho Kid. Hand it over. Second thought, set it down right there."

Jack Liffey slipped out of the tank harness and set it on the ground. "Why don't you just take off with the air supply and we'll wait here for the fire department?"

"No can do, my man, though I agree you *did* do me a big favor the other night. I don't really get that part of it, but life is full of surprises. Here I am, picture it, ninety years old, propped up in the old folks' home in Miami and still puzzling about what the hell grudge *did* that Liffey guy have against that cop that he wouldn't let the guy peach me up? I don't think I'll lose much sleep, though. I guess life is just a big wildlife show with the lions popping out of the bush and eating the gazelles. I'm afraid it's my nature to have the claws and a catlike character, and yours to favor the cloven hoof."

Jack Liffey noticed he had black gypsy eyes that remained expressionless no matter what he was saying, strange for someone with such fair hair. He decided there was no future in grabbing for the gun. That only worked in movies.

"Gentlemen, let us retreat into this room here and discuss a little field trip I've arranged to introduce you to the outside world."

He herded them into the big open office, where papers were strewn across the floor and across a half-dozen desks.

"Dad!" the boy cried. Milo Mardesich was gagged and duct-taped to a cheap desk chair, and in the redhead's usual style, much of his hair had been crudely shaved off. His skin was burned red, so he'd probably been out in the toxic cloud for a while. His eyes registered astonishment, and he mumbled something through the tape.

"*Dad*?" the redhead said. "My-my."

The boy strode across the room and began prying the tape off his father's arms.

"Get away from him," the redhead demanded.

"Go ahead, shoot me. Maybe you'll miss and blow out one of the windows."

"Not if I get very, very close." He came up and pressed the pistol into the meat of the boy's shoulder. "Okay, now, little son, since you're intent on freeing your old man, if it is your old man, let's do it quick as a cat." He grabbed the tape across Milo's mouth and yanked. Milo screamed when the duct tape came away and brought a lot of his mustache with it.

"That'll leave the lip sorer'n God. Have a seat," he announced, waving them to sit down. He hiked up his pants and perched on the corner of a desk facing them. Like a social-studies teacher, Jack Liffey thought. A dork, Maeve would say. He wanted badly to see Maeve again, to see her grow up and become something. He was really quite frightened, but doing his best to hide it.

The redhead's eyes were going crazy now, as if the stony facade had cracked away. Jack Liffey decided he was on something stronger than marijuana. Maybe he'd Shermed up his joint with PCP. Every now and again he would duck his head a little as if a large gliding bird was passing overhead, just missing him.

"Now I got your attention, I got to tell you the story of the grasshopper and the bees. I ever tell you this one? Naw, of course not. This grasshopper, he loves honey, and every year he buys a jar of it from the bees to eat over the winter, and the bees, they got their reasons, they sell him a bit of their honey every year, make some extra money, you know, and everybody's happy. It's all working out okay and the world's in its accustomed orbit.

"But little by little the bees take to jacking up the price and keeping most of the honey for their own kind. Still, since grasshopper's been a steady customer and all, they keep selling to him, maybe the price is a little higher and he gets a little less, but still he gets his honey.

"Now, one winter the price is double, and grasshopper, he finds out one of the queen bees is behind the cutbacks and price hikes. She's a real cunt, likes to see the honey lovers suffer, you know?"

"There's only one queen bee," Jack Liffey said.

The redhead ignored him. "Still, he's going to get his honey and no point rockin' the boat, they figure he's thinking, right? The workers show up at his door as usual to bring him his winter hit of honey. So what does the grasshopper do? Grasshopper fucking breaks the jar of honey over their heads, these bees standing there at his door with great big eyes, and all the bees come buzzing down to sting him to fucking death, and as he's shuffling off his mortal coil, about nine thousand stingers in his ass, one of these bee types asks him, 'What the fuck you do *that* for?' You know what he says?"

"These insects all speak English?" Jack Liffey said.

The redhead glared, but went on. "He says he just got in a bad mood. You know something? I don't believe it. I believe it's, like, he's the kind of grasshopper that don't take no shit. He don't take people fucking with what he wants."

"I hate honey," Jack Liffey said. He wondered if riling the man would serve any practical purpose, but it was better than doing nothing.

"Okay, wise guy. You get to lead the parade. Help Pops there to his feet. You three are getting a big break. You get to make a run for it."

"Out there?" the boy objected.

"There it is. Just hold your breath the first five miles or so and you'll be fine. I suggest north up Buena Vista."

"Why don't we all just make friends and wait for the fire department?" Jack Liffey said. "I gave you a break once."

"I worked at Tommy's Pizza once, too. Tommy didn't teach no one to stick around where there's a bunch of evidence of murder one. Maybe that's why Tommy's didn't pay so fucking good."

Jack Liffey decided not to point out the logical inconsistencies the redhead kept sprinkling through his little exemplary tales.

"Up-up, dudes."

The redhead marched them back down the hall to the cafeteria, where a horrible yellow light flooded in the sliding-glass doors from the hostile world outside. He marched them right up to the doors. They could see Nick Giarre tied to his black leather office chair, still staring off into the burning yellow fog.

"Feets, don't fail you-all now. I count five and anyone not out the door gets shot in the dick. One."

"Let's go folks," Jack Liffey said. He wrenched the door open, and as the redhead fought at pushing the other two out, he made a beeline for Giarre and rammed his hand down in the man's pants' pocket. There was nothing but change and a Chap Stick on the left, but the right had what he wanted, a little plastic box with a single key attached. The siren was still hooting over and over, and the roar in the distance seemed to have picked up a notch.

"*Hasta la vista,* dudes." The door slid shut behind them.

"Cover your face with your shirt and follow me," Jack Liffey yelled.

He took a breath and his lungs filled with fire. He had to fight the drowning panic as he climbed the wall. Once he was over, he pulled a flap of his shirt up over his nose and mouth. He guessed Milo would have a worse time because he'd already had a big dose, and he glanced back as he was rounding the corner of the building to see Jimmy helping his father over the block wall.

"Around front!" he called.

There was one button on the plastic box and the parking lights of the big black Beemer flashed at him as he pressed it. With all the other noise in the air, he couldn't hear whatever unlocking signal it gave. The door came right open and he jumped in and jammed the key in the ignition and cranked. The big engine roared to life along with the insistent *clang-clang* of the seat belt warning. It was an automatic transmission, he noticed. *What a wimp.* He rammed it into reverse, and backed until he saw the boy half carrying his father around the corner, then he got out and opened the back door, feeling dizzy and sick. Jimmy pushed his father into the backseat and fell to his knees, vomiting.

"Get in *now*."

He got back in the driver's seat and reached across to tug the boy in. He pulled the car forward until he could see the front window of the executive building. The redhead was standing there, wearing the aqualung with the mouthpiece dangling like a necklace. Jack Liffey hesitated a moment, then picked up the steering-wheel lock that lay beside the seat, got out, and hurled it with all his strength at the big front window. Things went into slow motion for a few moments and he watched the steel bar with its red neoprene covering tumble end over end through space and strike the lower corner of the picture window, which vanished all at once in a shower of glassy gems. The last sight he had of the redhead, the man had really big eyes and he was fumbling for the mouthpiece of the aqualung. You put me in a bad mood, too, Jack Liffey thought.

He coughed for a while, uncontrollably dry-heaving, and then tumbled in, slammed the door, and made sure all the vent levers were off before he floored the pedal. The big beast slammed them all back into the seats.

"Jesus Ka*beez*us," the boy said.

Two turns and he would be on Victory Boulevard, which ran west for twenty straight miles across the Valley floor. He knew he was sitting behind a five-liter V-12 engine. It had forty-eight valves and far more torque and horsepower than anything he'd ever driven in his life and he'd always wanted to open up something like that and feel it crank.

He came around the first turn and skidded to avoid a

woman lying in the street. He couldn't see very well in
the fog and he just hoped no one had abandoned a cement truck in the middle of the road. There was the last
turn, Victory. He straightened the wheel of the big beast
out into the middle of the road, right over the center
line, a part of his mind calculating that if sixty miles per
hour was a mile a minute, a hundred and twenty would
be two miles a minute.

Try and catch me, highway patrol.

"Yoweeee!" The boy grimaced and straight-armed the
dashboard as the automatic roared up through the gears
and the horrible yellow world flashed past their windows.

"Open it up!" Jack Liffey bellowed. In fact, despite
the nausea and the burning sensation all the way down
his throat to his lungs, he was pretty excited and pretty
proud of himself.

Epilogue

THE RATTLE OF MORTALITY

"**DADDY ALWAYS CHEATS**," **MAEVE BLURTED OUT. SHE WAS** getting pretty competitive, and he wondered where it was coming from. He'd always thought of himself as a good loser in games like this, and he knew he was, though it was mainly only true when he was among people he liked and trusted.

"I know," Marlena agreed with a grin. "Jackie's a big cheat."

He frowned. "That wasn't cheating. Actually I prefer a game with more possibility of cheating, like poker." All he'd done was add *I-T-Y* to the word *mortal,* but the four-point *Y* had come out on a triple-letter square and given him a total of thirty-two points. Marlena was only passable at Scrabble and kept trying to sneak in Spanish words, but she was happy to play with them and regularly come out a hundred or more points behind because she and Maeve enjoyed joking with each other and Maeve really loved the game.

Maeve played Scrabble recklessly, laying words out into open areas to offer possibilities for her opponents, while he played with a merciless defensive caution that tended to crab everything into one tight corner as he waited for a big killing, and still Maeve managed to beat him once in a while.

"Mor-tal-i-ty," he repeated to himself, as if the word might lose some of its mystery to a careful enunciation.

It had certainly been dogging him recently, though he supposed it wasn't that strange to be a bit obsessive about death after almost 2,300 people had died in the catastrophe that had become known as the Burbank Gas Cloud, or in the manner of disasters the world over, just *Burbank*. On the international-league standings of disasters, however, Burbank wasn't even in the first division, as the newspapers kept pointing out in ghoulish little tables. Bhopal had killed over 6,000. Even a simple ferry sinking in the Philippines in 1987 had killed 3,000. Every twenty years or so a typhoon rolled into Bangladesh and killed 100,000. Earthquakes in China, Japan, and South America did the same every decade or so. And a 1931 flood in China had killed almost four million people. But it was a pretty big event in a country like the U.S. that had insulated itself so successfully even from its wars.

Burbank seemed to have changed him and made him warier, he could feel it. Afterward, he'd been in the hospital getting his lungs Hoovered out for almost two weeks, and he hadn't liked it one bit that gas victims had died in beds on either side of him. These days he found himself reading the obits in the L.A. *Times,* which he'd never done before, and relating each item directly to himself: Oh, this one's only forty-two, younger than me. This one was sixty. Eleven years to go.

In fact the *Times*'s instant paperback on the disaster, *Deadly Summer Smog,* was tented open on his coffee table. It was propped onto the page that mentioned him and his hell-bent drive out of the yellow cloud, an escape that had killed a lumbering mule just west of the 405 as he sideswiped the poor beast at 127 mph. A piquant traffic footnote to the catastrophe. But not nearly as celebrated as Schatzi Groening, who had died of the spreading gas cloud while chained to a foldout sofa in Van Nuys, or the redhead, Tim O'Connor, who had died trying desperately to hot-wire an old AMC Concord with plastic taped over the right side windows. Both shared billing in a chapter entitled "Blood Will Tell," which was devoted to the shady enforcers of GreenWorld Chemical, though the *Times* got most of the details badly wrong.

Marlena's radar picked up his eyes on the book. "You was almost famous, Jack."

"*Were*," Maeve corrected automatically, and then she ducked her head in a signal of chagrin at her impertinence.

"I'm locally famous," he owned, indicating his two Scrabble opponents. "That's plenty for me." Outside, the interminable basketball bounced on and on as the kids from the Astaire sat on the retaining wall, chatting and dribbling, a kind of mindless fidget of conversation for so many of them. In fact, it was a basketball player who'd almost made him famous for real. A minor pro star who'd played in Chicago in the eighties and then become a small-time Hollywood producer had called him up and pestered him to death about his story. Jack Liffey had finally agreed to talk to a man the ex-point guard called "his screenwriter" about his experiences. The screenwriter, a boozy old hack with bad body odor and a plastic hand, had been sharp enough to fasten like a hawk on the possibility that Jack Liffey might have touched off the whole disaster by digging into GreenWorld's dirty work, but nothing had ever come of their talk. Thousands and thousands of dollars had been in it for him—the only reason he'd put up with the screenwriter's horrible body odor—but the money was always somewhere far down the road.

He remembered suddenly to record his score—distraction was another trait that had slipped up on him since Burbank—and he rotated the board toward Maeve. She'd been thinking for some time.

"How's that family doing?" Marlena asked.

"They're all just super-duper. The boy fell off the Holy Boy Road and decided to take himself to college at Northridge this fall. The dad taught himself Java and is making a killing designing Internet Web sites. And the mother is working for the Red Cross or something like that, caring for victims of the gas. It's another family saved from the brink of doom by the timely intervention of Jack Liffey, always standing at moral attention over the world. Wire Palladin, Culver City."

He noticed that Marlena watched him closely whenever Faye's name came up, but he was not going to make any concessions to irrational jealousies. There had never been anything between him and Faye.

He knew that there were broader effects of the gas cloud, too, harder to articulate, difficult even to notice in the urban muddle of the world city. In a peculiar way, the disaster seemed to have burned off some of the excess religion that had lain heavily over the basin. That's the way it felt to him, anyway. The Broom Closet in North Hollywood and an ashram in Burbank had shut down for good in the wake of people who had died taking shelter within. It was like one of those borderline camel-straw-broken-back changes—just enough of a change, the ecumenical babble retreating from some critical mass of competing versions of holiness, until the city became livable again for the secular.

Maeve was making all kinds of faces at her letters, canting her head this way and that, as if the little wood tiles were purposely defying her.

"And we're all onto the next phase of our lives," he concluded.

"I seen too many phases already," Marlena said. "I like this one."

"Ha!" Maeve cried. "Diet-*ician*. I'll make cheat words just like you."

"Perfectly legal."

He watched Maeve slap down her letters and scribble her score with triumph, and then discreetly he watched the masses shift under Marlena's blue print silk blouse as she slipped a hand in at the neck to readjust her bra straps in the heat. His mind was on her big, ultrasensitive nut-brown breasts, where it seemed to be spending a lot of its spare time lately. The idea of the ardent and affectionate lovemaking that awaited him was like a bright lantern in a dim valley.

Thut-thut, the basketball went on and on outside, an atomic clock kept out in the condominium's courtyard by the Bureau of Standards. A yardstick for setting all the other instruments that measured the gnawing away of their minutes. In fact, a strange form of mortality had crept up on him that very morning when he'd gone to the supermarket and found people staring left and right in puzzlement. He'd ignored whatever it was, left it sizzling at the corner of his consciousness, until he went to the cornflakes and found, where the familiar yellow boxes should have been, a phalanx of Liquid Plummers. His hand had frozen in midair. The vengeful modernizers had got to the supermarket and reshelved everything following some obscure new logic. In that moment he'd had the vivid insight that knowing where things were and where they belonged was one of the very few methods of fending off death, and like all of the others, it could be taken away far too easily. He'd broken out in a cold sweat.

"Twenty-six points," Maeve announced. She looked up and glanced from one to the other of them. "You know, since Mom went and married Butt-head, why don't *you two* get hitched?"

His eyes went to Marlena and he could see her distancing herself quickly in self-protection—the animal inside backing away from the deep brown eyeholes. Maybe it was an artifact of that insistent timekeeper that bounced away out in the courtyard, over and over, or the obits in the paper, the unsettled arrangement of the supermarket, all the rattles of mortality reminding him that there wasn't all that much time left to him, that there wouldn't be too many more brass rings drifting past, and none of them would ever be absolutely perfect.

"Sure," he said, smiling as he watched the big earthy kindly Latina stare fretfully back at him. "Why not?"

PENGUIN PUTNAM INC.
Online

Your Internet gateway to a virtual environment with
hundreds of entertaining and enlightening books
from Penguin Putnam Inc.

*While you're there, get the latest buzz on
the best authors and books around—*

Tom Clancy, Patricia Cornwell, W.E.B. Griffin,
Nora Roberts, William Gibson, Robin Cook,
Brian Jacques, Catherine Coulter, Stephen King,
Jacquelyn Mitchard, and many more!

**Penguin Putnam Online is located at
http://www.penguinputnam.com**

PENGUIN PUTNAM NEWS

Every month you'll get an inside look at our upcom-
ing books and new features on our site. This is an
ongoing effort to provide you with the most
up-to-date information about
our books and authors.

**Subscribe to Penguin Putnam News at
http://www.penguinputnam.com/ClubPPI**